Dreams of Bread and Fire

ALSO BY NANCY KRICORIAN

Zabelle

NANCY KRICORIAN

Dreams of Bread and Fire

a novel

For Brenda
with much
affection
xo

Grove Press
New York

The author would like to acknowledge the authors and/or publishers for use of lines
from the following works: Louise Bogan, "Fifteenth Farewell," *The Blue Estuaries: Poems:
1923–1968* (Ecco Press 1988); Elizabeth Bishop, "One Art," *The Complete Poems, 1927–
1979* (Farrar, Straus & Giroux 1983); Diane di Prima, "More or Less Love Poems," *Pieces
of a Song: Selected Poems* (City Lights Books, 1990); Nahabed Kouchag, "Thoughts" in
Armenian Poetry Old & New, compiled and translated by Aram Tolegian (Wayne State
University Press, 1979); Dora Sayakan, *Armenian Proverbs: A Paremiological Study with an
Anthology of 2,500 Folk Sayings* (Caravan Books, 1994); E. A. Yeran, *Pocket Dictionary or
Pocket Companion, English-Armenian* (Hairenik Press, ninth edition, 1960).

Published simultaneously in Canada
Printed in the United States of America

FIRST GROVE PRESS PAPERBACK EDITION

Library of Congress Cataloging-in-Publication Data

Kricorian, Nancy.
    Dreams of bread and fire : a novel / Nancy Kricorian.—1st ed.
      p. cm.
    ISBN 0-8021-4123-4 (pbk.)
    1. Americans—France—Fiction.   2. Armenian Americans—Fiction.
3. Women—France—Fiction.   4. Paris (France)—Fiction.   5. Historians—
Fiction.   I. Title.

PS3561.R52D74 2003
813'.54—dc21   2002044681

Grove Press
841 Broadway
New York, NY 10003

04   05   06   07   08   10   9   8   7   6   5   4   3   2   1

For Eddie Baba and Irene

1965

The grandparents' apartment smelled of spices and lemon furniture polish. Ani took off her shoes in the front hall and put on pink slippers that slid across the Oriental carpets. This was her new home. She wasn't to touch the blue vase or the china figurine of the girl driving a flock of geese. Baba sat in the wine-colored plush armchair with a tall lamp beside it reading his newspaper. Ani could sit on the couch, on the hassock, or in Grandma's lap. There was a glass bowl filled with hard candies on the coffee table. A red and white peppermint spun like a pinwheel in her mouth.

Grandma kept candy bars behind the balled-up plastic bags in the breadbox. She read their names to Ani off the bright paper wrappers: Almon Joy, Milky Vay, Tree Musketeers. Ani and Grandma sat on the couch on the back porch spitting watermelon seeds over the railing onto the grass. Then they went to the garden to pick mint and parsley. Auntie Alice called from the second-floor porch—it was a two-family house—for them to send up some mint. Ani dropped the sprigs into a basket hanging from a long cord and watched as Auntie Alice pulled it up.

When the neighbor's dog started to bark, Ani looked through the hedge and saw his jerking blond head. He growled and bared his sharp white teeth. Grandma yelled, Hush up, *char shoon!*

In the bedroom that she shared with her mother, there was a framed photograph of Ani's father, David Silver. At night, long after bedtime, Ani imagined she heard his footsteps approaching in the hall. It had all been a mistake. He wasn't dead after all. Ani pretended she was asleep and lay in the dark listening to her mother crying.

In the morning Baba said, Let's go shopping, *anoushig.*

At the market a large man with a white apron and hairy arms spoke in Armenian to Baba. The man cut a sliver of halvah, offering it to Ani. It crunched and melted on her tongue. In the bakery Baba bought some rolls and round cracker bread from a woman with a gold tooth. She also spoke Armenian. So did the tailor at the dry cleaners and an old woman whom they met on the sidewalk.

Is this Armenia? Ani asked, slipping her hand into her grandfather's.

This is Watertown, Massachusetts, Baba said.

Is your last name Silver?

Baba shook his head. Your last name is Silver. Our name is Kersamian.

The old elementary school was being torn down so Baba took Ani to watch the wrecking ball crash into the brick building. Dust rose as the walls fell in jagged sections, leaving empty classrooms exposed and floors sagging into the rooms below. The next day, just yards from the demolition, Ani's kindergarten class met for the first time in a room with an accordion divider in the modern wing of the junior high school.

During recess Ani hooked her fingers in the chain-link fence separating the schoolyard from the work site, imagining the rooms as they had once looked with desks, chairs, and children. The teacher was at the blackboard writing letters with yellow chalk when the wrecking ball came hurtling through the wall. The children screamed and tumbled through the collapsing floor.

It was Ani's fifth birthday. She didn't have any friends, but Grandma invited the grandchildren of her friends. On the morning of the party, Grandma brushed Ani's hair into a ponytail cinched high with a red velvet ribbon. The red polka-dotted dress was made of fabric stiff as waxed paper and underneath she wore a red tulle petticoat that scratched her legs.

They played a game called Button, Button, Who's Got the Button with a large black coat button on a circle of green yarn.

Then they put on party hats with white elastic that cut into Ani's neck. They sat at the dining room table with the lights out waiting for the cake. The candles glowed in a semicircle and Ani blew them out with one breath.

She stood in the front hall with a chubby girl named Carol Hagopian who was in Ani's Sunday school class at Grandma's church. Carol's eyebrow was a long black caterpillar across her olive forehead. There was a fine black down on the sides of her face.

Carol said, You don't have a father, do you?

My father was run over by a car when he crossed the street. He went to heaven, Ani told her.

Your father wasn't Christian, so he didn't go to heaven, Carol replied. He's burning in hell.

Ani knew that her father's ashes were in a cylindrical tin in the bedroom. Ani believed that his spirit was in heaven, which she understood to be a place near the moon where good people went when they died. She imagined that hell was at the center of the earth where the devil chased bad souls around with a pitchfork while hot lava rained down on them. Her father was not in hell.

Carol's eyes were almond-shaped like a cat's and she wore a half smile, curled at the corners.

You want to see something really neat? a boy asked Ani.

Ani hadn't noticed him come into the hall.

In the middle of his extended palm rested an egg-shaped rock the color of smoke.

He said, It's gray quartz. I found it at the beach this summer.

What's your name? Ani asked.

Van Ardavanian, he said. My grandmother and your grandmother are cousins.

His eyes and hair were black and his smile burned like a candle.

Ani told him, Come on. I want to show you something.

Van followed her to the bedroom, where she reached under her bed for a white cigar box. She opened the lid and surveyed her treasures: six acorns, a bottle cap with a rebus inside, a bead bracelet, and a soft brown cloth bag filled with marbles. When she dumped the marbles on the chenille bedspread they clicked against each other, then stared up expectantly.

Those were my father's, Ani explained.

Van selected a green cat's-eye shooter and rolled it between his palms. Trade you, he said.

For what? Ani asked.

The rock for the marble.

Okay, Ani said, sealing their friendship.

Ani was in the backyard playing tea party at the picnic table with her Penny Brite doll. Ani poured water from the teapot into Penny's cup and dropped a pebble in for a lump of sugar.

Her mother called from the back door: Ani, come get a sweater.

Ani reluctantly climbed the steps to the house.

When she returned two minutes later the tea set was still on the table, but Penny Brite was missing. Ani checked under the table, under the bench, and behind the metal lawn chair. Then she peered through the hedges. The neighbor's big dog had Penny in his mouth.

A loud scream rose up from inside Ani, circling out of her mouth into the air.

By the time Baba pried the doll out of the dog's jaws, her red dress was nothing but wet scraps and there were deep teeth marks in her belly and dents in her legs.

Ani ran to her bedroom and hid under the bed. It was a small tight world where nothing bad could happen.

Later Ani's mother knelt down by the bed and poked her head in. She had just returned from Woolworth's, where she had bought a new Penny Brite that she slid toward her daughter. There was a stupid grin on the doll's face and it smelled of plastic. Ani turned her face to the wall.

Soon the smell of cooking butter, onions, and peppers drifted out of the kitchen. Ani heard Grandma's sewing machine in the dining room. Finally Grandma, without saying a word, slid Penny

Brite under the bed. Ani recognized her doll by its damaged legs, but Penny was wearing a different dress that was navy with white pleats instead of red with white. Ani lifted the dress and ran her thumb over the teeth marks in the doll's belly. Then she reached out for the new doll, which was still lying on the floor.

Penny Dark and Penny Bright, Ani whispered.

1982–1983

Ani Silver was afraid of flying. But she was afraid of many things, including dogs, hypodermic needles, parallel parking, and public ridicule. She was afraid of sleeping alone because as an adult of twenty-two she still had dreams about Satan and his hordes of fallen angels who glared at her from the corners of the night.

As she buckled her lap belt and put her seat into the upright position for takeoff, Ani was thinking about her boyfriend, Asa Willard. She had waited until the jet's door was firmly secured before allowing herself this indulgence. She feared that during her absence, despite his recent promises of undying love and fidelity, he would replace her. She believed he subscribed to the algebraic theory of love—another available woman could easily carry out the functions that Ani performed as his girlfriend. To her he was unique and irreplaceable.

Ani had met Asa three years earlier while she had been working her financial aid job at the desk in the library's reserve room. The long oak tables in the cavernous basement room were full of frat jocks reading photocopied articles for government and economics classes. She barely glanced up when a guy asked her for an article for Govy 42. She fetched the manila folder, took his ID card, and read the name on it, covering the photo with her thumb. It was a game she played to relieve the tedium: trying to guess what the guy looked like based on the name. Asa Willard, Class of 1980. Asa, an Old Testament name. Either a prophet or a king. She imagined dark curly hair, coffee eyes, and a long sad face.

As Ani handed the card back to Asa Willard, she confronted a pair of indigo eyes patterned with black diamonds. His skin had the smooth warmth of ivory and his hair was the color of the fine sand above the surf line. Her face must have registered some kind of dismay because he asked, Are you okay?

I'm fine, she said. She had watched him walk away with the grace of someone whose bones were strung together with purple satin.

A few days later Ani was sitting on the carpet in the poetry room of the English library reading through a pile of new books. Asa Willard surprised her by bringing her tea at four o'clock.

You want a cookie? he asked.

No, thanks, Ani said.

I'm Asa Willard, he said, sitting cross-legged on the floor across from her. He was wearing gray rag socks, baggy jeans, and a red plaid flannel shirt.

I remember you from the reserve room, she admitted.

Now you're supposed to tell me your name, he prompted.

Ani Silver.

Nice to meet you, Ani. What class are these for? he asked, gesturing to the books.

No class. It's what's left of my spiritual life, Ani told him.

Lapsed Catholic? he asked.

Armenian Evangelical, she told him. She hoped he wouldn't ask for an explanation of what that was. How to describe the old Armenian aunties in the front pews singing "Onward, Christian Soldiers" under the direction of Southern Baptist Pastor Duke? She saw tiny cubes of white bread on one silver-plated communion tray and thimble-sized glasses of Welch's grape juice in the other.

I'm a lapsed half Catholic, he told her.

What does that mean? You go to mass every *other* Sunday?

Mother's Catholic, Father's Episcopalian. I have pagan leanings.

Ani reluctantly glanced at her watch. Damn. I'm late for work. Thanks for the tea. She scrambled to her feet.

What time do you get off work? he asked, smiling crookedly.

When he walked her home that night they paused under the lantern over the dorm entrance. It was snowing. He pulled off his mitten and brushed the snow from Ani's hair. He kissed the tip of his forefinger and touched it to the center of Ani's forehead. That's your third eye, he said. The seat of wisdom. Good night, Ani.

Ani peered out the plane's window at the city's lights falling away beneath her. The Kersamians' car sped along Memorial Drive toward home. Her grandmother was in the front seat rubbing the lenses of her glasses with a lace-trimmed handkerchief. In the backseat her mother Violet bravely sniffed back tears. Baba kept a firm grip on the steering wheel and admonished the weeping women, "*Vhy babum,* you two. Save your tears for somebody's funeral."

The man in the seat next to Ani was flipping through a magazine about motorcycles. His knees were jammed into the seat in front of him and his shoes poked out into the aisle. Ani believed that if she didn't say a word to him the invisible wall between them would hold firm. She'd never have to see the snapshots of his children or hear about his new girlfriend or the reason for his trip to Paris.

After the flight attendant cleared away the dinner tray, Ani closed her eyes. He loves me, he loves me not, he loves me, he loves me not, the plane's ventilation system hissed. Soon it had shifted into the noise of rolling surf.

She was startled awake by the pilot's voice over the intercom. They had begun their descent into Orly Airport. In a windy cloudbank, the plane bucked slightly and Ani's stomach swooped toward her ribs. She gripped the armrests. Ani hated the landings most of all. What if the wheels didn't descend? What if the brakes didn't work? On her first flight to France a few years before, Ani had thrilled at the sound of the passengers clapping as the plane's wheels touched down. We should all applaud our miraculous, death-defying arrival on the tarmac.

At the baggage carousel Ani waited for her cobalt-blue backpack, the one Asa had bought for her. It was an internal frame mountaineering pack, now crammed with clothes and shoes. She had used it on a miserable canoe trip they had taken to Acadia National Park. After paddling in the bow until the muscles in her arms burned and her palms blistered, she had stumbled under the weight of a sixty-pound pack during the portages. They hadn't seen another soul for days and the mournful call of loons made Ani want to cry. Asa accused her of lily dipping with her paddle and took it as a personal offense when she lay coughing in the tent during the fifth consecutive day of pouring rain. When they got back to town she was diagnosed with a bad case of bronchitis.

Ani hoisted the pack to her back and made her way out of the terminal past pink-faced French soldiers standing guard. The soldiers' boots were black and they had big guns slung over their shoulders as though ready for combat with a deadly enemy. Ani nervously hurried past them.

The taxi driver didn't seem to understand when she repeated the address for the second time, so she handed him the slip of paper. He nodded gravely and pulled from the curb. They sped along a highway until they entered Paris via a broad boulevard lined with shops. In the heart of the city they wound through narrow cobbled streets. Finally the driver pulled onto the sidewalk in front of a glass-paned double door. Ani handed the driver some colorful notes as he propped her pack inside the front hall. The concierge, eyeing Ani up and down as though inspecting a horse, gestured toward the elevator. Ani rode it to the second floor.

The apartment door swung open. A blond woman dressed in a lime-colored knit dress and a matching headband smiled broadly. Her teeth were as regular and white as Chiclets. She extended a hand on which glittered a diamond the size of a chickpea.

"Hello, Annie. I'm Tacey Barton. And this is Sydney," the woman said, gesturing to a thin sour-faced child at her elbow. The girl had honey-colored hair and was dressed in a smaller version of her mother's outfit.

"Hi," Ani replied. "My name is pronounced Ah-nee."

The mother said, "Well, Ah-nee, we're thrilled to see you. Just in time. John and I are leaving on a trip to Vienna and Budapest tomorrow morning. We'll be back on Tuesday. Sydney has been looking forward to meeting you, haven't you, honey?"

The child grimaced. Ani guessed it was a smile of some kind. She knew the Bartons had another child, a boy named Kyle who was at boarding school in Connecticut. Ani had negotiated with Tacey Barton over the telephone: in exchange for room, board, and one hundred and fifty francs a week Ani would see Sydney off to school each morning and watch the child four afternoons and three nights a week. This arrangement with the Bartons would supplement Ani's meager student fellowship and leave plenty of time for classes at the university.

"Drop your bags by the door, Ani, and I'll show you around." Tacey turned on the heel of her lime flats.

The apartment had twenty-foot ceilings and French windows overlooking the Palais-Royal garden. Although it was bigger than any house Ani had ever been in, she pretended that it wasn't anything out of the ordinary.

Sydney accompanied Ani to the top floor of the building to the servants' quarters under the eaves.

"Do you spend much time up here?" Ani asked the child, as they made their way down the windowless hall.

"No. But I always take the au pairs upstairs on the first day."

"Have you had a lot of them?"

Sydney shrugged. "I don't know. About six, maybe." The child pointed to a door on their right. "This room is for the housekeeper. But right now we have a lady who comes four mornings a week and lives someplace else. Her name is Beatrice."

They turned a corner and faced a door at the end of a short hall.

"This is your room," Sydney said.

Ani inserted the long jagged key in the lock and turned it once. The door wouldn't open.

"That's the wrong way." Sydney pushed Ani's hand aside and turned the key twice in the other direction.

It was called a *chambre de bonne,* and it appeared to Ani that the maids in the Palais-Royal had lived pretty well. The room was spacious and airy with white walls and a high ceiling—especially for a garret. On the twin beds under the dormer windows the white sheets had been cuffed neatly over yellow wool blankets. A couch and two armchairs were grouped on one side and a small round kitchen table with two stools sat in the far corner. There was a washbasin in a tiled alcove in another corner of the room.

"Where's the rest of the bathroom?" Ani asked.

"Out here," Sydney said, opening the door and pointing to the hall.

Sydney and Ani stood on one of the beds so they could look out the window at the long rectangular garden below. A fountain cast up sparkling jets of water as couples strolled along the tree-lined allées.

Sydney asked, "You know how to make pancakes?"

"Sure do," Ani answered, making an effort to sound cheerful. She needed a shower and a nap.

"Our last au pair was this nasty English girl who smoked cigarettes and always had a hangover. She made pancakes one time and burned them. One night she was supposed to be baby-sitting when she left me alone in the apartment to go meet her boyfriend. My mother fired her." Sydney stared at Ani expectantly.

"That's too bad," Ani said feebly. Her energy level was dropping precipitously.

Sydney asked brightly, "Are you poor?"

Ani had no idea where this question came from or where Sydney was heading. "What do you mean?"

"What class did you fly on the airplane?" the child asked eagerly.

"Coach."

"You're poor." Sydney nodded with satisfaction, a small smile on her lips. "*We* fly first class. *We're* rich. But I suppose it wouldn't make sense for an au pair to be rich. I mean, why else would you work as somebody's servant unless you were poor?"

As Ani examined Sydney's fine symmetrical features, she understood that this was one of those animal moments where if she didn't assert her authority she'd suffer for the rest of her tenure with the Bartons.

"Listen, Sydney," Ani said, "let's get this straight. Your mother hired me, but she doesn't own me. I'm bigger than you are and you have to do what I say. You got it?"

Sydney stared. As Ani turned back to the scene outside the window she saw from the corner of her eye that the child's small pink tongue had flickered out and in with defiance. Ani pretended she didn't see the gesture.

"So, you know how to make pancakes?" Sydney launched the conversation anew.

"Sure do," Ani repeated.

"I love pancakes," the girl said.

At dusk, when the sky was blue-gray nearing black, Ani went down to the garden. The fountain was idle and the place was empty except for two boys kicking a soccer ball. After righting a metal chair, Ani sat in a pool of light with brittle leaves skittering at her feet. A woman's heels clicked historically along the tiles of the lighted arcades. Ani propped a stiff-backed notebook on her lap and pulled out a thin sheet of writing paper.

Dear Asa,
I wish you were here right now so the dark garden would be romance instead of loneliness. Missing you is like the deep ache in my bones I have with a fever. When you get here in December I'll show you the garden and the streets, and everything that seems like shadow now will be vivid and solid because we're seeing it together.

Ani crumpled the paper, tossing it into a nearby trash can. She wanted to be cheerful and resolute. I hate it when you're clingy and dependent, Asa had said to her. Pretend you're a sunflower, Ani told herself, instead of a grapevine. But the face of a sunflower couldn't help but turn toward the sun. And wasn't that a bit much: making Asa out to be a celestial body at the center of the solar system and herself to be a lowly plant?

Early the next morning Ani leaned against the sill of the Bartons' kitchen window. Under the glowing red and white TABAC sign on the corner store, a gaunt African in royal-blue coveralls swept the flooded gutters with a twig broom. Ani turned from the window to forage in the cupboards and the refrigerator. She wondered where in Paris Tacey Barton had managed to locate individually wrapped slices of Kraft American Cheese. There was no flour, but Ani found a box of pancake mix, some milk, and a carton of eggs.

By the time Sydney padded into the kitchen in her fluffy slippers and quilted bathrobe, Ani had a stack of pancakes to offer her. The child was on her second plate when her father burst into the room in his running clothes. He was a trim, handsome man with the energy of a coiled spring.

"*Je vous en souhaite bienvenue,* Ani," John Barton said, with a strong American accent. Not waiting for Ani's reply to his welcome, he turned to his daughter. "*Comment ça va ce matin,* Sydney?"

"*Assez bien, merci.*" The child's response was barely audible.

"*Qu'est-ce que tu as dit?*" the father barked.

Sydney carefully wiped the maple syrup from the corners of her mouth with a napkin. Ani saw a flicker of disdain pass across the child's otherwise impassive face.

"*Je t'ai demandée une question,*" he snapped.

Sydney pulled at a thread on her robe's cuff.

Ani sat frozen in her chair, hoping that the man she had instantaneously christened Le Con wouldn't address her again. The father's face grew redder and the child looked more miserable and obstinate by the second.

Ani had envied the kids she knew with the good fortune of having a father. When they made Father's Day cards in elementary school, Ani addressed hers to her grandfather. Occasionally there were father-daughter events at school or at church, but Ani felt self-conscious about Baba's filling in so she stayed home. Now, watching Sydney and The Asshole, Ani knew there were worse things than having lost your dad at a young age.

"What are they teaching you at that school?" John Barton demanded. "At your age you should be speaking French like a native."

"Starting so early in the day, John?" Tacey appeared, puffy and pale in her yellow dressing gown. "Go take your run. The driver will be here in two hours."

Tacey poured herself a cup of coffee and washed down an assortment of vitamins and pills. "I'm going up to put my face on." As she reached the kitchen door, Tacey turned and said, "By the way, Ani, you should sleep in the guest room while we're gone. Also, it would be a big favor if you ironed a few of John's shirts. The housekeeper uses too much starch and I scorch them. Be careful if you run the washing machine. It's overflowed three times and the Comédie Française Library is below us. They're suing us for zillions of francs."

Later in the day Ani took Sydney to the Tuileries Gardens for a ride on the carousel. After watching a puppet show they bought sandwiches and Orangina from a kiosk. An old woman with a grizzled lapdog about the size of a loaf of sandwich bread sat down next to them on the bench. The old woman struck up a conversation with Sydney, who chatted in flawless French.

In the late afternoon, Ani and Sydney made their way back to the Palais-Royal garden.

"I'm bored," Sydney whined. She was dragging her feet across the gravel, intentionally scuffing the toes of her red leather shoes.

The muscles in Ani's neck tightened in response to the pitch of Sydney's voice, but she made an effort to be pleasant. "If you could do anything in the world, what would it be?"

Sydney replied, "I don't know. Go to a ski resort. Or go on one of those big cruise ships. There are stores and lots of kids around. And swimming pools. And a movie theater."

"Do you want to pretend we're on a cruise ship?" Ani asked.

Sydney brightened. "Okay. We're on a cruise. And I'm the princess and you're my maid. I yell at you because you're stupid and never do anything right."

Ani forced a smile. "I have a better idea, Syd. How about we pretend I'm the evil stepmother who forces you to scrub the ship's deck with a toothbrush and then locks you in a broom closet for the night?"

"I don't think I like that game," Sydney said doubtfully.

"Oh, no," Ani said, "I promise you're going to love it."

In the kitchen that evening from a cabinet lined with all manner of American canned goods, Sydney selected SpaghettiOs for supper.

"You know, Sydney," Ani said, as she stirred the congealed mass in the pan, "if my grandmother saw this stuff she'd say, 'Food not fit for no dog.'"

"I guess your grandmother can't speak English very well, can she?" Sydney sneered.

"Geez, Syd," Ani said, "we've managed to have a pretty nice time here today. Why do you want to go and say something rotten like that?"

"You're the one who insulted my dinner," Sydney said defensively.

At bedtime Ani offered to read Sydney a book, but the girl said she wanted a story.

"What kind of story?" Ani asked.

"A true story. About when you were a little girl," Sydney said.

She was lying in her bed with her newly brushed hair gleaming on the white pillow. She was sleepy and the pinched look was finally gone from her face.

"Okay," said Ani. "Let me think." She paused and shuffled through her catalog of memories. "My Rabbit Mr. Babbit" was the one she chose.

"There was once a little girl named Ani Silver. That was me. My grandfather came home one afternoon near Easter with a ball of fur hidden in his jacket pocket. It was a small white and brown rabbit with a pink nose. I named him Mr. Babbit. Baba built a cage—"

Sydney interrupted. "Who's Baba?"

"My grandfather," Ani said. "He built a cage out of wire mesh and wood and put it next to the garage. Baba would help me take Mr. Babbit to the basement, where we let him hop around. He liked to sniff everything, just to see if it might be delicious. I tried to get him to chase a marble, but once he found out you couldn't eat it he didn't want to have anything to do with it. He liked to hide behind the furnace and sit on old newspapers. Wherever he went he left a little trail of poops behind him."

"That's disgusting," said Sydney.

"That's a rabbit. One morning a girl from across the street came over to play. Her name was Brenda O'Malley. She brought some carrots for Mr. Babbit. I told her not to open the cage because Mr. Babbit wasn't allowed out in the yard. She could drop the carrots through a hole in the top. But Brenda O'Malley was stubborn and she opened the door. Mr. Babbit shot out and rocketed across the garden. We chased him around and around until he bellied under the hedge into the neighbor's yard. I called for Baba and my mother, but it was too late. The neighbors' dog growled and then I heard a weird scream. Not a person's scream. I didn't even know rabbits could make a sound like that. My grandfather pushed through a gap in the bushes and then he yelled, 'Ani, go to the house *now*.' I shouted at Brenda, 'Murderer!' Then I ran into the house and slammed my bedroom door." Ani paused.

"Is that the end of the story?" Sydney asked.

"There's a little more. Baba hammered together a wooden box and put Mr. Babbit inside. He nailed the cover down so I never saw the blood. But even without seeing it I knew poor Mr. Babbit was in wet scraps of fur. I hated that dog. His name was Wolfie and he had great big teeth. My grandmother's cousin and her grandson were at the house for the funeral. Van and I—"

"Who's Van?"

"The grandson. He was a friend of mine. We dug a grave behind the garage with a big spade. Baba played 'Taps' on his harmonica. Van and I painted a sign on a piece of plywood. It said, HERE LIES MR. BABBIT. A GOOD RABBIT. WE SHALL MISS HIM."

Sydney yawned and rubbed her eyes. Ani turned out the light.

Classes at Jussieu, the university's science division, met for the first time on the day of the Bartons' return. Ani was enrolled in the Department of the Science of Texts and Documents, but her afternoon started with a modern dance class in a drafty gymnasium. In the locker room after class she changed quickly and dashed to a building a few blocks from the central campus. She slid into a seat in a large amphitheater filled with long benches and tables anchored to the floor.

Professor Sofia Zed, the world-famous semiologist, swept into the hall wearing a voluminous black cape. She stood at the lab table searching through a black leather bag from which she pulled a compact and a gold tube of lipstick. The entire class watched in rapt attention as Zed applied a coat of lacquer red to her mouth.

Then the lecture began. While Ani scribbled notes on the social context of Mallarmé's work, the students around her unwrapped sandwiches and candy bars. Someone threw a paper airplane across the aisle to get a friend's attention. Several women in the back row were carrying on an animated discussion, and a student seated a few feet away from Ani fell asleep with his head on his arms. Ani was surprised that Zed didn't reprimand the class.

At the end of the lecture, Ani rushed to the campus for a seminar with Michel Sondage. The professor sat at a small table in the front of the classroom shuffling through yellowing lecture notes, his gray wirelike hair a stiff wreath around his head. The room was crowded with pale thin students dressed in black. Everyone was smoking, including the professor, who lit each cigarette from the butt of its predecessor in a long train of nicotine and smoke. Sondage let the ashes droop on the end of his cigarette until gravity pulled them to the desktop. Then he brushed the ashes from his papers to the floor.

"The Infinite, what is the Infinite?" moaned Sondage. He tugged mightily on his hair as though trying to pry the wreath from his head. His cigarette dangled from his mouth as he spoke through a blue haze. "We will see, my dear students, we will search together for the Infinite. We will define its lack of frontiers. Where will we find the Infinite? It is in the poetry of Baudelaire, this we know, and the work of 'Opkins. We will be reading these poems. But it is also in the films of Joseph Mankiewicz. All of you, I would like you to go see *Suddenly Last Summer*. There you will come face-to-face with the Infinite."

As Ani left the classroom her clothes and hair reeked of smoke. On the WC door someone had scrawled, *We are all prisoners of the state*. In the pitch-dark bathroom—the lightbulb had burned out—Ani searched in vain for toilet paper. She thought wistfully of the white clapboard buildings at the college she had attended.

When Ani arrived back at the Bartons' apartment, Tacey called for her to come upstairs. Sydney was at a friend's house for a play date.

"Give me that sad little thing," Tacey said, unknotting the handkerchief-sized cotton scarf at Ani's throat. "You can't do anything with that." Tacey pulled open a dresser drawer that held a colorful array of neatly folded scarves. She extracted a scarlet one. "This is the perfect color for your dark hair and fair skin."

As Tacey demonstrated eight different ways to tie the scarf, Ani tried to appear attentive although she had absolutely no intention of arranging a scarf even two different ways. Tacey Barton was a grown woman of reasonable intelligence who spent most of her days shopping, lunching, and doing tricks with scarves. Ani thought of Asa' s mother, Peggy, who was a woman of the same social class as Tacey Barton but with different inclinations. Peggy wore a floppy straw hat and leather gardening gloves while pruning her prized roses.

One evening when Ani was visiting the Willards on Cape Cod, Peggy had invited Ani to join her in the garden. Seated amid the hydrangeas and wisteria vines they had discussed, among other things, Peggy's decision to drop out of college in her junior year in order to marry Ben Willard, Asa's father. She had explained. Ben's five years older than I. He was done with law school and ready to settle down. If I hadn't married him right then he would have found somebody else.

There it was again, the algebraic theory of love. It ran in Asa's family.

Tacey was saying, "I insist that you keep this scarf, Ani. And take this lipstick. It's just the right shade of red."

"Thanks," Ani said weakly.

Tacey gave Ani an appraising glance. "All you need is a bit of makeup, a haircut, and some new clothes."

Asa's first letter arrived the next day. Written on yellow paper with blue lines, it was full of news about law school, the weather in Seattle, his weekly tennis games with a new friend named May. He said he missed Ani and looked forward to seeing her in December. He wanted to take her to Le Meurice for dinner, a place he had stayed with his parents. He hoped she was being good. There was a little smiley face after this sentence. Because she loved him she pretended it was endearing. Then he had signed it, *I love you! Asa.*

Ani pored over the letter as though it were a coded document whose meaning resided in the gaps and spaces between the words. Roland Barthes had described the lover as a semiologist in his savage state. Who was May? What did she look like? At such a distance Ani's advanced skills in ferreting out betrayal were of no use to her.

Asa had given her plenty of opportunity to hone those faculties. The way he flirted with that woman on the ski team for most of a term. The time when they were both home in Massachusetts on Christmas break and Asa had slept with an ex-girlfriend. It made her ill to think about it. He was at his family's house in Cambridge in the sack with somebody else while she was less than two miles away in Watertown, all trusting and full of holiday cheer. But once they were back on campus he had dropped enough hints that she had rooted a confession out of him. When he went to India he had sex with three women, one of whom was a hooker. He explained, But I didn't know she was a prostitute until afterward. Oh, please, Ani had said, spare me the details. Unfaithful *and* delusional.

From the beginning his feelings for her were like a pendulum on a grandfather clock. When she tried to walk away he chased after her. Then, when he had her full devotion, he turned his back. Come here, go away, come here, go away. It was a hopeless wrangle.

Ani thought, But I love him and he loves me.

He had invited Ani to come to Seattle with him for the summer before he started law school. At the end of the summer she had offered to stay on. She had told him, I don't have to go to Paris, you know. I can give the fellowship money back. I could work full-time at a bookstore and apply for graduate school here.

He said, It doesn't make any sense, Ani. This first year of law school is going to be a grind. I have to stay focused on my work. You go to Paris, and if everything works out, I'll come visit at Christmas.

If everything works out?

Ani, it would be crazy to commit to each other right now. I love you, but we're going to be thousands of miles apart. Who knows what might happen?

Ani had felt the floors inside her body collapsing on top of each other. She started crying.

I'm afraid I'll never love anyone the way I love you, she said.

I'm afraid no one will ever love me the way you do, he replied.

That night after Asa fell asleep she studied his handsome face and watched his chest rise and fall. She wanted him dead.

She returned to Boston and prepared for Paris, sure that his eye had already locked onto a new target, some pert law student from California. But then the night before Ani left town he had called her family's house. With passion in his voice, he said he wanted to make a commitment because he loved her and didn't want to lose her.

What were the other words he used? Monogamy. Fidelity. Trust.

Ani's dumb, greedy heart had opened like a lily.

you cannot teach a donkey to become a horse

When Ani arrived at the Saint-Ambroise Cinema, Michael, a German film student who was in the Sondage seminar, was waiting outside. Her new friend had blond hair, a black leather bomber jacket, and a girlfriend in Munich.

"*Bonsoir,*" Michael said, kissing her on one cheek, then the other, and repeating this gesture of friendly greeting again.

This whole business of social kissing made Ani nervous. She either pulled away too soon or left her face hanging out there too long. In France the older generation grazed each cheek once. In Amsterdam, as she found out from a Dutch acquaintance, the custom was three times. Among young Parisians it was four. *Quatre bises,* it was called.

They went into the theater. In the black-and-white film, Katharine Hepburn played Elizabeth Taylor's aunt and Montgomery Clift's eyes glittered in his gaunt face. Under a burning sun, Elizabeth Taylor's dress flared white against a stone wall. Then came the boys with sharpened tin cans, or were they knives? Ani felt dizzy when they emerged from the darkness into the street. Michael insisted on walking her home. He had his hands shoved deep in his jacket pockets, but they were walking so close that ' his elbow brushed against hers.

Michael wondered out loud about how this movie had to do with what Sondage called the Infinite. Ani thought Sondage's notion of the Infinite was akin to Zed's idea of the Semiotic, by which she meant the maternal body, the chaos and cacophony of somatic experience. Michael disagreed. He thought it had more to do with the traditional idea of the Sublime. He began to elaborate on the concept. Ani tried to listen, but he lost her when he plunged back to Ancient Greece.

They reached a large intersection where Michael, who was still lecturing, steered Ani by the elbow across the street. His fingers sent little pulsing messages to various points in her body. She gently withdrew her arm as they reached the sidewalk. She had an understanding with Asa.

The first time Ani and Asa had sex it was out at a ramshackle log cabin on the river. Asa was sharing the place for the summer with some friends who were climbers and Outward Bound instructors. Earlier in the week, Asa had taken Ani to the Outward Bound ropes course. Tied onto a rope that Asa secured from below, Ani made her way through a series of maneuvers that landed her on a platform high in the branches of an oak. She was now expected to jump to a platform on another tree.

Come on, Ani, Asa called. You're doing great. Don't think about it, just jump.

She guessed she was higher than the rooftop of the family house. It seemed that the space between the two platforms was the same as the length of the Oriental rug in the front hall. She imagined her grandmother saying, *Vhat you doing up tree like some kind of crazy squirrel?*

Asa squinted up at her. Come on, Ani. Trust yourself. Trust me.

He looked so handsome and small down there. She took a deep breath and jumped. Alighting on the other platform, she wrapped her arms around the tree and felt her pulse against its rough bark.

A few days later she went to the campus infirmary to get birth control. She tried to be cool, but her palms were sweating as she listened to the various options and watched the nurse pointing to a model of the female reproductive organs. Ani took the prescription to the drugstore on Main Street, mortified at the appraising glance the pharmacist gave her when he handed her the box.

There was a big gathering at the log cabin that night. Ani didn't recognize many people at the party, but she wanted to show Asa how self-sufficient she was. She stood barefoot in the yard listening to a burly mountaineer describing the aurora borealis over Alaska. Everyone clutched a beer bottle, but Ani hated beer. She thought it tasted like coins soaked in yeasty water. Joints circulated. Somebody was stuffing hash into a wooden pipe. Night had fallen, and there were fireflies signaling across the meadow.

Asa beckoned to her from the river's edge. He and his friend Joe had dragged a silver canoe to the shore and were about to go for a paddle. Asa took the stern, Joe manned the bow, and Ani sat cross-legged on the canoe floor as they glided off.

There were no clouds and the stars stretched like a net across the inverted bowl of the sky. Asa and Joe smoked a joint that Ani handed between them. She leaned back to take in the constellations. The only ones she recognized were the Big and Little Dippers, but Joe had been an Eagle Scout and pointed out a dozen others. A streak of light dropped across the starlit fabric and disappeared.

Look, Ani said, a falling star.

Another star plummeted, and another.

When they returned to the cabin, people were sitting in a circle on the braided rug in the living room. There were candles all around, their flames flickering in the breeze coming off the river. Asa and Joe sauntered to the kitchen and began to forage in the fridge. Ani went to the bathroom, where she wrestled with the diaphragm. It kept springing open at the wrong moment, and she almost dropped it into the toilet.

She passed through the kitchen, where Asa and Joe were at the counter eating chocolate ice cream from the carton with spoons. Ani said she was going to bed and glanced at Asa, but his eyes were dull. When he smiled at her his lips caught on his teeth.

Just as well, she thought. He's still stoned.

The cotton sheet felt cool against her skin. She heard laughter coming from the front room, thinking she recognized Asa's voice in the tangle of sounds. A crack of light glowed at the bottom of the door. Ani rolled onto her side and listened to crickets pulsing in the tall black trees outside.

She had no idea what time it was when Asa slipped onto the futon beside her. It seemed as though she had been asleep for hours. His hand brushed the crest of her hip and found it bare. Usually she wore a T-shirt and panties. They had been sleeping in the same bed for a while, teetering between passion and frustration.

He struggled out of his boxers, pressing toward her. His mouth tasted of pot and felt like warm, honeyed velvet. Then he was on top of her and inside her and Ani thought with relief, Finally it's done. He pulled out suddenly and she felt a thick wet gob slide down the inside of her thigh.

What did you do that for? Ani wiped her leg with a corner of the sheet.

Asa leaned up on one elbow. What do you mean?

It was so dark in the room she could barely see his face. I have a diaphragm in.

Why didn't you tell me? he asked.

I thought you knew, she said.

I'm supposed to be psychic all of a sudden?

You mean you did that thinking we had *no* birth control? You jerk. She flopped over so her back was to him.

He began to massage the base of her skull and neck. You want to do it again?

The next morning Ani studied Asa's perfect sleeping face on the pillow beside her. Her heart contracted with fear.

Nothing has changed, she assured herself.

In a subterranean recess of Ani's mind was lodged the belief that she and Asa were now married.

Ani and Michael turned into the Palais-Royal. They strolled along the stone arcade, past the shop that sold lead toy soldiers, the interior design boutique, the tearoom, and the restaurant where Napoleon and Josephine had dined. The gilt letters painted into the black wood above the entrance said LE GRAND VEFOUR. Ani wondered if she'd ever be able to afford to eat there. Maybe when Asa visited in December she'd be able to convince him to take her there instead of to Le Meurice, the hotel restaurant his father favored.

The next day Ani had no classes. Reading through a pamphlet listing the smaller metropolitan museums, she came across a description of the Musée Arménien de France. Just the place to go on a cloudy homesick afternoon. Ani rode the metro to the Porte Dauphine and walked along stately avenue Foch until she found a small plaque affixed to a tall wrought-iron fence. She pushed open the gate, crossed the graveled yard, and entered the grand building, climbing a broad staircase to the second floor.

"*Bonjour, mademoiselle,*" said an old man sitting behind a desk. He had flying gray eyebrows, a long curved nose, and thick wire-rimmed glasses. He looked like one of Baba's friends, but oddly this made Ani feel shy. Maybe he would speak to her in Armenian and she would fumble around for words. She wasn't in the mood for speaking French with him either.

"*Bonjour, monsieur.*" Ani moved quickly past the desk so as not to engage further conversation.

The museum consisted of two rooms, the high walls covered with oil paintings by Armenian artists, mostly portraits and landscapes, among them a number of representations of Mount Ararat. The dark wood display cases were filled with artifacts and typed white labels describing them: gold earrings from Urartu, an embroidered wedding towel from Moush, lace doilies made in Ainjar by survivors of the defense of Musa Dagh. Ani lingered over the illuminated manuscripts. She studied the old black-and-white photographs of Armenian revolutionaries, or fedayeen, from the end of the Ottoman period.

In the photos the fedayeen were posed in various groupings, some holding rifles, their chests encircled with or crossed by bullet-filled bandoliers. There was one figure she was drawn to, a military leader in a white sheepskin cap, a rifle in one hand and binoculars in the other. His handsome face radiated intelligence and resolve. The caption below explained that he had been killed in battle defending his town from Turkish assault. A hero and a martyr.

As Ani passed by the desk on her way out of the museum, the old man said to her in French, "Excuse me, mademoiselle. Are you Armenian?"

Ani thought, My grandparents are Armenian. My church was Armenian. Most of my friends growing up were Armenian. But my aspiration was to be upper-middle-class American. So what does that make me?

"My mother is Armenian," is what she said.

He nodded and smiled. "You look Armenian."

Dear Ani,
I'm writing to say that I won't be coming to Paris for
Christmas. I feel bad doing this by letter, but it would be too
painful to talk with you right now. This has nothing to do with
anyone else. May is still going out with her boyfriend at
Stanford, so I'm caught in a triangle. Nothing is stable at this
point. It's just that I don't think I can take the roller coaster you
and I have been on these past few years. My needs have changed,
and I can't deal with my own ambivalence anymore. I still love
you. I had to stop writing for a few minutes because I was
crying. I think we'll both be happier this way. I will always be
your friend.

Love, Asa

Ani read the letter twice before the words began to sink in.
Dumped by mail. What an ignominious ending. Asa had probably felt off the hook since the moment that he dropped his cow-
ardly letter in the mailbox. She checked the postmark on the
envelope. Eight days. For eight days he had enjoyed an Ani-less
existence while she played the chump.

Ani raced to the nearby post office, shut herself into a telephone
booth, and dialed Asa's apartment in Seattle. She gripped the receiver tightly as the line rang. She had no idea what she would
say when she heard his voice.

"He's asleep right now. May I take a message?" the young
woman who answered the phone asked politely.

"This is an emergency. You need to wake him up," Ani said.

A groggy Asa came to the telephone. "Hello?"

"Asa Willard, you gutless creep," Ani said.

"Ani?" he asked.

"That was May who answered the phone, wasn't it?"

"This has nothing to do with her. I love you, Ani, but we're no good together."

"You said you wanted to spend the rest of your life with me," Ani reminded him, as though he were an amnesiac. "Are you in love?"

He paused before answering. "I'm in love." There was not a trace of guilt in his voice.

"You asshole." Ani slammed down the phone. Her face bunched up as she squeezed back the tears. I will not, I will not, I will not cry.

She crawled back to her room and let the heavy air plaster her to the bed. She couldn't lift her arm to turn on the lamp after dusk fell. When she woke in the middle of the night, rain was drumming on the skylight windows. There was no radio in her room, no television, no telephone, just the ticking of the wind-up alarm clock and the desolate rain. She moved to the couch, wrapping herself in a blanket. She opened a novel but read the same page six times without understanding it. She stretched out on the couch and stared up at the ceiling.

When the alarm went off, Ani dragged herself to the shower, too tired to care about the puddles she left on the tile floor. In the mirror her eyes were hollow and there were purple smudges beneath them. At least she didn't have to face the Bartons this morning. She had told Tacey she needed the morning off to go to the police prefecture for her *carte de séjour*.

She rushed to meet Michael at a café on the rue de Rivoli at 7 A.M. He was living in the same district and needed to get his permit from the police as well. As she silently sipped her tisane across the table from him, Ani was grateful for the company and for the fact that she didn't know Michael well enough to have to tell him anything. She watched him stir sugar into his espresso with a tiny spoon.

By the time they reached the police station there were about fifteen people ahead of them, and the line snaked longer behind as the minutes passed. Ani pushed up the collar on her coat against the cold and shifted from leg to leg. Michael turned his body, standing in front of her to block the wind. Finally at 9 A.M. the doors opened and they filed inside.

A man from the Ivory Coast, who was just ahead of Ani in line, was subjected to long hostile questioning. From a distance of six paces, Ani couldn't quite make out the words, but the pantomime of the white officer's disdain and the black man's attempt to maintain his dignity brought a taste of bile to the back of Ani's throat.

I considered all the oppressions that are done under the sun: and behold the tears of such as were oppressed, and they had no comforter; and on the side of their oppressors there was power; but they had no comforter.

Ecclesiastes. That was the Preacher for you. Worrying about comforting the oppressor as well.

The cop glanced at Ani's student identification card, flipped through her passport, and waved her away. He followed the same procedure with Michael.

Ani returned to her room, put on a flannel nightgown, and climbed into bed. She pitched across an ocean of dreams and woke up a few hours later with a throbbing headache. She stared vacantly through the skylight at a rectangle of blue with strolling fleece. Then it became a blank screen onto which she projected scenes from the past.

In Yosemite the cold skies were blue. Asa had paid for Ani to fly out and meet him for Thanksgiving one term when they were both on leave from school. They had hiked the Mist Trail toward Vernal Fall. Asa climbed steadily up the stairs ahead of Ani, and she panted behind him like an asthmatic mountain goat. They passed several other hikers, but that late in the season the park had few visitors. After the first hour Ani silently cursed with every footfall. Onion head, she thought, taking a line from Baba's book, the donkey is following the ass yet again.

The next day in Tuolumne Meadows after a breakfast of trail mix, rye bread, and reconstituted dehydrated eggs, Asa suggested they try some peyote.

What is peyote? Ani asked.

Holding out some dried, furry things the color of thistles gone to seed, Asa said, Native American shamans used these in their rituals. They can bring on fantastic visions.

Ani watched him doubtfully as he wedged a bud between two apricots and handed it to her.

She spat the first mouthful on the ground. It tasted vile.

Don't waste good shit, Ani. Do you know how much I paid for these?

I don't care how much you paid for them. I'll vomit if I eat that.

Sure, everybody throws up. Then you get the high.

Forget it, Asa, she stated.

Not to be dissuaded, he brewed some peyote tea and added honey.

It will go down easy like this, he assured her.

Ani choked down a quarter cup and then he drained the rest.

Now what happens? Ani asked.

Let's hike up that ridge. Looks like we'd get a great view from there.

Twenty minutes later they sat on an outcropping of stone with their legs dangling over the side. Most of the trees were bare except for some distant pines. The moss on the rocks around them gave off a pulsing light.

Do you see that? Ani asked.

What?

The light coming out of the moss. It's neon.

He crowed with delight. You're tripping, little girl.

His laugh unnerved her. Also being called little girl. She saw two small horns sprout from his sandy head, and there was an unsettling glint in his eyes.

Asa lay on his back, saying dreamily, I can feel the life spirit surging through the trees and rocks. If God is anywhere He's here in the mountains, the trees, and the earth on this very spot. I'm glad you're here with me, Ani, to share this.

An emerald lizard lashed its tail in Ani's skull. The night before, he had confessed to her that he slept with several women while on the valley floor before Ani had arrived. There should be a punishment for that kind of betrayal. She scrambled on top of Asa and sat on his stomach, pinning his hands to the rock.

With her face six inches from his, she asked, Asa Willard, will you marry me?

Fear flickered through his blue-faceted eyes, and she saw a muscle twitch in his jaw. The devil had taken her to the high mountains and tempted her with power. Ani realized that if Asa jumped up suddenly she might fall from the ledge. She laughed and climbed off him.

He sat up, rubbing his forehead. Ani, you shouldn't fuck with me like that when we're tripping. It's dangerous.

Sorry, Ani said.

He talked slowly. You know sometimes I love you . . . but sometimes . . . I'm not sure if I'm in love with you.

What's the difference? she asked, sensing a kind of sophistry.

He explained. Being in love means projecting yourself into the future with that person—you know, marriage and kids and the whole thing.

The lizard flicked its small split tongue.

Nancy Kricorian

Ani said, Don't worry, Asa Willard. I wouldn't marry you. You've done so many drugs our children would be mutants.

Ani observed with interest as his face flooded with hurt.

Asa asked, How can you say that? Don't you take our relationship seriously? Someday I want to marry you. I'm in love with you, Ani.

"I'm in love with you, Ani," she mimicked out loud in her Paris garret. "What a lame-brained weasel he is," she said to no one. He played her like a yo-yo on a string. But who gave him the string?

After Asa had graduated from college he went to India. Ani was in New Hampshire, holed up in a senior fellowship office with her books while Asa was trekking in Nepal and Kashmir. Before he left he told her they should leave things open, not make any promises. He suggested that she should expand her sexual horizons. She suspected his motive was to keep himself free to fuck any woman that came across his path. But, as with all his recommendations—read the books on his top-ten list, learn to do a pull-up, lose a few pounds, and try this or that drug—she had taken this one on as well.

During the third week of the term, there was a knock on Ani's office door in the library. She assumed it was her friend Elena but opened to find a tall thin guy in a blue work shirt and loose jeans. A shock of straight black hair covered his forehead.

Sorry to disturb you. Do you by any chance have a pencil sharpener in there? he asked.

No, Ani said, but there's one on the windowsill in the main room.

Thanks. He ducked his head as he retreated.

Two minutes later there was another knock.

Didn't introduce myself, he said, extending his hand. I'm Will Jeffers. My office is next door.

She shook his hand. Ani Silver.

38

What's your project? he asked.

Feminist literary theory, she said.

So you're a feminist?

She smiled. At least in theory.

What does that mean?

There's an old saying: *Between talking and doing there are mountains and valleys.* What are you working on?

I'm writing a manuscript of poems.

What kind? Ani asked.

You know contemporary poetry?

Some.

New York School kind of stuff.

Ashbery?

Chattier, more narrative. Along the lines of O'Hara with the Snyder nature thing thrown in.

A few minutes later, Ani and Will were standing in line in the snack bar sliding plastic trays along the silver counter. Ani had taken a yogurt and a fruit salad. She was on a diet. When they got to the register Will drew a wad of crumpled ones from his pocket. He handed them to the cashier, who smoothed and counted them. The cashier told him he was sixty-five cents short. After he rummaged in his pockets, producing only another quarter, Ani gave him a dollar.

Where are you from? Ani asked.

He pushed his hair off his forehead. Connecticut. Stuffy suburb with more country clubs than grocery stores. My family owns a greeting card company. American Cornucopia. Heard of it?

Ani liked the warmth of his smile. She asked, Cards with nature scenes on them and poems that don't rhyme?

That's right. Hallmark cards have end rhymes and ours don't. My dad employs a freelance staff of starving poets. I started writing ditties when I was nine.

Precocious kid, Ani said.

When I began to read real poetry, I felt sick about the crap on those cards. Haven't had a thing to do with the company since I was fifteen.

Does it influence your writing?

It's like this, he said. When I finish a poem I ask myself, Could this be an American Cornucopia greeting? If I answer, Not in a million years, I'm happy.

As they walked back to the library, Ani noticed a dull coin embedded in the dirt. She bent to pick it up.

What's that? Will asked.

A penny, Ani answered.

Lucky penny?

Ani explained. Picking it up might not bring you luck, but not picking it up will definitely give you *bad* luck.

Will laughed. Where did you get that idea?

My Old World grandmother. She believes in omens and curses. When I was nine she caught me and a friend playing with a Ouija board and almost had a heart attack. She told me that Satan was the power that moved the indicator. She said she knew a girl in the old country who was possessed by demons and threw herself into the ocean. She didn't want me to end up like that.

Demons, huh?

Ani shrugged. There's a lot of magical thinking in our house. When I was little I believed that Satan was hiding in the sheets at the foot of my bed and my guardian angel slept behind the headboard.

Will said, I thought my shoes turned into crocodiles in the dark. Just the usual.

Ani and Will closed themselves into their separate offices. Ani had just settled into her chair when there was a quiet knock.

Sorry to bother you again. Will hesitated. I have a question.

Yeah? Ani asked.

Are you engaged in some type of serious situation, or could we go out on an ostensible date this Saturday night?

Ani paused. There is a boyfriend, but at the moment he's in India. We've left things open. What about you?

I've been seeing someone for three weeks, but I like you better.

What if you meet someone you like better than me three weeks from now?

He grinned. Not likely.

The next day as Ani was crossing the campus she heard someone calling her name. From the backseat of an aging station wagon taxi Will beckoned, then opened the door.

Hop in, he said.

Where are we going? Ani asked, as the car pulled into traffic.

Where are you taking us, Eugene? Will questioned the heavyset, balding driver as they moved down the hill toward the Connecticut River.

Well, Eugene answered deliberately, see, it's like this. I thought we'd go by my son Dell's farm. Take a look-see at the cows. I know you like those cows, William. They are very poetical. Then my wife Wanda will be giving us some tea and Vanilla Wafers, if that suits you and your lady friend there.

Sounds good, Eugene. Sounds very good, Will replied.

This one's better looking than the one you brought last time, William, I can tell you that, Eugene said, winking at Ani in the rearview mirror. What's her name?

Ani, said Will.

She should be called Nelly, Eugene commented. Don't you think Nelly suits her, William? She has the same mane as my son's horse, called by that very name.

I like it, Eugene. I like it very much, Will responded.

Wait a minute, Ani protested. You're going to call me Nelly after a horse?

There are many noble Nellies, including the horse, Will told her.

On Saturday evening Ani and Will met for dinner at a restaurant on Main Street. Will put away an enormous amount of food for someone as thin as he was. For dessert he ordered Mississippi Mud Cake and plunged in with gusto.

He glanced over at her. You know, Ani, you're eyeing this cake with a strange combination of fear and longing. Have some. He extended his fork toward her.

She took the bite. Delicious. It's weird. I'm used to Asa—

The itinerant, erstwhile, so-called boyfriend?

The human calorie counter. I don't measure up to his physical ideal. He's a rock climber. He wants me to lose weight.

Must be something the matter with the man's eyes, Will said gravely.

Afterward he pulled her to a stop in the middle of the sidewalk, bending his face toward hers. Tasting of chocolate with a hint of beer, his kiss was lighter and quicker than Asa's. She let him walk her home but didn't invite him into the apartment. He lingered on the front steps until she agreed to see him the following evening.

The next night Ani crossed the rickety porch of an old house. Someone had painted THE ARGOSY in crooked letters on a piece of board and nailed it above the door. When Ani knocked, Will opened with a flourish and a grin.

Nelly, he said. Welcome to the Argosy. The crew has shore leave tonight. Come upstairs to my cabin.

She saluted him. Aye, aye, Captain.

They navigated a cramped, cluttered kitchen, up a flight of warped stairs, and down a narrow hall. She knew they were heading to his bedroom. As she followed she calculated that this was their third date—fourth, if you counted lunch. It seemed like a respectable number. His small room was painted a daffodil yellow and there were scraps and sheets of paper tacked to the walls from the low ceiling down to the dusty baseboards. They were poems, some of them photocopied from books, some written out in Will's sloping hand. As heat rose from the registers, poems fluttered like leaves.

Any of these yours, Captain? Ani asked.

Not a one, he said, flicking back the fallen lock of hair. You want to dance?

Here? Ani asked. There was about a foot of bare floorboard bordering his mattress.

Pointing to the mattress Will instructed, Step out of your shoes.

With the cassette player blasting Talking Heads, Will took Ani's hand and they pogoed around the bed. After he unbuttoned his shirt, Ani followed suit, and soon their clothes were on the floor. They twirled and hopped and swayed.

As Ani danced, the list of prohibitions in the cave of her skull withered until it was illegible, until it disappeared and she could do anything she wanted. She fell to the mattress laughing.

You're crazy, you know, she told him.

He dropped down next to her and said soberly, Crazy about you.

During a thunderstorm the following afternoon Ani expected God was going to strike her dead with a bolt of lightning as she stood on the street corner. Or that a car would careen out of control and mow her down as she crossed the campus green. What was the Old Testament punishment for adulterers? Death by stoning. *Let him who is without sin cast the first stone.*

For the next few days Ani startled every time the phone rang, sure it was Asa calling from Kashmir. He was feeding coins into a slot in a little glass phone booth set in the side of a snow-capped mountain, telepathically alerted to her treachery. But he didn't call.

Ani stopped in the bookstore to buy a copy of Frank O'Hara's poems. She found what she was looking for on the shelf and then stood reading from a new collection by a favorite poet. She wanted both books, but she didn't have the money. Glancing around from the sides of her eyes, Ani checked that no one was watching. She unzipped the large center pocket of her anorak and slid one book inside. The zipper redone, she carried the other book to the regis-

ter and paid for it. Her heart was thumping just above the purloined volume as she exited the store. She was on the road to
becoming a career criminal. What was worse, Ani wondered,
adultery or shoplifting?

One afternoon Will slipped a typewritten note under Ani's
office door.

Dear Nelly—In point of fact I believe I love you.
This feeling has nothing to do with roses, hearts,
or any of the usual. More along the lines of that dark
mare in Dell's pasture grazing in rye grass and chicory.
I'll say your eyebrows are vaults of the night sky
and your gray eyes the first stars, at the risk
of sounding poetical. I'll say I love you, but you
already know this alleged fact. Your Captain Will

That night Ani and Elena met for supper at the student center
café. Ani and Elena were sharing an off-campus apartment where
their respective boyfriends drifted in and out. Ani had had only
one boyfriend before Will. Elena was the one who played musical
beds.

So you and Will are a hot item? Elena asked.

Ani admitted, I'm a little in love with him. He makes breaking up with Asa seem possible.

Does Will know he's a human can opener?

Ani imagined herself trapped in a can of New England clam
chowder. She shrugged. I told him about Asa.

He any good in bed?

Elena!

Oh, don't be a prude, Ani. Is it better or worse than with
Asa?

Six of one, half a dozen of another, Ani answered evasively.

Ani wasn't even sure what the question meant. Were some people
better at sex in the way that some people were better tennis play-

ers? She had to guess that Asa and Will were probably evenly matched. Kind of weird to think about sex as a competitive sport.

At the end of the term, Ani and Elena were in the kitchen drinking tea from steaming mugs when the phone rang. Will was asleep in Ani's bed so she dashed to still the ringer.

Ani, is that you? It's great to hear your voice. Asa sounded so close he could have been calling from next door.

Where are you, Asa? Ani asked.

Home. Got back last night. When are you coming down?

In a few days.

Can I drive up and get you?

Asa. I've been seeing someone for a couple of months.

His voice was tight. Anybody I know?

No. Her voice was flat.

You can't do this to me, Ani. I love you, he whispered hoarsely.

Later Will counseled her. He's going to put you on a diet of Wheat Thins and water, Nelly. Don't let him do it. Your breasts are pleasing the way they are.

Elena shook her head and warned, As soon as Will is out of the picture, Asa's going to be up to his old tricks again.

Ani refused to allow Asa to come fetch her. She also wouldn't make a date to see him in Boston. She knew she was weak.

She took the Vermont Transit bus south and Baba met her at the depot. On the way home when they drove right past Asa's street in Cambridge, Ani forbade herself to glance down the block at his house. Asa called four times within hours of her arrival, his voice whittling at her resolve until it was less than a matchstick. She finally agreed to meet him the next afternoon at a café in Cambridge.

When he walked into the Algiers Coffeehouse and she saw his handsome face she knew she was lost. Twenty minutes later she agreed to go home with him. She fell into his arms as soon as they made it back to his family's conveniently empty house.

The next day he came to Watertown, where they sat chastely on the living room couch. At his behest Ani had taught Asa a few words of Armenian so he could win over her grandmother.

Medz mairig, inchbes es? Asa asked. His accent was atrocious.

Lav em, lav em, char dghah, Grandma said, breaking into a smile. *Toun inchbes es?*

Kesh chem, he replied. Not bad at all.

Ani was invited to the Willards' New Year's Eve party. Asa introduced her as his girlfriend to his pals from prep school and to his parents' well-heeled friends. Asa, his sister Lizzie, and some of the younger set put on coats and fled into the winter garden to get stoned. Ani ended up at the kitchen table talking with the caterer and the student waiters, who hustled in and out with trays of canapés.

When Peggy discovered Ani she pulled her aside. We're all so happy that you can be here with us, Ani. Asa loves you very much. She stared at Ani meaningfully. Then Peggy led Ani by the hand back to the party.

In the New Year she returned to school, and even though Ani told Asa she wouldn't stop seeing Will he moved in with her and Elena. At night Ani trudged down the snowy hill to the apartment where Asa was waiting. He cooked supper. He read her poems. He gave her a massage.

When she arrived at her office in the morning there was a note on the floor just inside the door:

Nelly,
I may go bald from tugging on my hair and tossing
against the white pillow that still smells of you.
Please come back to the Argosy and sail
with me under the prayerful sighs of the poets.
The moon is a laughing fool and the stars broken
shards of a jam jar in my hands when you are not.

Love, Will

Minutes later Will knocked on her door, and they had sex on the leather armchair in her office.

After a month Asa said, I can't take any more of this shit, Ani. It's me or him. And she understood. She called Will and told him to meet her at the Inn.

Ani and Will left the Inn and walked across campus. They passed the library and headed toward the pond, where snow along the roadsides gleamed under tall streetlights. Beyond the pines there was a sheet of mist hanging over the frozen water. Ani and Will moved through fog onto the snow-covered golf course. In the slow dark Will reached for Ani's hand, but she withdrew it, shoving it into her jacket pocket.

I can't do this anymore. Ani's voice was muffled and sad.

It's King Asa, isn't it? He's been bullying you. Damn him, Nelly. He doesn't deserve you.

I'm tired, Captain. I can't get any work done. You should be seeing other people.

Now that you mention it, I've taken a liking to this girl. Name's Sissy.

A long hatpin of jealousy shot through Ani. Sissy? she asked.

Will eyed her slyly from under a lock of fallen hair. Freshman, he said. Blond. Awful cute. He flicked the hair out of his face.

Ani said, Okay, so I'm jealous. But that doesn't change anything. I can't sleep with you anymore.

The thing is, Nelly, Will said, I love that black mane of yours. I love the soft skin right here. . . . He leaned in close, running his finger under her chin and down her neck.

She almost relaxed into his caress, but then she remembered. Stop it, Will, she admonished.

He leaned forward and tried to kiss her.

I said stop it. There was steel in her tone and she pushed him firmly with the heel of her hand.

Goodbye, Nelly. Will turned from her, walking deeper into the fog toward the woods that ran the edge of the golf course. Ani watched as he vanished into the night.

He slid a final note under the door:

Oh Nelly,
When Eugene heard about us he said, William
that was a beautiful girl you had there, won't
find another quite like Nelly. But then there's
a lot of fillies in the pasture. Damn all this talk
of animals is what I say. Damn your ersatz
boyfriend. If love had any sense it would shoot
itself in the head and bleed in the goddamn snow.
Remember me, Nelly, and don't much mind
the girl you see on my arm; she knows nothing
about how I am always your Captain Will.

Will and Sissy hadn't lasted past spring, but then he had a new girlfriend, a redhead. And a month after graduation Ani had gone to Seattle with Asa.

"Played me like a yo-yo," Ani repeated bitterly. It was late afternoon, she hadn't eaten since breakfast, and she was still in her nightgown. She savagely brushed her hair and jerked on some clothes. Little Sydney was waiting.

Ani found Sydney in the bathtub arguing with her dolls. Tacey
called to Ani from her bedroom, where she was applying magenta
lipstick at her dresser.

Glancing at Ani in the mirror, Tacey asked, "What's the matter with you? You have big circles around your eyes. You look like
a raccoon."

"Asa dumped me," Ani blurted out. She hadn't meant to dis-
cuss her misery with Tacey, but she had no one else in whom to
confide.

Tacey raised her plucked eyebrows in the mirror. She blotted
the lipstick with a tissue and wiped a fleck of pink from her tooth.
"From what you told me, you're better off without him, aren't
you? You're a beautiful girl, Ani. And you're in Paris. What would
you say if we got you a telephone up there? I mean, how else are
you going to arrange dates?"

Dating? What a dismal prospect. But Ani liked the idea of a
telephone.

"Okay," Ani said.

"I'll call the phone company tomorrow. They have them in all
colors. We'll order you something cheerful, like yellow or orange.
Listen, could you get Sydney out of the tub? I'm late. John's waiting for me at the office."

At bedtime Sydney said, "Tell me a story. About when you were
a kid. But no dead animals."

"Okay. No dead animals." Ani pondered a few seconds. "Right.
Once upon a time there was a girl named Dana Grimaldi—"

Sydney protested. "No. It's supposed to be a story about *you*. A
true story."

49

Ani explained. "This is a true story about me, and there are no dead animals, but it starts with a girl named Dana Grimaldi, in my hometown. Dana was a thick, bearish girl with brown curly hair. She had small eyes and crooked teeth. Her nostrils flared like a bull's when she was angry. She used to pick fights in the school parking lot, and a big crowd of kids would stand around in a circle chanting 'Fight, fight, fight, fight!' Every few months she would find someone new to bully. In sixth grade she picked an Armenian girl from Beirut named Pearlene Gosdanian. She hated Pearlene."

"Why did she hate her?" Sydney asked.

"Dana hated her because Pearlene wore a flowered shirt with plaid pants. She hated her because Pearlene spoke English with an accent and because she came from a foreign country. She hated Pearlene because she didn't like the sound of her name. So Dana waited for Pearlene outside at the end of the school day. Dana walked up to Pearlene and shoved her back and said, 'So, DP, what do you have to say for yourself, you Armo rugbeater, you stinking camel driver.'"

"What's a deepee?" Sydney queried.

"Displaced person. A refugee. Fresh off the boat from the old country. Pearlene Gosdanian was no pushover—she was scrappy. She wasn't going to take that kind of talk from anybody. But Dana just hauled back and punched her right in the nose. When Pearlene saw the blood on her hands she ran. My friend Lucy Sevanian and I chased after her to make sure she was okay, but Pearlene turned on us, spitting. She yelled all kinds of curses at us in Turkish."

"Is that the end of the story?" Sydney asked.

"No," said Ani. "A few years later, when we were in junior high, Dana went after a girl named Manoushag Ovsanian. Usually Dana found someone almost as tough as she was, but this Manoushag was small and timid. Fresh off the boat. Manoushag backed up toward the school fire escape when Dana came at her. I was standing to one side of the fire escape with my friend Lucy. We were halfway between Manoushag and Dana. Without thinking, I stuck

Dreams of Bread and Fire

out my foot and tripped Dana. She smacked down on the pavement and jumped up, bellowing, 'Who did that?'

"She turned back to Manoushag. I thought she might kill the girl, she was so mad. So I said, 'Leave her alone, Dana. She's half your size.' And then I ran. The crossing guard yelled at me to stop, but I ran and I ran until I slammed the front door behind me at home."

"Then what happened?" Sydney asked anxiously.

"Then Dana told everyone at school she was going to kill me. She said she was going to grab me by the hair—I had very long hair at the time—and swing me over her head and throw me up against the school's brick wall."

Sydney inhaled sharply.

Ani continued. "I was so scared I didn't know what to do. My grandfather wanted to give me boxing lessons. My mother wanted to call the principal. My grandmother prayed to God. The next day I scuttled along the halls like a small green crab. I sneaked out of school by the side entrance. I made it halfway across the field before she spotted me. Then she came charging at me with her head down. A pack of kids followed at her heels. They wanted to see the fight.

"I stopped running and turned around to face her. I mean, she wasn't going to give me any peace until she got her revenge. So I stood there waiting and she barreled into me. The breath was knocked out of me as I hit the ground. I was lying in the grass staring up at a circle of faces, feeling Dana's sneaker kicking into my leg. Then I saw Van."

"He helped you bury Mr. Babbit?"

"The very same. Dana said to him, 'You know this sack of shit?'" Ani paused. She had been excising the curse words as she went along, but this one slipped out. "And Van said, 'She's my cousin.' He grasped my hand and pulled me to my feet. He plucked a leaf out of my hair. So Van, Dana, and I walked over to the bench to talk it out. She wanted an apology. I said I was sorry, although I

51

didn't really mean it. As soon as it was out of my mouth, I silently prayed for God to forgive me for lying."

"Then what happened?"

"Van told us to shake hands." As she said the words Ani felt Dana's hot, meaty palm against hers.

"What happened after that?"

"Then Van walked me home. The end. Now it's time for you to go to sleep." Ani turned out the light.

"Can you sing to me?" Sydney asked.

This little light of mine, I'm gonna let it shine,
This little light of mine, I'm gonna let it shine,
Let it shine, let it shine, let it shine. . . .

As Ani sang, she heard Grandma's voice in her ear.

Akh babum, *Ani, vhy are you so sad,* aghchig? *Forget about him. Peh! Spit from you mouth.*

Baba would agree with Grandma. He said, *What does the donkey know of the almond,* anoushig?

Ani could see her mother's melancholy face. *I'm so sorry, sweetie.*

And Elena Torino? What would she say? *You should have dumped that drug-addled white boy before he dumped you.*

Asa wasn't drug-addled. He was a pothead. Okay, she admitted to Elena's specter, he also dropped acid from time to time, snorted coke, and tossed back flaming shots of whisky. He sometimes made vodka blender drinks for breakfast.

In August, Ani herself had done half a tab of acid at a Grateful Dead concert in Seattle. The place was like a Renaissance carnival, complete with troubadours, jugglers, and dancers. Vendors hawked everything from bootleg tapes to quaaludes. Ani and Asa ran into someone they knew from school, a sweet guy named Barry who had dropped out to follow the Dead.

Doe-eyed Barry wore loose bright clothes and a rainbow band around his forehead. He was painting faces and selling LSD. When

Asa and Ani joined him on his blanket, Barry painted a chain of red roses down one side of Ani's face.

Barry told them, Last year when I was out at Red Rocks for a show, this storm blew up just at the right moment in "The Wheel." Man, it was intense. Lightning splitting the sky. Then when the song was over the storm went on by. It was amazing. The boys can control the weather. It's like the crack in the cosmic egg, I'm telling you, man. They're trying to put Band-Aids on the abyss.

Asa attempted to pay Barry for the flowers, but Barry wouldn't take the money.

Sell me a blotter then, Asa said.

You need two? Barry asked.

Asa gestured at Ani. This woman gets drunk on half a glass of wine. One is enough.

After they walked away, Ani commented, The poor guy's brain has turned into steamed cauliflower.

What about it, Ani? Half a blotter? Asa asked.

Do you think this is a good place? Ani asked.

Where better than a Grateful Dead concert? Half the audience is tripping.

So Ani put the tiny slip of paper on her tongue and they entered the Coliseum. By the time they found their seats, Ani couldn't make any sense of the music, which was loud and discordant. She gazed at colored beams of light playing above the stage. She stared at the people around her as they clapped their hands. Their bodies swayed and their mouths opened, sending out shiny bubbles that drifted toward the high roof.

Asa asked, Are you okay?

Ani nodded yes.

You're all right? he asked again.

She nodded.

Can you talk?

She shook her head.

Try to say something, Asa ordered.

There were words in her head, but Ani couldn't seem to transfer them to her tongue. It was as though the connection between brain and vocal cords had been severed. Ani wondered if she would ever speak again. She'd have to carry note cards and a pen to communicate with people. Or she'd have to get a horn like Harpo Marx. She could wear a curly wig and an oversized man's suit.

Asa said anxiously, Don't flip out on me, okay?

Ani had forgotten about Asa. There he was with his diamond eyes, white teeth, and that smooth flawless skin. Under the gold lion on his black T-shirt beat a fickle heart.

Suddenly Ani felt the need for the toilet. Pushing past the people in their row, she ran up the aisle to the circular gallery. She approached the railing and peered down at the long drop to the stadium's ground floor. Glancing up she noticed several uniformed police officers eyeing her warily. Ani backed away and turned toward the LADIES sign.

The white-tiled bathroom was filled with lovely girls who undulated like undersea plants. Ani surveyed the room, selecting the ones she thought Asa would like best: the slim long-haired ones with fine features. After using the toilet she stood before the washbasin running her hands under cold water and staring at herself in the mirror.

A stranger to herself, she considered the black hair done with tiny braids, the chain of roses painted along her cheek, and the long line of her neck. In seventh grade social studies a boy—an Armenian boy from Beirut named Arsen—was handing out paper for a quiz. He leaned down and said, You have a beautiful neck. It was probably the nicest thing any boy had ever said to her, up to and including Asa Willard. Except for Will. Will Jeffers and Arsen Arslanian knew how to talk to a girl.

She shut off the tap and wandered into the corridor, where tie-dyed figures were leaping and cavorting under the benevolent watch of the cops. Asa materialized at her side.

Jesus Christ, Ani. You scared the shit out of me. Where were you?

She pointed at the rest room.

You still can't talk?

She shook her head.

Come on, you. Asa laid hold of Ani's arm and towed her back to their seats.

The music went on and on. But Ani's mind was a many-petaled flower. She remembered lying under the lilac bushes with her cheek on the soft emerald moss that grew on the shady side of the house. Perfumed French lilacs bloomed near the front walk in early spring. In their bedroom Violet was spraying cologne on her wrists. Baba played his harmonica while Grandma pinned laundry to the line on the porch. Held up by a wire hanger, the clothespin bag was one of Ani's childhood dresses with the hem sewn shut. Ani wanted to hide in her grandmother's apron pocket.

When the concert ended, Ani and Asa joined a throng of people streaming over glittering sidewalks. Asa raised his arm to hail a cab.

Let's walk, Ani said.

It's about five miles, Ani. I don't think you're in any condition to walk. Hey, you're talking!

Then she couldn't stop talking. The words poured out of her in a torrent. By the time she finished a sentence her mind raced to another thought entirely, her tongue barely able to keep up with the flow.

Wouldn't it be incredible if the president and all the senators were tripping on acid? It would toss them out of the narrow boxes they're trapped in, Ani said to Asa.

Ani, that's not an original idea, Asa replied.

Who cares about original? I'm part of humanity.

When they got home, Ani lay in the big bed gazing at the oval streetlight just outside their window. An ersatz moon, as Captain Will would have said. Whoa, Nelly, what are you doing there, girl? Ani closed her eyes and watched Day-Glo geometric patterns swirling behind her eyelids while Asa moved on top of her. Miles of starless space stretched between their bodies. She fell asleep and dreamed that she was being chased inside an enormous pink snail's shell by clowns in polka-dotted suits and black-clad soldiers with bayonets.

Ani sat in Sydney's darkened room while the little girl slept. She heard the front door open and went downstairs.

"You're home early," Ani said to Tacey. It was minutes before eleven.

Tacey dropped her fur coat onto the hall carpet. "Early and alone. The Czar decided to take everybody to Crazy Horse. I just wasn't up to all those prancing tits."

Ani lifted the fur and hung it in the closet.

Tacey asked brightly, "You want to have a nightcap?"

"How about I make you a cup of tea?" Ani offered. She was hoping that Tacey wouldn't turn out to be either a mean or a maudlin drunk.

Tacey followed Ani to the kitchen. "You know, John has no idea about life, Ani. He sits at his desk, insulated from the world by his lackeys. He doesn't know how to talk to the fellow who parks the car, let alone his daughter. It's sad, really."

Ani filled the kettle from the tap and set it on the stove.

Tacey slumped into a chair at the table. "You're lucky, Ani. You had a bad boyfriend, but you didn't marry him, did you? When I was your age, I was already married. Mrs. John Barton. Did I ever tell you the secret of a successful marriage?"

"No, you didn't," Ani replied, sitting down across from Tacey.

Tacey leaned forward and whispered dramatically, "The secret of a successful marriage is that the man has to love the woman more."

"Why is that?" Ani asked, not sure she wanted to hear the response.

"Isn't it obvious? Otherwise the asshole is feeling up his secretary and treating you like a doormat."

Ani didn't say anything.

Tacey continued. "When you get married you start out dewy and fresh and full of hope. His comments are amusing and his gestures are sweet. Then as the years go by his jokes turn mean. And the way he flicks the dandruff from his shoulders makes you want to crack him over the head with a golf iron."

Ani heard the wall clock click from one minute to the next.

"Jesus." Tacey sighed, her face suddenly haggard. "I'm so goddamned tired."

Sitting in the first-class compartment of the train, Ani rode the metro to its far northern end. If the police checked her ticket she would pretend not to speak French and play the ignorant American. Liberté, Egalité, Fraternité. It rankled her notions of democracy that there should be separate classes in the subway. It also appalled her that people were required to show identity cards if the cops requested them. It was one thing to be asked for a driver's license if you were in a car, but the notion of having to produce official documents for merely ambulating in public was bizarre. No one had yet requested to see either her *carte de séjour* or her passport. This ordeal seemed reserved primarily for young men whose skin tones ran to shades of brown: copper, cocoa, and coffee.

Ani walked the last half mile to the university at Saint-Denis. There was a network of star professors whose seminars and lectures American university students flocked to in a kind of cerebral tourism. She had vowed not to do it herself, but here she was, making the pilgrimage to Saint-Denis to hear Professeur Julien Cafard, the renowned philosopher. Both Zed and Sondage made frequent reference to Cafard's work—they belonged to the same intellectual constellation—so Ani felt compelled to hear the great man's words coming out of his own mouth.

Thirty minutes before the seminar began students jammed the classroom, standing along the walls when all the seats at the tables were taken. Julien Cafard entered, surrounded by an entourage of acolytes. The white-haired professor chain-smoked his way through a lecture on Truth while Ani jotted down phrases she hoped were at the heart of his argument. Suddenly Cafard stopped mid-sentence and went into a spasm of ragged coughing.

The student next to Ani whispered into her ear, "He has only one lung. Philosophy is a cruel mistress."

Ani glanced at her neighbor. With enormous dark eyes and a drooping mustache under a prominent nose, he looked like a reincarnation of Marcel Proust. At the end of the lecture he introduced himself as Philippe and invited Ani to come to his home for tea. His place was only a short walk from the campus so Ani agreed.

The apartment's shutters were drawn, thick drapes covered most of the windows, and the wallpaper was ruby red. The place had a dark womblike atmosphere. Philippe, switching on an antique floor lamp over which hung a red silk shawl, explained that he suffered from severe asthma, hence the sealed windows. There were two side chairs in the room, a box spring leaning against one wall, and towering stacks of gray cardboard egg crates.

"What are those for?" Ani asked, gesturing at the egg cartons.

"Follow me," he said.

They went into the next room, which was dominated by a large bed with a red velvet headboard. An upright piano stood nearby. Overhead, the ceiling was lined with egg crates.

"The neighbors complain about my piano, so I put up the cartons against the noise. Let me play for you," Philippe said.

He settled himself onto the piano bench as though he were in a concert hall. He closed his eyes and began awkwardly to play a Satie nocturne. His nostrils dilated, his brow furrowed, and when a black forelock fell over his face he tossed his head like a stallion.

Freezing his hands above the keys, Philippe gazed at Ani with longing.

He breathed, "*Je suis fou. Je veux follement te faire l'amour.*"

Then he flung himself at her.

Just as they were getting each other's clothes undone, Philippe leaped up shouting, "*Mon dieu!* I'm late for my job."

Hurriedly buttoning his shirt, Philippe hustled her out of the apartment. When he asked for her coordinates, she gave him a number that was correct except for the final numeral. With any luck she would never see him again.

On the metro home, Ani marveled at how close she had been to having sex with a complete stranger, and a completely bizarre stranger at that. Only the guy's eccentric behavior had brought a halt to their ill-advised encounter. And it was Asa's fault, the foul betrayer. She thought of his narrow face and his slightly calloused hands. She had loved those hands most of all.

Men started buzzing around like flies, although Ani felt more like carrion than honey. Was she sending out secret signals of which she herself was unaware? When a medical student from Pau followed her home one afternoon, she agreed to go out with him that night to hear Argentinean music. He corrected her French and droned on about the details of his family's prune farm. She lied and said she didn't have a telephone. Then he lurked outside the back door several days in a row until Ani told him to get lost.

She went on a miserable date with a Greek actor who showed her his portfolio of head shots. She sat in a café with a disheveled Polish painter who told her that American culture was primitive but that he loved the enthusiasm of American women. She disliked the glint in his eye when he pronounced the word *enthusiasm*. She didn't sleep with any of them.

Ani and Michael went to see *The Philadelphia Story* at a cinema near the Odéon. After the movie a chill wind blew bits of newspaper and trash along the boulevard. They went to a nearby café for a hot drink. Then Michael invited her to his place to play backgammon. She had played the game with her grandfather a few times—he called it *tavloo*.

They sat on the bed in Michael's one-room apartment—it was a real apartment, though, with its own bathroom and minuscule kitchen—and he set out the pieces. He beat her twice and then let her win the third time. It was getting late and they both knew she'd miss the last metro if she didn't leave soon. They set up for another round.

Michael executed his next move on the board as he said casually, "You know, you can stay here tonight if you want. There's a new toothbrush in the medicine cabinet."

She went to the bathroom and put in the diaphragm she had impulsively thrown in her bag.

After she slid between the sheets of Michael's bed the sex happened fast, without any conversation. His body was foreign and unfamiliar. She was afraid to look at his face. Now she understood what Elena had meant when she asked if sex was better with Asa or with Will. It had generally been good with both of them, but sex with Michael wasn't good at all. Odd how the mechanics of the thing could be more or less the same, but the sensations so different. Did this mean he was a bad lover or did it mean that they made a dismal combination?

Thankfully, it was over soon enough and she settled her head into the crook of his arm. The mood was companionable despite the stale sex. It occurred to her that he was probably as lonely in this foreign city as she was.

Michael fell asleep and Ani listened to his slow, steady breath. *If two lie together, then they have heat: but how can one be warm alone?* She drifted into sleep feeling calmer than she had in days.

In the morning, Michael insisted on accompanying her home on the metro. He kissed the back of her hand as they sat watching the stations go by. She could barely meet his gaze.

She was worried that she might have ruined their friendship. Companions were hard to come by in Paris. Aside from Michael, Ani had one prospective friend, a woman in her modern dance class. Even though Tacey and Sydney filled her hours, they weren't exactly comrades. Would she still be able to go to the movies with Michael after this?

After Michael left her at her door, she ascended to her silent room. She followed a rectangle of sun as it inched across her bed. She listened to the slow slide of her breath. In its rhythm she heard the echoes of a favorite poem.

You may have all things from me, save my breath,
The slight life in my throat will not give pause
For your love, nor your loss, nor any cause. . . .

Asa Willard had emptied her pocket. He had stripped the walls. He had taken a hacksaw to her leg and amputated it above the ankle. She would hobble around, remembering what it was like to walk on two good feet.

Even at the worst moments with Asa—when she was scared or he was deliberately unkind—she had never been bored.

The previous summer they had hitchhiked across the country to Seattle, stopping in Boulder for a few days, where they had climbed one of the Flatirons. Sure, Ani was afraid of heights and had panicked during the crux move of the climb, but at the end it was worth it. They had feasted under the blue banner of the sky at the top of the world. Hawks had circled around so close that Ani felt as though she could have touched a tail feather. When would she ever do something like that again?

The day after their climb, a friend of Asa's had dropped them off outside the Rio Grande freight train yard in Denver, where they had sneaked past the NO TRESPASSING signs. The sky was overcast and it began to drizzle. Train whistles blew sharp and high over the desolate yard. Ani and Asa pulled rain ponchos from their packs and crouched between the fence and some rusted red boxcars. Nearby a dirty triple-decker was loaded with new American sedans streaked with dust. Tracks stretched into the distance.

Asa whispered, You wait here while I scope out the scene.

He was tense and wired for action, as though they were partisans about to blow up a bridge ahead of an occupying army.

Our mission depends on you, Asa Willard, Ani whispered back.

Crouching low, he trotted into the dark.

Two minutes later a watchman ambled by holding a large flashlight. When he aimed its stark beam on Ani, she had visions of spending the night in the Denver jail.

Where are you headed? he asked, not unkindly.

Salt Lake, Ani replied.

You're not alone here, are you, young lady? the watchman asked with concern.

My boyfriend's looking for the next train out, she explained.

The man gestured to a line of cars several tracks over. That'll be the jackrabbit to Salt Lake. He nodded at Ani and went back to his rounds.

When Asa returned he said, Damn. I have no idea which train we should take.

Ani pointed. That one over there is the jackrabbit to Salt Lake.

How do you know that? he asked skeptically.

The bull told me.

Ani and Asa crept alongside the train until they located an open boxcar door and clambered in. The yard lights cast a parallelogram of brightness on the grimy wooden floor. They found several large sheets of heavy cardboard and pulled them to one end of the car. As they were settling into their corner two figures climbed in.

Hello, people, said a tall lean man. He was wearing soiled jeans and a denim work shirt rolled to the elbows. Don't mind if we share the accommodations, do you?

No problem at all, Asa responded. He stood and pulled Ani to her feet.

This here is Ray, the taller one said, pointing to his short sidekick, and I'm Wiley. Ray bobbed his head while Wiley extended his hand.

Asa shook Wiley's hand. I'm Asa. This is Ani.

Wiley's face cracked into a smile that cried out for a dentist. I haven't seen a girl riding the rails in a good long time.

As the train rattled out of the yard, the men set up in the opposite end of the car while Asa and Ani retreated to theirs. The train picked up speed, dashing along the tracks.

Ani whispered, Did you catch the naked woman tattooed on Wiley's arm? I think there's something the matter with the short one. He looks like an ax murderer.

Will you please calm down? Asa whispered back.

Great. We're in a boxcar with a couple of deranged derelicts and he tells me to calm down. What are you, some kind of *dahngahlakh*?

Asa said, I'm not going to let anything happen to you.

Thanks, Superman, Ani said.

Ani drew her knees up and closed her eyes. She pretended to relax, but actually she was envisioning Asa wrestling Wiley to the floor while Ray chased her around with a knife.

After a while, Asa and Ani moved to the boxcar door and saw a tunnel through the mountains looming ahead.

A lineman standing near the track waved frantically and shouted at them, Get inside! Cover your faces!

As they entered the tunnel, Asa and Ani lay on the floor with sweaters over their noses and mouths. Wiley and Ray pulled their shirts over their faces as well. It seemed like a long time that they were hurtling through the dark with thick, acrid air around them.

Asa drew her close with his free arm. Ani lay in his embrace, sure that their dead bodies would be discovered in the car when it arrived in Salt Lake. Her mother had begged Ani to take the bus. She claimed she wouldn't get a wink of sleep until Ani called from Seattle. Her family would weep over Ani's open casket. The Kersamians would forever curse the name of Asa Willard for leading Ani to an early demise. That ruled out joint burial in the family plot in the Ridgelawn Cemetery.

Finally, light and clean air flowed into the boxcar.

The four of them moved to the doorframe, where the clustered lights of small mountain towns passed by. Soon there were only isolated houses and then they were in the craggy wilds of the Colorado Rockies. The moon cast a creamy carpet of light over the angular peaks.

Wiley said, Me and Ray broke out of a work camp near Lubbock a few days ago.

What were you in for? Asa asked.

Picked up for vagrancy. Sent us out to the farm. Barbed wire all around. The foreman had a whip and kept at us from dawn till dusk.

To Ani it sounded like something out of a fifties chain-gang movie.

I didn't think that kind of thing was legal anymore, Ani said to Wiley.

Wiley laughed. Honey, you wouldn't believe the things that are legal in Texas.

Asa and Ani unfurled their sleeping bags on top of the cardboard and crawled into them for the night. It felt as though she had barely dozed when Ani was shaken awake by a length of bad track. As the car rattled from side to side her head scrubbed back and forth over the cardboard until her hair was matted in the back. Asa somehow slept through the lurching. Ani sat cross-legged by the door watching the sunrise. The red cliffs and mesas of Utah spread spectacularly for miles.

The train slowed as it entered the Salt Lake yard. First Asa tossed their packs out and then Ani jumped out after them. Asa was at her heels seconds later, with Wiley and Ray behind. They all shook hands farewell at the yard's entrance.

Ani's stomach was pinched with hunger. Down the road she and Asa found a pancake restaurant. It was Sunday morning and the restaurant was filled with well-groomed Mormon families breakfasting before church. Ani noticed that the family in the adjacent booth was inspecting them as though fearful of contagion. She imagined herself from their perspective: wild black hair, wrinkled flannel shirt, soiled parachute pants, and sneakers.

Sorry pair of sinners, we are, Ani whispered to Asa. But she was happy.

Missing Asa swept over her like an illness. Ani skipped class several days in a row and took long naps. Her dreams were long and complicated with casts of thousands. The boy who sat behind her in first grade—the one with the jug ears and the sloppy smile—was made to sit in the wastepaper basket by the teacher yet again. Dana Grimaldi chased Lucy Sevanian around the school parking lot while Ani stood on the hood of a car shouting for help. Then Ani was in a house by the shore looking for Asa. Curtains fluttered in the windows and sunlight streamed in silver white. Ani heard the sound of Asa and May's laughter coming from a bedroom down the hall.

When Ani arrived in the dance studio's dressing room, her new friend Odile was sitting on the bench pulling on her leg warmers. Ani unbuttoned the wool coat under which she was wearing dance clothes and a sweater.

Odile gasped. *"Tu n'as pas honte, toi?"*

"Shame about what?" Ani asked her.

"Of walking around dressed like that. What if someone should see beneath your coat?"

"Nobody's going to see anything," Ani told her. "Besides, I have no shame. I'm American."

Odile laughed, showing small white teeth. She had a graceful neck and porcelain skin. Her fawn-colored hair was upswept in a loose bun.

Ani and Odile sat on the floor in the middle of the classroom with their legs in first position. To the left, to the right, to the center. And once again. A sea of arms moved in unison and legs scissored closed with a swish over the wooden floor. At a flick of the teacher's palm, Ani folded down, resting her face on her knees.

She was six years old, climbing a narrow staircase with a black patent-leather bag banging against her leg. The changing room was aflutter with girls and their mothers, clothes strewn on benches along the wall. At home after the first class, Violet and Grandma quarreled in Armenian over Ani's head, but she understood what they were saying.

Amot. Shame, said Mariam Kersamian.

I'm not going to talk about it with you anymore, Violet replied.

My granddaughter is walking around before everyone with no clothes on.

I'm not listening. Violet walked out of the room.

The body is God's temple! Grandma called after her.

Sitting on the back porch, Violet sewed silver sequins onto the edge of Ani's tutu. Ani and Baba spread newspaper on the driveway and spray-painted the tap shoes silver. Grandma watched these preparations grimly without a word.

The day before the recital Ani modeled the whole outfit, including a silver tiara. She pirouetted around the living room, where Baba, Grandma, and Violet were sitting. Ani tied on her tap shoes and moved to a spot of bare floorboard between two carpets to make a series of clattering taps.

Grandma muttered loudly, Amot.

Baba said, Those shoes sure make a racket.

Amot. Amot kezi, Grandma said, a little louder.

Violet demanded, What is shameful about it? Would you tell me?

You let you daughter on stage in naked legs with his vorik hanging out? Grandma spoke in English so Ani wouldn't miss her meaning.

Violet heaved a sigh. Ma, she's six years old. All the girls are dressed like this.

How should child have no shame unless mother teach him? Mariam Kersamian asked darkly.

Ani puzzled over her grandmother's sentence. What was the mother supposed to be teaching? That the child should have shame or have no shame? Was Ani's bottom really hanging out of her costume? Ani suddenly felt like her torso was made of big, yeasty dough rising from the leotard in all directions.

She didn't take another dance class until she was in college. The first day of the term she had arrived twenty minutes early to the makeshift dance studio on the stage of the old assembly hall. Stripping to her leotard and tights, she stood in front of the mirrors.

Amot. Amot kezi. She shook her head, but failed to dislodge the whispering voice from her ears. *Anamot.* Shameless.

In the dressing room after class, Ani told her friend, "Don't worry, Odile, I'm going to change out of this leotard. It's soaked."

Odile asked, "You have time for a coffee?"

Seated in the café, Odile talked quickly while her thin hands were as stately as swans. Her family would spend the upcoming holidays at their farmhouse in the country. She would be out of town for ten days. She and her boyfriend Pierre were throwing a party—*un boum,* she called it—at their apartment on New Year's Eve. She hoped Ani would come. What was Ani doing for Christmas?

The Bartons had left for Connecticut that morning so Ani would be alone in the palace for two weeks. Christmas dinner would be brown rice and a chocolate bar. Ani cast around for a story.

"My friend Michael and I are going to Bretagne for a few days," she lied.

Since the backgammon night, Ani had avoided Michael. She had even gone so far as to unplug the telephone. The day after her conversation with Odile, she arrived late to Sondage's seminar. Michael, who was at the other side of the room, tried to catch her attention. Ani tucked her chin and scrutinized her notebook. After class he chased down the hall behind her.

"Come drink a coffee with me," he said, piloting her by the elbow. "I'm taking the train to Munich in the morning. You want to go to the cinema tonight?"

"I can't. I have to baby-sit." She looked pointedly at her watch. "I've got to run or I'll be late."

"As you wish." He gave her the Parisian *quatre bises.* "But we should talk after the holidays. I'll telephone when I get back."

Ani sat on the metro glancing at the people around her, their faces very French and inexplicably sad. Everyone seemed to be on

No

Nancy Kricorian

the verge of tears. She put her head against the window and peered out at the dark tunnel.

During her final term in the college dorm a basketball player who lived in a single in the basement had died in his room. He had returned drunk late one night and thrown up, choking on his own vomit. After about four days, when the smell had begun to seep up the stairwells of the dorm—Ani had noticed it in the hall—a janitor had traced the odor to the guy's room. His name was Bob. He was a friend of a friend, and Ani had once eaten lunch with him in the dining hall. She found it strange how people's lives might intersect at one point and then, like billiard balls, bounce off each other and go in different directions. Bob had dropped into God's side pocket.

It was while she was living in that dorm—not long after Bob's death—that Ani and Asa had started going out. About a month into their relationship they had hitchhiked to Cambridge for the weekend. It was the first time she had met his parents. Peggy Willard, a thin fair woman with long copper hair tied back with a blue velvet ribbon, smiled brightly at Ani and warmly shook her hand. Ben Willard was tall and sallow with a handsome lined face. The four of them sat at a long oak table in a formal dining room with oak wainscoting and salmon-colored walls. Asa and Peggy did most of the talking. There were long quiet pauses during the meal that Ani didn't dare fill with chatter. She observed Ben Willard refilling his glass with wine until the bottle was empty. He went to the pantry to get another.

Asa tells me you're from Watertown, Ani, said Peggy. You're Armenian?

My mother's Armenian.

Ben returned to the dining room. You know what George Orwell says about Armenians, son? he asked, winking at Asa.

Ani's breath halted in her throat for a few seconds while she waited for Ben to drop the blade.

Don't trust them. They're worse than Jews or Greeks. Ben Willard smiled.

Asa colored deeply. Dad, what kind of thing is that to say?

Ben, that's not very nice. Peggy's voice was edged with false cheer.

Can't anyone around here take a joke? Ben asked darkly.

In the library's stacks Ani had scoured Orwell for the line and found it: *Trust a snake before a Jew and a Jew before a Greek, but don't trust an Armenian.*

She wrote the phrase in the small notebook of quotations she carried with her. But even before she copied it down she had committed it to memory.

As she passed the gilt café on the place Colette, Ani noticed couples leaning over small white cups. Long shadows striped the garden. Ani's heels struck the cold stone arcades and then hushed across the runner in the hall. In the attic she swiftly turned the key in the lock, switched on a lamp, and opened a book. The room was silent but for the clock. Ani felt condemned by its small judgments.

Christmas Eve was a lost day. Ani stayed in her nightgown until late afternoon, when she threw on some clothes and headed across the river. In an austere macrobiotic restaurant not far from the university she treated herself to a meal of brown rice and vegetables. The only condiments were toasted sesame seeds and tamari. It was early, she was the sole customer, and the bald waiter gazed at her sternly as she chewed. She felt like a loser.

The art of losing isn't hard to master.

Christmas alone in Paris isn't any disaster.

An unlucky star.

Baba said, *The star of some is bright, of others blind.*

Ani had harbored the idea that when she left for college she could make herself into a new person. The house on Spruce Street with its fractured English and coupons clipped from the newspaper was far away. No one would know anything about her past except what she related. She didn't have to mention that she was on financial aid. And in her freshman term she was lucky to be assigned to the hidden dish room in the dining hall where none of the other students—except other charity cases like herself and Elena—would see her in the beige polyester work shirt scraping garbage into the pit.

At the end of her first shift, Ani stopped into the basement lavatory near the gray locker room. As she sat in the stall two local women who worked the cafeteria food line entered the room. Ani caught a glimpse of them through the door crack.

Those goddamned stuck-up kids with their wiseass cracks, one said.

If I didn't need the money, the other one responded, I would have fucking spit in that shit's eye.

Ani slowly unwound toilet paper from the roll.

They're looking for chambermaids at the Inn, the first offered.

Same fucking pricks there, just thirty years older, the second quipped.

Ani flushed the toilet and unlocked the stall. She kept her head down and strode out of the room, hearing their chuckles behind her.

With money she had saved up from her summer job, Ani went shopping on Main Street near the campus. She bought a fine-gauge red cardigan with gold buttons and a pair of wide-wale corduroy pants. Her mother would have gasped at the price tags, but Ani hardened herself against guilt. Next she stopped at the shoe store for a pair of clogs and rag wool socks.

Ani wore this outfit on a date with a junior from a suburb of New York City. Steve Hecht was surprised she had never heard of Scarsdale, where his family belonged to the country club. When she mentioned that she lived near Boston, he suggested Newton and she didn't argue. It didn't work out with Steve. He stopped calling when she wouldn't have sex with him after the third date.

Asa had disliked the corduroys and the yoked sweaters. Once he asked her, Why are you pretending to be somebody you're not? He preferred the peasant blouse and a red flowered Afghan skirt: bohemian chic. He also liked her in flannel and jeans: woods woman. It turned out, though, that changing identity wasn't as easy as changing costume.

The word for destiny in Armenian is *jagadakir:* what is written on your forehead. God inscribed your fate on your brow in vanishing ink while you were yet in your mother's womb. You cannot erase what is written on your forehead.

Not only had she now lost Asa, but also gone was the life he would have given her. She would never have a refrigerator that dispensed ice cubes. She would never drive a silver Volvo station wagon. Soon she'd be living on Spruce Street, using the bus to commute to the dull job she would need to pay back her student loans. But for now, she was in exile. Ani felt faceless and almost invisible, as though the filaments attaching her to the surface of the world had torn loose. She was a kind of ghostly balloon bobbing through a translated sky.

Ani pushed the plate of tasteless food aside and opened her bilingual copy of Rimbaud's poems. She had purloined it from the campus bookstore during her final week as an undergraduate.

Je suis au plus profond de l'abîme, et je ne sais plus prier.

Rimbaud had renounced his faith when he was young. His life and his writings were about transgression. But he had been a sinner who finally repented on his deathbed, calling for a priest. Will there come an hour when you pray for forgiveness, Ani Silver, or will you die an outlaw?

A light snow was falling as Ani emerged from the restaurant. She drew a paisley wool shawl—a Christmas gift from Tacey Barton—over her head. People hustled by carrying baguettes and bright shopping bags. Ani turned off the boulevard onto a side street, walking without a destination.

On the other side of the street she saw a bookstore with a buttery light spilling out its windows. The sign across the storefront said LIBRAIRIE SAMUELIAN: an Armenian name. Crammed shelves spanned from floor to ceiling, and there were several customers with their heads bent over display tables. Ani had stepped off the curb toward the store when a dark-haired man strode out of its front door and hurried down the sidewalk.

His head was down and his shoulders were hunched against the cold. He wore a dungaree jacket over a bulky cable sweater, jeans, and running shoes. His gait reminded her of someone familiar, but who? She was always seeing people who reminded her of far-off friends. Only a few days before, she was certain she had seen Elena in a passage of the metro. But even as she hurried to overtake the woman Ani knew that the face would be a stranger's.

Was it loneliness that conjured up resemblance? Who was this man a stand-in for?

Suddenly she smelled the waxy smoke of blown-out candles, tasted pink sugar roses, and heard the laughter of children.

"Van!" she called.

When he paused and glanced back, Ani could almost make out his features. He didn't see her in the dusk and continued on his way.

"Wait," she called, as she ran after him. "Van. It's me. Ani Silver."

He turned. "Ani?"

They stood under a streetlamp, the falling snow dissolving on the pavement at their feet. He was shorter and darker than Ani remembered. His shiny ebony hair was cut close to his head and he no longer had sideburns. She studied the black eyes under jet brows and the strong, straight nose. His jaw was shadowed by a day's growth of beard. He looked like a man now, serious and grown.

"What are you doing here, Van Ardavanian?" Ani asked.

"Me? I was looking for a book. What are you doing here, Ani?" His broad smile had a warmth that came from the depth of his eyes.

Éblouissant, thought Ani. Dazzling. On a dark December night his smile is like the sun.

They went to an old-fashioned café with a gleaming mahogany bar and lace curtains in the windows. Ani hadn't seen Van since high school, and now they were sitting at a corner table in a Paris café.

Ani said, "Last thing I heard was that you went to Beirut after you graduated. Your grandmother wasn't thrilled about that."

Van shrugged. "Nobody's grandmother would be happy."

"What were you doing?"

"Working for a relief agency. Armenian Refugee Aid Association: ARAA."

"What are you doing here?"

"Same thing. ARAA has a Paris office. It's been around since World War One. First they helped Genocide survivors. Now it's Lebanon and Syria. But what about you, Ani? What have you been up to?"

"Nothing so noble. I got a BA. Hopped a freight train. Climbed a mountain. I'm studying literature at the university."

"What are you doing for Christmas?" he asked.

"My boyfriend—ex-boyfriend—was supposed to be here, but that fell through. So I'm on my own."

"Too bad," Van said, shaking his head with a sympathetic frown that turned into a wry smile. "I've got no plans either."

On Christmas morning in the Bartons' kitchen Ani tied an apron over her skirt. By the time the buzzer rang at minutes after one, the fish was in the broiler and the rice pilaf was steaming in its pot.

Van followed her through the grand apartment. She had assumed he would be impressed, but his brows moved closer together and she sensed his disapproval.

"This place is huge," he said. "What's that garden?"

"Palais-Royal garden," Ani told him.

"You live in a palace?" he asked incredulously.

"I live in a *chambre de bonne* that comes with the apartment. The Bartons live here."

"How do they pay for this?"

"He works for some bank. It's a company apartment."

"A French bank?"

"No, a big multinational. They were in the Philippines before Paris, and before that in South America." Ani didn't mention Tacey Barton's nostalgia for Manila, where she had been able to afford a full-time staff of six. And they were happy servants. Apparently the dollar didn't go as far in France. Beatrice, the current part-time housekeeper, was neither cheerful nor servile enough to suit Tacey.

"Roving predators," Van said bitterly. "They get their wealth from exploiting Third World countries."

Ani was surprised by his harshness. The Bartons weren't Ani's people, but she hadn't thought of them as evil.

She looked around the room, trying to see it through Van's lens. On the gleaming twelve-foot table where Ani had set two places with the Bartons' ornate silver and china, the crystal wineglasses glittered with menace.

Still, she couldn't view either Tacey or Sydney as a roving predator. They were consumers. Tacey was a professional shopper and Sydney was a shopper in training. Ani had gone with them once to the avenue Victor Hugo, where the minks and sables outnumbered the little dogs shivering in their sweaters. In an elegant boutique Tacey had opened her leather wallet and dropped a fan of francs on the counter.

Tacey's money came from her husband, and her husband's money came from his work at the bank, and the bank's money came from extracting wealth from poor countries. Or at least that's what Van had just said. Ani had no idea what banking entailed and had little interest in the subject. What exactly did Le Con do all day at his office? Ani avoided him as much as possible, but when he passed through the apartment he left behind an ill will that almost smelled.

Van asked, "What's it like being a servant to the ruling class?"

"I'm not a servant. I'm an au pair."

"Seems like a question of semantics to me."

"Maybe it's just an attitude. I couldn't afford to be here if I didn't have this job. The kid's kind of sweet."

"This room gives me the creeps," Van said.

"Okay," Ani said. "We can eat in the kitchen if the décor bothers you that much."

"It's not a question of aesthetics, Ani."

"I know, I know. It's a question of ethics."

They set the everyday dishes on the table in the long narrow kitchen. The room was large by Parisian standards, but it was the smallest in the apartment. Ani opened a bottle she had filched from the Bartons' wine cellar. As she went to pour some into Van's glass he covered it with his hand.

"Not even a little wine on Christmas day?" she asked.

He shook his head. "Since when do you drink?"

She shrugged. "A glass of wine on a festive occasion seems okay to me. What are you, a teetotaler like my grandparents?"

"All right," he said. "I won't be dogmatic. Give me a splash so we can make a toast to old friends."

"I thought we were cousins," Ani said.

He raised his glass. "Friends, cousins, compatriots."

Ani had once asked her grandmother how she and Van were related.

Grandma had answered in Armenian. His grandmother Sophie is Sourpouhi Nahabedian. My family name was Nahabedian. Sourpig's husband's father and my father were first cousins.

The blood tie was remote. It occurred to Ani that only an Armenian would think of Van as her cousin.

This conversation had taken place in the Ardavanians' crowded living room. It had been Van's high school graduation party. Ani roosted next to her grandmother on the couch while Baba sat in a corner with Van's grandfather, Vahram. The two old men leaned their heads together like conspirators.

In the car on the way home Baba said fondly of Vahram Ardavanian, That guy is a hard-boiled egg. Still a Hunchak.

What's a Hunchak? Ani had asked.

Baba said, There are three main Armenian political parties: Dashnak, Hunchak, and Ramgavar. The Hunchaks are Communists. The Dashnaks go to Saint Stephen's Church and the Ramgavars go to Saint James.

Ani asked, Where do the Hunchaks go?

Straight to hell, Baba said.

When he had stopped chuckling at his own joke, Baba continued. Van's family goes to the First Armenian Church. They're *poghokagan,* but not so Protestant as your grandmother.

What are we? Ani queried.

Chezokh, he replied.

What's that?

I vote Democrat and your grandmother votes Party of God.

Grandma had swatted at him with her handbag. God's listening to you, Mr. Smart Pants, she had said.

"You want some tea?" Ani asked, beginning to clear the plates from the table.

"Sure," Van replied.

As Ani filled the teakettle from the tap, Van asked, "So who was the boyfriend?"

"Asa Willard: mountaineer and pothead. He dumped me for someone more exotic."

"Sounds bad," Van said.

"Yeah, well. In upbeat moments I comfort myself with the fact that I'll never have to listen to the Grateful Dead again."

Van laughed.

"You have a girlfriend?" Ani asked. She wanted him to say no.

"Had one in Beirut. Maro. She died about a year ago." Elbow on the table, he put his chin in his hand and frowned at the floor tiles.

Ani envisioned an Armenian girl with long raven hair lying in the road as a dented black car sped away. Blood pooled on the pavement as people crowded around her lifeless body. That was how Ani's father had died. But this girl Maro, whom Van had loved, had her own story.

Into Van's long silence Ani cast the question. "How did she die?"

"Sniper. She was standing by the window in her parents' apartment. A bullet through the head."

Ani blocked this image from her mind's eye. She didn't want to see it.

"I'm sorry," she said, regretting the pale blandness of her remark.

"She died for nothing," Van said bitterly, placing emphasis on the final word.

Nothing, Ani repeated silently.

"There are things you would die for?" she asked.

His eyes met hers like a shot. "Yes. What about you?"

She looked away from his fierce gaze. "I don't know."

During Ani's freshman year, her European history professor had asked each student in the discussion section whether he—there were only two girls in the group—would have gone to the barricades during the French revolution of 1848. Ani, who had been called on first, had said no. She was suffering from mono at the time so the idea of walking up the block was overwhelming, let alone heaving paving stones at firing loyalist troops. Much to her chagrin, everyone else in the class had earnestly answered yes. Ani looked around and was unable to imagine the white boys at the table joining any kind of insurrection other than a cafeteria food fight.

"You want some more tea?" Ani asked.

"No, thanks," Van said, glancing at his watch. "I've got to head out. I'm staying at a friend's place in Ivry until I find something in town."

As Van was leaving, there was an awkward moment at the door. Should they shake hands? Should they exchange *quatre bises*? Should they hug? Ani couldn't decide what gesture was appropriate and Van wasn't helping. He seemed to have curled in on himself like one of those potato bugs that Ani used to find under the marble stepping-stones in the back garden. She wrote her phone number on a scrap of paper, and he said something vague about getting in touch after he had settled in.

Ani went to her empty room. She missed her family. At home her mother was probably gathering up the shredded wrapping paper while her grandfather leaned back in the armchair digesting his meal. Grandma would be at the kitchen sink, her yellow rubber gloves plunging through the soap bubbles while she hummed "Amazing Grace." Ani dialed the number on her orange telephone. There was no answer in the downstairs apartment so she called Auntie Alice and Uncle Paul's place.

When Auntie Alice answered, the receiver was handed all around. Ani's cousin Mike and his wife had produced the first great-grandchild, whose wail could be made out in the background. Grandma couldn't hear anything so Ani had to shout into the phone. Her mother sounded distracted, but Ani couldn't tell if it was just the long-distance connection and the din in the apartment. Every member of the family wished Ani a merry Christmas and asked about the weather in Paris. Overcast and seasonably cold with light flurries.

She forgot to mention Van.

An old Judy Garland record was playing on the stereo when Ani arrived at the party. Odile, dressed in a vintage black gabardine suit, dragged Ani through the crowded front room toward her boyfriend, Pierre.

"Finally we meet," Pierre said. "Odile has been telling me about you."

"I hope she's been saying nice things," Ani said.

"Of course, only magnificent things," Odile said.

After Pierre went to change the record and Odile drifted off to attend to other guests, Ani searched the front room for familiar faces. For a moment she was sure she would spend the next hour haunting the edges of the party, eating finger food and sizing up the other misfits who were nervously moving around the perimeter of the room. With relief she spotted a cluster of Sondage groupies near the window. One of the women recognized Ani and waved for her to join them. Ani gave silent thanks as their conversation eddied around her.

After a while she dropped onto the couch to duck the haze of smoke. A narrow-faced guy with wire-rimmed glasses settled beside her, his wineglass in hand.

"*Un boum comme ça, c'est épuisant, quand même.*" He sighed, running his fingers through dark curly hair.

Ani answered in French. "Totally."

"But you're from Toulouse?" he asked.

"Toulouse? Why do you think that?"

"The accent, of course."

"Thanks for the kindness. I'm American."

"What's your name?"

"Ani Silver."

"I am Jacques Stein." He shook Ani's hand. "With a name like
Silver I suppose you're Jewish, which explains why you don't look
American."

"I'm half Jewish, half Armenian."

"Do you feel twice blessed or doubly cursed?" he asked.

Ani said, "I feel American."

He gave a curt nod. "It's certainly simpler that way."

This sounded vaguely dismissive to Ani. "Is that bad?"

He shrugged and grimaced, simultaneously tipping his head
to one side and turning a palm up. "You're fortunate you have
the choice."

"And you don't?"

"Can one forget who one is for an hour with a name like Stein
in a country like this? Open your eyes, Mademoiselle Silver." He
drank deeply from his glass.

After a pause he said, "You will excuse me. I'm tired and must
go home before I get into an even blacker humor. It was a pleasure to have met you."

Ani watched him retreat across the room and make his apolo-
gies to Odile at the door.

Open your eyes, Ani Silver. It felt like a biblical injunction. Ani
thought of the black leather Bible she had been given by her Sunday school teacher. The Bible had provoked a fight between her
mother and grandmother about Armenian school.

Most of the Armenian kids that Ani knew attended Armenian
school part-time. Lucy Sevanian went to Saint James Church on
Monday and Wednesday afternoons. Van Ardavanian attended
Saturday school. Grandma pleaded with Ani, but when the girl
saw the hard look on her mother's face, she said no.

Why should she go, Ma? Why? Violet asked. What does she
need it for?

Because it's her language, Grandma said in Armenian.

Her language is English, Violet replied. She's American.

She's Armenian, Mariam responded in Armenian.

She's half Armenian, half.

While they argued over her head, Ani imagined a black dotted line drawn down the middle of her face that ran down her torso. Her right arm and right leg were on the Armenian side. Grandma had her right arm, Mom had the left arm, and they were jerking her back and forth across the boundary between Armenia and America.

You don't care, Grandma scolded in English. You don't teach you daughter nothing. You vent to New York to smoke cigarettes vith beatnuts—

Beatniks, Ma, beatniks. And I wasn't hanging around with beatniks. I was in college.

Grandma said bitterly, You drop out college to marry that *herya.*

Ani's mother went pale. He's dead. Isn't that enough for you? she yelled. She ran to her bedroom and slammed the door.

Grandma sank into her armchair and put her face in her hands. *Bidi mernim, bidi mernim,* she moaned. I'm dying.

Ani didn't think her grandmother was dying; at least it didn't appear that way. She stood wondering whether to pat her grandmother's back or to search out her mother, paralyzed by the fear that both of them hated her. She was, after all, the source of the trouble. At that moment Ani was relieved to hear Baba entering the front door.

What's all the yelling? Baba asked. I could hear you down the block.

Without a word, Grandma went to her bedroom and slammed the door.

They got into a big fight, Ani explained. Baba, what does *herya* mean?

He looked at the girl knowingly. Your grandmother's tongue is a razor, eh? *Herya* means Jew, honey.

What's a Jew? Ani asked.

The Jews are God's chosen people. Like the Armenians, they were chosen for a lot of suffering.

Are they Christians?

They have their own religion.

Do they believe in Jesus?

He sighed. Not in the way you mean, *yavrum*. But Jesus was a Jew. Listen, why don't you go out in the yard and play for a while.

On the swing, Ani pumped harder and harder until one side of the swing set lifted from the ground at the top of each arc. Silver must be a Jewish name, she thought. Her grandmother referred to non-Armenians by nationality: the O'Malleys were known simply as "the Irish," the Narbonis were "the Italians," and the Pappases were "the Greeks." Grandma rarely pronounced a surname, unless it was Topalian, Hagopian, or Bardazbanian.

At school, even though the kids never talked about it, everyone knew who belonged to which ethnic group. In school and at recess, kids could play with anyone, but after-school socializing was often organized along national lines. Ani was counted as an Armenian.

Ani slowed her swing. Was she American or Armenian? But now there was an added quandary: the left side of her body was American *and* Jewish. Would Jesus have to squeeze into the right side of her small heart? What about Ani's father, the *herya*? Were there different sections in heaven for Jews and Christians? Did Jews go to heaven?

In her grandmother's bedroom behind the armchair hung a bright picture of Jesus knocking at a heavy wooden door framed by ivy, and under the picture, in Gothic script, were printed the words:

Behold, I stand at the door, and knock: if any man hear my voice, and open the door, I will come in to him, and will sup with him, and he with me. Rev. 3:20

Whenever Ani had looked at this picture she envisioned her father standing on the other side of the door, about to open it for Jesus. Her father's face as he was in life had faded from memory, so the black-and-white photo Ani kept on the shelf in her room was the father she imagined. It was this monochrome David Silver, with black hair, gray eyes, and a fixed smile, who greeted God's son.

Pastor Duke's wife was Ani's Sunday school teacher. Mrs. Duke, a pretty, bird-thin woman with prematurely white hair, told the kids about her conversion.

One night, when I was nine years old, children, I was lying in my bed praying for forgiveness and asking Jesus to enter my heart when I heard Jesus' voice. He said, Rebecca, I will wash away your sins, and I will never forsake you. The next morning, children, when I opened my eyes, the world was changed by my love for Jesus and His love for me. Outside my window the grass was greener, the flowers brighter, and the birdsong sweeter. This happiness can be yours, children. God loves you and wants you at His side.

The pastor's wife instructed them to bow their heads and ask Jesus into their hearts. Ani imagined her heart was a fist and she had to loosen the fingers so Jesus, as small as a slip of soap, could take up residence. She made a chapel with her hands and squeezed her eyes closed to silently issue the invitation.

Ani stopped breathing for a moment to listen for Jesus' answer but she didn't hear anything except for Charles Hairabedian, who was sitting next to her, cracking his knuckles. She looked around, hoping that the basement Sunday school would be gleaming with Christ's light, but it appeared just the same. The blackboard partitions around them were covered with chalk dust. The graying dropped ceiling had yellow watermarks on it from when the pipes had leaked.

Ani glanced around the crowded Parisian apartment. One minute that dusky childhood was around her like a cloak and the next she was transported back to the present. Here she was in France,

Dreams of Bread and Fire

thousands of miles away from anything she could call home. She saw herself from above, a tiny speck on the face of the planet.

Odile alighted on the couch next to Ani. "I hope Jacques didn't bother you."

"He says he can never forget for one minute who he is in this country," Ani reported.

"Oh, he's a paranoiac like most Jews. But when he isn't grumbling he can be quite droll," Odile replied.

Ani lifted her eyebrows slightly. Obviously, Odile thought of Ani as an American.

"Here," Odile said, pushing a plastic champagne flute into Ani's hand. "It's only minutes until the New Year."

87

"In Connecticut we had Pop-Tarts for breakfast." Sydney wrinkled her nose. "Lots of frozen dinners and SpaghettiOs."

"Your dad was eating SpaghettiOs?" Ani asked. She slid a stack of pancakes onto Sydney's plate.

"They went out for dinner. Kyle and I ate food that wasn't fit for no dog."

Ani said, "I missed you too, Syd."

"What did you do for Christmas?" Sydney asked.

"An old friend came by. You want a cheese sandwich or peanut butter and jelly for lunch?"

"Cheese. Boy or girl?"

"I've known him since I was five."

"A boyfriend?"

"No."

"Mommy said to be nice because your boyfriend dumped you. You should send him a stink bomb. Kyle showed me how. We have all the ingredients."

"I'm not into revenge, Syd."

A stink bomb didn't seem like a bad idea to Ani, although her own fantasies ran toward letter bombs. It made her sick, thinking about Asa's exciting post-Ani life. Only that morning she had dreamed that Asa had insisted on showing her photos of him and May on the beach. He was red-eyed stoned. She woke feeling like a dishrag that had been laundered until it was threadbare.

At least with Sydney and Tacey back Ani had a reason for getting up in the morning. Then seminars at Jussieu resumed, and dance classes provided more distraction. Odile and Ani were choreographing a piece that came out of their improvisation sessions. One afternoon Ani met Michael at the Pompidou Center to watch four hours of ethnographic films. She fabricated an excuse for why she couldn't go to his place to play backgammon.

When Ani had given up hope of hearing from him, Van finally called. They made plans to go to the movies later in the week. Ani selected an old comedy and they met outside the cinema. In the darkened theater clear black-and-white frames rolled over the screen, dialogue played out crisp as newly minted bills, and Ani laughed until tears slid down her face. She was still smiling when they emerged onto the street.

"That was entertaining," Van said.

"I've seen that movie at least five times on TV."

"You were laughing before the lines were out of their mouths."

"I know some of the dialogue by heart."

They strolled through throngs of tourists on the place Saint-Michel and headed across the river. After passing beneath the massive blackened walls of the Palais de Justice, which gleamed under stark floodlights, they paused on the Pont au Change to survey the facade of Nôtre-Dame.

An image flew like a bat across the back of Ani's skull: a torn gap in the chain-link fence at the edge of the country club.

Watertown. Ani was sitting on a flat stone under a tree, having spent all her tears. She had fled the house after a fight with her mother. She squeezed her eyes shut and rested her cheek on her knees. When she heard footfalls approaching she lifted her head.

Van had said, Ani? Is that you?

What are you doing here, Van?

I come up here a lot. That rock you're on is my thinking spot. And then I line these up and knock them off with stones. He scooped up a half dozen empty beer bottles and cans, nimbly arranging them at the foot of the fence. With a precise hand, he hurled a stone at the first bottle, shattering its neck. You want to try?

Ani lobbed a rock, missing a can by about a foot.

He handed her another stone. Look at it and aim for it.

Have you heard about my mother? Ani asked. She pegged the can.

Good job. . . . What about her? He pitched rocks in quick succession, knocking down the row.

She's going out with a guy named Harry Vosdanian. His wife's running around town weeping and calling my mother a whore.

Van grimaced. That's too bad.

It sucks. Ani sat down on the flat stone.

He sat beside her. Must have been hard on her, coming back to Watertown after your father died.

Her grown-up life disappeared and she was in her parents' house again, Ani said. Now she's acting like a teenager. I'm the one who's supposed to be running around with the boyfriend that everyone despises.

They sat in silence, listening to the wind in the trees and the occasional passing car.

Ani replayed the scene from earlier that morning when she had entered the kitchen. Her bleary-eyed mother, hair crushed on one side and billowing wildly on the other, was sitting at the table in her housecoat nursing a cup of coffee. Baba hid behind his newspaper. Grandma noisily stirred her coffee while spying Violet out of the sides of her eyes.

Mariam Kersamian's face was like the time and weather display that hung in front of the bank in Coolidge Square: 8:50 A.M., 48°F, CLOUDY WITH CHANCE OF THUNDERSTORMS.

As Ani sat down with her breakfast cereal she felt the air pressure plummet.

Grandma said accusingly to her daughter, You out late last night.

Don't start, Ma, Violet protested wearily. I have a headache.

You have hang-in? the old woman asked with contempt.

A hangover, Violet corrected.

Ahnbeedahn. Married with tree children she take my daughter and get her drunk.

He, Ma. *He* took your daughter out and got her drunk.

Grandma inhaled sharply. You admit it! Vith a married man.

He's separated, Violet said.

The old woman flipped into Armenian. Separated? He has separated from his senses? Have you also separated from your senses?

Baba carefully folded his paper, rose from his chair, and headed out of the room.

Where are you going, coward? Grandma shouted after him. Tell your daughter what you think about this squash head she brought to our house last night.

From the dining room Baba called, I'm not jumping into your cooking pot.

Violet pressed her temples with her hands. Ma, don't.

Amot kezi. Aren't you ashamed? Do you know what people will say? Look at your daughter. How can you shame her?

Hold on, there. Leave me out of this, Ani said.

She fled the kitchen and went down the basement stairs. She put a pillow over her head so the bickering was unintelligible.

In the late afternoon, Violet called Ani into her room. She patted her bed, indicating that Ani should sit next to her.

So, what did you think of him? Violet asked almost shyly.

Who? Ani asked.

You know good and well who, Ani.

Ani didn't respond, but thought, You mean that fat rich guy with the mouth like a split cherry and the tacky white Cadillac?

Violet ignored her daughter's silence. We've known each other for years. I was surprised when he asked me out on a date a few months ago.

Do I need to know this? Ani muttered.

Why are you so mean? It's bad enough that my mother treats me like a criminal. After ten years of living in this convent, I have a boyfriend. What crime is there in that?

Is this supposed to be girl talk? Ani asked deliberately.

Get out! her mother shouted. Just go away!

So Ani stormed out of the house and headed to the golf course, where she had been discovered by Van. He was sitting next to her now on the thinking rock as stars were beginning to appear in the sky beyond the hill. Ani realized her mom would be worrying. Her own anger was spent and she could almost remember having been fond of her mother.

It's getting late, Ani said to Van, looking across the darkening green of the country club.

Van stood and took Ani's hands, pulling her to her feet. For a second they were facing each other, only inches apart. A feather of anticipation brushed along the inside of Ani's skin. Did she want him to kiss her? It was confusing. But then he stepped back and they turned to go.

Leaving the golf course, Ani and Van walked under the broad canopy of summer trees down Bailey Road as the asphalt glittered under the streetlights. Across plush carpets of lawn, they saw the gold glow of table lamps or the stuttering blue glare of televisions from living room windows.

I can't believe you're going to California, Ani said, when they reached the bottom of the hill.

What's the matter with California? he asked.

It's about as far away as you can get without leaving the country.

Leave the country, now there's an idea, he said. I've never been on an airplane.

Me neither, Ani said. So where to?

Moscow, Tokyo, Buenos Aires, Istanbul, Delhi.

How about Paris? Ani asked. That's where I want to go.

Sure, why not? Van had replied.

That was the last conversation between them before he left town. How many years ago was that? Almost six. Now here they were on an old stone bridge in a foreign city as black water flowed beneath them, long streaks of light playing across its surface.

"You hungry?" he asked.

"Ravenous," Ani said.

"Let's go," he said, putting his hand at her elbow. "There's a good couscous place a few blocks from me."

When he dropped his hand to his side Ani still felt the pressure of his fingers on her arm. It was a phantom touch that ached. She glanced over at Van's profile, and her heart fluttered in its box.

This was how it began: a hunger that was indifferent to food and averse to sleep. The feelings frightened her, because they reminded her of the early days with Asa.

The first night she went to Asa's apartment he had cooked supper. After the meal with his housemates, Ani and Asa had retired to his bedroom. There were stacks of paperbacks under the window and several yellow plastic milk crates filled with ropes and climbing gear. Ani and Asa sat across from each other on his mattress on the floor, both of them cross-legged.

Thanks for dinner, she said.

My pleasure, Asa said.

Ani looked into his blue irises patterned with black. She felt a flickering near her ribs and a slight dizziness.

I want to show you something. Put your hand up like this, Asa said, holding his palm facing out at the level of his face.

When Ani imitated his gesture she noticed how perfectly proportioned his hand was—long fingers with a broad palm. The hand looked so gentle and sincere that she couldn't help but trust it.

Now, he instructed, move your hand toward mine. Stop when our palms are about an inch apart.

Ani did as he said. Their palms were parallel.

Now what? she asked.

Close your eyes. Stay like that and see what you feel.

It was as though light with the force of water flowed in the space between their two hands. Ani felt its warmth pulsing against her skin.

Open your eyes, he said. Can you see it?

Ani stared intently at their hands. No.

One time I saw the energy curling like little tendrils of smoke, he told her.

Were you in an altered state? Ani asked.

Tripping my brains out. He laughed, clasped her hand, and leaned toward her.

When they kissed it was black velvet; it was a cleft in the sky.

Wow, he said. Nice.

A confusing set of sensations danced through the nerves in her body.

That's the problem with bodies, Ani said. If you try to say what you feel, the words bounce off sideways. It's like smells. How can you describe a smell? I mean, the smell of white paste brings back first grade, but how can you explain what white paste smells like? Some combination of flour, sugar, the sourness of yogurt, and a Popsicle stick. I feel everything in that scent: the colored construction paper that we cut with small scissors, the rows of desks with children at them, the yellowing window shades on the tall windows.

Is how to describe it the first thing you think of? Can't you be in it? Asa asked.

Ani paused. What do you mean?

Try to empty your mind of words so the only thoughts are sensory perceptions.

They kissed again.

Falling, falling, Ani thought, down a dim stair with satin-lined walls.

Ani saw herself and Van reflected in a display store window as they walked.

There would be no more pitching headlong into the dark. *Gamatz, gamatz,* Grandma always advised. Slowly, slowly, one foot after the next.

A bell jangled as Van opened the restaurant's door and gestured her in. All the tables were occupied, but the *patron* assured Van in Arabic that it would be two minutes. Then a waiter showed them to a table and soon afterward a platter of fluffy couscous and a steaming tureen were set in front of them.

"How's your mother?" Van asked, as he ladled food onto Ani's plate.

"She's okay, I guess," Ani replied. "She writes me these long letters filled with news about people I don't care about."

"Whatever happened with that Harry guy?"

"He eventually went back to his wife and broke my mother's heart. I hated him so much it was hard to be sympathetic," Ani said.

The waiter came to the table and refilled their water glasses. A few minutes later Van excused himself to go to the men's room. Ani stared out the window, her focus turned inward. Another scene surfaced from the pool.

Violet switched on the table lamp. When are we going to meet this Asa, your mystery man?

I don't know, Ani said. Her voice caught in her throat. She and Asa had been arguing again.

Are you sleeping with him? her mother asked.

Yes.

Your father and I didn't sleep together until we were married.

I thought you guys were sophisticated hipsters. Grandma acts like you were practically a harlot.

Violet sighed. Ani, your grandmother believed any woman who wore a dress that showed her knees was a harlot. I was a nice Armenian girl. My vices were an occasional cigarette and marriage to an *odar*.

What about Harry? Ani asked.

That's different, Ani. I'm a widow with a grown daughter. This mess I've been in with Harry was guaranteed to disrupt my life alone.

What about his wife?

Harry moved out long before he and I started seeing each other. And if you'd like to know, Harry and Hasmig have been meeting with their priest for the past few months. They're talking about getting back together.

Oh, Mom, I'm sorry.

I could use a cigarette, Violet said, sniffing back tears.

You'll be okay, Mom. You'll find somebody better. Ani brushed her mother's hair back from her forehead. She noticed for the first time a few white strands threading Violet's black hair.

It wasn't so easy, was it? You loved somebody whether they deserved it or not, probably more if they didn't deserve it.

Ani glanced up to see Van approaching from across the room.

His face was clouded as he sat down, as though he were puzzling over some kind of a problem.

Ani commented, "You know, Van, you were never what anyone would call talkative, but now you're downright taciturn."

"Do you mind?" he asked.

"It leaves me lots of space for my thoughts, but sometimes I want to know what's going on in there."

"What are you doing next year?" he asked.

"I'm waiting to hear from graduate programs. What about you?"

Van shrugged. "At the moment, I'm satisfied with the work I'm doing."

"Any long-term goals?" she asked.

"I'd like to sail a small boat to Aghtamar—you know, the island in the middle of Lake Van."

"That's in Turkey, isn't it?"

"The Armenian homeland. I could see myself building a house on the shores of the lake. People from the Diaspora will come back to restore the community there."

"You think people are going to pack their bags in Watertown and Fresno to head to Turkey—I mean Armenia?"

"Some will. The ones who still have an attachment to the homeland."

"Even if you get a bunch of Armenians to go back, aren't other people living there now? I mean, it's been almost seventy years."

"After the revolution, Armenians, Kurds, and progressive Turks will live side by side and rebuild the region."

"After what revolution?" Ani asked.

"Ours. You want to join?" He asked this with a wry smile.

A sexy smile, thought Ani, with some kind of question in it. "I'll take a rain check. I'm not sure I want to go back to Watertown, let alone the Armenian homeland."

Ani was accustomed to riding the metro by herself at night and walking solo along dusky streets, but when Van insisted on escorting her home she felt grateful. They skirted the grand boulevards, making their way through narrow side streets. She glanced at his profile, which filled her with yearning.

These were the ways that Van was unlike Asa: his skin was olive, his eyebrows emphatic, his hands square with hair on the knuckles. His hometown was Ani's hometown. They had both traveled far from there.

There was a wall around him, but maybe there was a door in the wall. Was that the way all men were, walls and doors? The problem with Asa was that inside the door was another wall with another door.

They made a half circle through the place des Victoires past a floodlit statue of the Sun King on a rearing stallion. Ani glanced in the windows of designer boutiques. She admired a dress in the Kenzo show window, then worried whether Van would suspect that she coveted the dress. He would not approve, she was sure.

Van put his hand at Ani's elbow, shepherding her through the crossings. Again the sparks flowed from his fingertips up her arm. Here again the craving welled up inside her.

The man, according to Tacey Barton, should love the woman more. But Ani wasn't about to start taking advice from Tacey.

Maybe it was like walking across a frozen pond. She was on one side; he was on the other. Let him take the first step. Then she would take a step. Until they met in the middle or plunged into the icy water.

The night was chill. She pulled the shawl closer around her neck.

"Are you cold?" Van asked.

"I'm okay," she answered.

"Here, take my hat." He pulled a black felt beret from his coat pocket.

Ani pulled the hat on and tucked her hair inside.

It was such a thoughtful, friendly gesture. Asa was never Ani's friend. Van had been her friend for a long time.

Tell me who your friend is, and I will tell you who you are.

Don't spoil it, Ani told herself, by tumbling down the old stone well.

On Beaujolais they stood awkwardly near the building's back door.

"Ani," he ventured.

"Yeah?" Ani asked, looking at him quizzically.

There was something urgent in his tone. She studied the downcast lids with sable lashes and the planes of his shadowed face.

He stared at his upturned palms.

"There's a lot you don't know about me. . . ." His voice was edged with flint.

Was he angry?

She joked. "Our great-grandfathers were first cousins. You come from Dexter Avenue. The only other thing I need to know is your phone number."

He replied, "And that I can't give you. I don't have a phone."

The tension of the moment dissipated. In her nervousness she had slammed a door on whatever it was he had wanted to tell her.

"So how can I get in touch with you?" she asked.

"I'll call you. I've got to go now. Good night, Ani." He backed away. "Thanks for the fun. I don't get too much fun these days."

"How about an address?" she called after him.

He laughed, turning toward the dark. "I'll phone, I promise."

Every time the orange telephone trilled in her room over the next week Ani hoped it was Van, but he didn't call. One evening as she was preparing for Sofia Zed's class she plucked the receiver on the first ring.

"Where'd you get this phone number?" she asked Asa, her blood spinning in her temples at the sound of his voice.

"Mrs. Barton gave it to me," Asa said. "You busy?"

"I'm reading about tortured love."

"You taking a psychology class?'

"Literature, Asa. Novels are full of it."

"I found another one of your notes this morning."

Before she had left his apartment in Seattle in August she had hidden slips of paper with lines from poems on them. Ani knew that if she didn't tell him to stop he would recite the words.

He began, "'*So much space between us two / We kiss the planets when we kiss—*'"

She interrupted. She knew where it was going and didn't want to be dragged to the end of the poem. "Don't, Asa. Don't read it."

"You're mad at me, aren't you?" Asa asked.

"Did you have a nice Christmas with May?"

"I didn't call to talk about that, Ani. I miss you."

The muscles in Ani's shoulders tensed. She didn't say anything in response.

"I still love you, Ani," Asa said.

Candlelight flickered in the mirror of an old dresser. She smelled apricot oil and tasted whisky and pot smoke on Asa's breath. His body was the landscape she had wanted to travel. Oh, no, she thought, I'm backsliding. Then suddenly she jerked herself up. Don't let him reel you in like a fish on a hook.

"Can't talk to you, Asa. Please don't call again." Ani laid the receiver in its cradle.

Sondage stubbed out his cigarette, indicating that the class was over. As an afterthought he growled, "All of you. Go see *Ordet.* At the crossroads of the Infinite and the Sublime, the Verb will bring you face-to-face with your soul."

Michael, who was seated next to Ani, passed her a note: *Tomorrow?*

While she liked Michael, she had no interest in coming face-to-face with her soul while elbow to elbow with him in a darkened theater.

Ani scribbled, *Can't. Maybe the Musée Marmottan next week.* She slid the note back to him. Disappointment registered on his face.

She wished Elena were in Paris. Ani missed her women friends. They used to sit around in the student center café for hours talking about life and books and relationships. Ani now understood that *relationship* was a euphemism for *bad boyfriend.* Having Elena to complain to was one of the things that had made life with Asa bearable.

Ani was weary of boys. Jacques Stein had phoned her to apologize for his behavior at Odile's party weeks after the event and to ask her out. She had turned him down. She couldn't take any more strained conversations in French with men she barely knew. And she hadn't heard from Van in three weeks.

On the street a man had his arm hooked around his girlfriend's neck like a shepherd's crook. The woman's face was doleful and downtrodden. A man and a woman bickered in the aisle of the department store where Ani was buying lipstick. Asa hated lipstick, especially red, so she chose a color called Rouge Radical. A woman at the next counter was purchasing concealer for a blackened eye.

That evening Tacey and Le Con were having a loud argument in the master suite. Ani sat at the kitchen table with Sydney as the child ate her supper. The apartment's solid walls and floors muffled the words, but Sydney's face was drawn, the muscles in her jaw moving stiffly as she chewed, while the angry tones and the sound of slamming doors filtered down the stairs.

"Do you think they're going to get a divorce?" Sydney asked.

"Oh, Syd, people can argue without getting a divorce."

"I think my dad has a new secretary. That's usually when they yell," Sydney observed.

The next day Ani went to a late-afternoon matinee by herself. Shot in black-and-white in an austere landscape, the film was a drama about a gentleman farmer and his three grown sons. One of the sons, who had gone mad from reading too much Kierkegaard, believed he was the Son of God. A beatific daughter-in-law died during a gruesome childbirth scene. In the film's closing moments, the lost son returned and, in a Christlike gesture, commanded the woman to rise from the dead. Her eyes fluttered open.

Tears slipping down her face, Ani wanted to shout at the screen, It's not fair! You can't bring her back to life. The dead stay dead. And the dead are good for nothing.

The lights went up. The moviegoers spilled onto the bustling street, where Ani became a faceless exile. She had wanted to free herself from old attachments—her family, the old house, the forsythia in the garden, and the familiar streets—but now she was a pale shadow sliding through the apparent world. The connections she had wrought in her new life had proved to be frail. She saw herself dangling like a spider dropped from the ceiling on a fine filament. It reminded her of seeing Asa rappel down a cliff face on his rope—it was a sturdy rope, after all, but from afar it appeared as barely a scarlet thread.

She stared down at her small reflection in the night-lit water gliding under the bridge. No matter how they looped around, her thoughts always seemed to come back to Asa. What would become of her now that he was no longer the center of her world?

What will become of us, Ani? What will we do?

That's what Violet Silver had said after the news of her husband's death was relayed over the telephone. Ani was four at the time and she was scared to see her mother crying, the tears spilling out of Violet as though she were cracking apart like a leaky dam. Ani had started to cry as well, not because her father had died—it would take months for her to grasp what that meant—but because she felt like a leaf caught in the flood of her mother's grief.

Her mother had left Ani with a neighbor named Mrs. Donnelly who had white hair and a stiff-legged miniature poodle. The woman's living room was filled with glass figurines and crystal knickknacks. Ani's feet, in their white anklets and red patent-leather shoes, stuck out from the sofa cushion. It was summer. The fat white poodle sat panting next to Ani on the couch, its pink tongue hanging out. Mrs. Donnelly, who brought out a tray of lemonade and cookies, gave Ani sidelong glances that were filled with pity.

Over the next days Ani's mother came and went, leaving her with a baby-sitter, a college girl with pink lipstick whose name was Cindy. In the evening Violet clutched the telephone to her ear and talked Armenian to her parents. There must have been a funeral, but Ani wasn't invited. Her mother came home with an urn full of ashes—all that was left of David Silver. Baba and Grandma arrived in New York with a borrowed truck that they loaded with the Silvers' belongings. On the drive to Watertown, Ani had accompanied her grandfather in the truck. Violet and her mother had followed in the car.

Ani's father had whistled songs through his teeth; he had smelled like Old Spice aftershave and new pennies. He had taken her by bus to Central Park, where he bought her an orange balloon and ten tickets for the carousel. When she fell down on the sidewalk and scraped her knee he had held a clean white handkerchief to the spot until it stopped hurting.

That wasn't a hell of a lot of things to remember about your father.

The summer Ani was twelve, she and her mother had spent two weeks in a borrowed house on Cape Cod. One night as Ani lay in bed listening to the sea unfurling itself over the shore she heard jazz coming from the stereo below. She descended to the ground floor, where the orange tip of a lit cigarette was reflected in the sliding glass door. For a second Ani thought the shadowed woman in the wing chair was a stranger who had slipped into the house.

Mom! You smoke? Ani finally asked.

Violet switched on the table lamp beside her. I used to. This is the first one I've had in seven years. Watch this, Violet instructed. She made an O of her mouth and blew out a series of smoke rings that spiraled above her head.

That's cool, Ani said admiringly. But isn't it bad for you?

Vhy babum! Filt in God's temple! Violet said, imitating her mother. Once in seven years even God will forgive. Don't say anything about it, Ani, okay? It's our secret.

Ani sat in the other wing chair, tucking her feet under her tailor style. How did you meet Daddy? she asked her mother.

A smile played at the edges of Violet's mouth. I haven't told you that story?

No, Ani said. Violet hadn't told her many stories about her father at all.

Violet said, When I was in college, I used to go to a coffee shop on Broadway in the midafternoon to have tea and biscuits. It was a slow time of day, so I'd sit there at the far end of the counter and do my reading. One day this boy sat on the stool next to me. I felt him staring at me, but I kept reading. When he came back the next afternoon I knew it wasn't a coincidence. On the third day he said, Excuse me, miss. I know this is forward, but I'd like to introduce myself. That was your dad. He had this sharp way of looking at things. He was full of jokes and funny expressions.

We sat on those stools talking until it was dinner. Neither of us had much money, so we ordered soup and crackers. When we were leaving the coffee shop it had started raining. I had no umbrella so we shared his. One of its ribs was broken. I was nervous to walk too close to him, so one side of my skirt was wet by the time we reached the campus. He saw that I was cold and took off his jacket and put it around my shoulders.

Violet gazed past Ani toward the sea, where nothing and everything could be seen on the night's black screen.

Was he an orphan? Ani asked. She assumed he had been without family, since they had no contact with any Silvers.

He had a big family—two brothers and sister, aunts, uncles, and cousins.

Why don't we know them?

Well, Violet said slowly, as though measuring her words, his parents were very religious, and when he married me they disowned him.

How do you disown somebody? Ani asked.

They held a kind of funeral service for him, as though he had died, she explained.

Did they know about the accident?

His sister sent him a note once a year on his birthday, so I knew her address and found her phone number. I called her before we left New York.

Do you miss him? Ani asked.

Violet stubbed out her cigarette in the ashtray. All the time, sweetie.

True nostalgia—nostalgos, *as the Greeks called it—is an aching in the heart for the homeland because you know what the homeland is and what it isn't.*

After one of her college professors said this, Ani carried the sentence around with her like a talisman without understanding why it resonated so strongly. Now she wondered what the object of her heartache was. It wasn't Van's idea of homeland but rather some more intimate place of rest and comfort. She had imagined the longing was for Asa, but maybe he was only a surrogate for some deeper loss.

She was lonely here in Paris. But hadn't she chosen this foreign place, far away and unlike anything she might call home?

As she crossed the street, Ani followed a schoolboy wearing a bulky leather satchel who was holding his glamorous mother's gloved hand. A teenager on his scooter buzzed along the edge of the gutter past stalled traffic. In the cheese shop the *fromager* had arrayed his odorous wares on hundred-year-old marble counters. The *primeur* had labeled the fruit and vegetables with small yellow signs bearing their names and prices. Ani repeated the words *pomme de terre* and *pamplemousse*. She liked the way this other language made her own feel strange and new. She loved that streets were named for writers and that the mail came twice a day.

Shutting herself in her attic room, Ani found the silence comforting. She believed herself capable of a month-long confinement in one of those whitewashed rooms in a Zen retreat. The steady pulse in her neck would be company enough. She wasn't waiting for the scrape of a key in the lock. In fact, she had thrown the extra key away.

As she settled down to her reading for the following week's classes, the phone rang. It was Odile, inviting her to a family friend's art opening on the rue Jacob. Would she be at George's modern class in the afternoon? Of course. It rang again: Michael about the museum date. The next call was from an American whom Ani had met in Sofia Zed's class. She wanted to borrow Ani's notes and to tell her about a party a bunch of Yale students were throwing at their apartment on the rue de la Roquette. Did Ani by any chance have any hash connections? Too bad. Bring a bottle then.

Tacey phoned in a panic because Sydney was running a temperature and would have to be home from school the next morning. Tacey's schedule was full—a salon appointment and a luncheon at the American Women's Club—and could Ani possibly cover Sydney through lunch? Ani's duties and hours had been creeping up without any increase in pay. This latest request was her bargaining chip in negotiations about spring vacation. Ani told Tacey she could baby-sit in the morning and took the opportunity to definitively decline the family trip to Switzerland.

The phone rang again. Who was left? Ani wondered.

It was Van. "Sorry I didn't call sooner. I went out of town for work. I just got back this afternoon."

Think fast, Ani. What to say? Lucky you caught me at home. It's been a real social whirlwind. This is the first night I haven't gone out in three weeks. It feels like only yesterday that we saw each other. I've been waiting by the phone for three weeks, you jerk.

"Ani, are you there?" he asked.

"Yeah, yeah, I'm here," she said.

"Listen, I'm a couple of blocks away. You want to meet for coffee?"

"Why don't you come over here."

After Ani hung up the phone she looked down at herself. She was wearing a pair of gray sweats, cut off at the knees and inside out, with an oversized T-shirt and a dance sweater. There were dusty wool socks on her feet. It was an updated version of the faded housecoat and ratty slippers her mother wore when she was down in the dumps. Ani jumped out of the rags and pulled on a pair of jeans and a sweater.

As Ani stood in the entrance hall Madame Spinelli, the concierge, opened her door. "May I be of some assistance, mademoiselle?"

"No, thank you. I'm waiting for a friend." She hoped the woman would go back inside her curtained door before Van arrived.

Madame Spinelli glared at Ani suspiciously as she retreated. A moment later Van was standing on the sidewalk grinning at Ani. At the sight of him the underside of her skin contracted with a tingling pinch. When he entered the building Ani put her finger to her lips, gesturing toward Madame Spinelli's door.

Ani backed into one corner of the elevator. Van's presence made the space seem cramped and close. Once they had passed the second floor she explained, "The concierge watches the door like a hawk. I guess that's part of the job description."

In the upstairs hall, Ani pressed the timed light switch and opened the door to her room.

"Nice place," Van said. "My *chambre de bonne* is the size of a closet. I put the chair on the desk so I have floor room for push-ups." He pulled off his jacket and dropped it over the arm of the couch.

"You want some tea?" she asked.

"Sure."

She filled the electric kettle from the washbasin's tap.

"I have my own sink too," Van said. "Toilet down the hall?"

"First door on the left. The shower too."

"You've got a shower? Now that's what I call luxury. I go to the municipal bath."

Ani winced. "Hate to even imagine it."

"It's not so bad. The spray got rid of the athlete's foot," he said, snapping his fingers, "just like that."

"And you have a real job. Don't they pay you?"

"Don't feel bad for me. I like living this way. It builds character."

"But you don't eat out of Dumpsters."

"Why would I do something like that?"

"I had this friend in college. This guy liked eating out of trash bins, hitchhiking, and panhandling. He used to like sleeping in Salvation Army shelters. A few times when he was bumming around he sold plasma to get money for food."

"Let me guess. He had a big trust fund."

Ani laughed. "You're right."

"Yes, and I can tell you something else. This friend was actually your boyfriend."

The teakettle whistled. Ani poured water over the tea bags in the two mugs. "It's that obvious, huh?"

"Let's just say I recognized the tone."

"You mean that bitter, resentful, bitchy tone?"

Van laughed. "I wouldn't have put it that way, but I won't argue with you."

Ani sat down across from Van at the round table. He was more talkative than the last time and funnier. His face appeared relaxed and open. She was more at ease with this side of him than with the somber, brooding Van of their long walk home, although that aspect of him was compelling too.

He put his hands around the warm mug. "I'm going to be working pretty hard in the next few weeks. Have to go out of town a couple of times. Fun isn't on the current agenda. But I had an idea. I'm taking a vacation in April: Corsica. I'm borrowing a car from a friend. There's an overnight ferry from Marseille. I have some friends in Bastia."

His face tensed as he talked. She wondered where this disjointed narrative was leading.

He continued. "I was thinking that maybe you might want to, you know, come along, if you can get away." Here he turned one palm up on the table. It was an unconscious gesture, more candid than anything he was saying.

The Bartons would be in Switzerland for twelve days, and Jussieu would be shut down for the Easter holiday. There was no reason not to go, except that she wasn't sure what kind of invitation Van was extending. Was this to be a romantic getaway or a companionable vacation? His face was indecipherable.

"When do we go?" she asked.

He left soon afterward, saying he had to get up early. Once the door closed behind him her mind whirred again. She had thought she had felt a zinging tension between them at the door, but maybe it was her imagination. A week with him on the island of Corsica might clear things up, one way or the other.

The next morning in the Bartons' kitchen, Tacey sat at the kitchen table looking at Ani over the rim of her coffee mug. "Sydney's still asleep. She was up in the night. I gave her some aspirin around four A.M. By the way, Madame Spinelli knocked on the door this morning. She wanted to tell me that you were sneaking Arab men into the building at night. Thank God I was the one who answered the door. John left early for work. You can imagine what he would have thought."

Ani explained. "A friend of mine stopped by last night for a while. That's the first night I've ever had anybody upstairs."

"Madame Spinelli told me he stayed almost an hour."

"I hope the poor woman at least pulled a chair to the door. I hate to think of her standing there for all that time," Ani said, the sarcasm embedded deeply in her voice.

"Imagine if he had stayed overnight. That would have been a scandal. Not an Arab, though, is he?" Tacey asked.

Ani disliked the tone Tacey was using. "No, not an Arab. Somebody I grew up with in Boston. An Armenian."

"Well, that's a relief. I didn't think it could have been an Arab, what with you being a Jew and all. That's what I told Madame Spinelli. But let's be more discreet, shall we? Why don't you go to his place next time? By the way, where *is* Armenia?"

Ani studied Tacey's face, which Ani usually saw as benign if somewhat rabbity. Now there was a decidedly ratlike expression about the mouth.

"It's part of the Soviet Union," Ani explained.

Tacey raised a well-plucked eyebrow. "Your friend isn't a Communist by any chance?"

Now they had ventured into the realm of the surreal.

Attempting to keep her tone even, Ani answered, "No, Tacey, he played in Little League and was a Pop Warner captain. As far as I know he's a registered Democrat."

"Well, just be careful, okay? There are all kinds of men around trying to take advantage of an impressionable girl like you. I've got to run. Check Sydney's temperature when she gets up, will you? The children's aspirin are in the cabinet in her bathroom."

Ani sat on the velvet couch in the grand salon with a book while Syd slept on. Van was right. The Bartons were rich white people, living in a palace apartment paid for by corporate thievery, and she was their employee. *What with your being a Jew and all.*

John and Tacey Barton had everything—the large home, the posh vacations, the offhand ease of buying what they wanted. Ani envied them and at the same time wished she could spit that envy out like a bitter seed. She had often felt this conflict in the Willards' home. Asa's sense of entitlement was both seductive and repellent.

One afternoon Ani and Asa were sitting on the couch in his family's living room talking about a point of geography. Asa had hunted the shelves for an atlas, and when he couldn't locate one he said, Damn. Let's go to the bookstore and get one. Just like that he went out and bought a leather-bound atlas, putting it on his father's charge card.

For some reason, this detail—more than the two sets of silver, the second home on Cape Cod, or the trust fund—had dismayed Ani. Shouldn't he go to the public library and look up the information he needed? Ani thought of her grandfather reading his Armenian newspaper at the library because the subscription was too costly. She herself had owned fewer than a dozen books by the time she finished high school. The other thousands she had read were borrowed.

When the Kersamians opened gifts, Grandma painstakingly peeled off the tape and refolded the creased wrapping paper, saving it for future use. She collected rubber bands from the daily paper by putting them on the neck of the kitchen doorknob. Before worn shirts were cut into polishing rags, the buttons were carefully removed. The Willards had no idea about this kind of economy.

In college, Ani had noticed that there were a number of students who came back from midyear vacation with deep tans. She had never before known people who used the word *winter* as a verb. She secretly wished to belong to this class of people. But at the same time, when given an opportunity to sneak in—whether through winning Asa's heart or being invited to join an elite secret society—her ambivalence had checked her.

Lizzie Meadows, whom Ani knew from the French department, had approached her in the library one evening. Lizzie said she needed to speak to Ani privately. Mystified, Ani followed her into the hall.

Lizzie surveyed the corridor to make sure no one was within earshot. Then she said, Ani, you're being tapped.

You mean someone's bugged my phone? Ani asked.

Not like that. I'm tapping you to join Terrapin.

Ani was still perplexed. Terrapin?

Terrapin is a secret senior honor society for women, Lizzie explained. Every year the seniors choose juniors to join. We've chosen you.

What do you do in Terrapin?

I can't tell you.

What do you mean you can't tell me?

Ani, the whole point is that it's secret.

So I'm supposed to join without knowing anything about the group's purpose? What if it turns out you're the women's branch of the KKK or Hitler Youth or something?

Lizzie smiled at Ani with indulgence. Trust me. You have to believe I wouldn't ask you to do anything that was bad for you.

Okay, Ani said slowly. So what next?

Be by the mailbox halfway down the hill toward the river at eleven P.M.

Ani hunted for Asa at his usual spots in the library to no avail. When she called the house they shared there was no answer. She hoped he was off having a beer with his friend Joe and not sneaking around someplace with the toothsome skier named Gretchen Woodbridge that she'd seen him flirting with at teatime in the library. Ani tracked Elena down in the library's stacks.

Do you think I should go? Ani asked.

Elena said, Are you crazy? Out of sheer anthropological curiosity you have to go.

I'm not the one with the anthropological curiosity, Ani reminded her.

Of course you are, Ani. These secret societies are the invisible glue that holds the Establishment together. Every CIA director in history was a member of Skull and Bones at Yale. I didn't know there was a secret society for women here. My God, what an opportunity.

Ani waited at the appointed spot. A beat-up Ford LTD crammed with women stopped in front of her. Before she had an instant to register the face that appeared out of the car door, a blindfold was placed over her eyes and Ani was dragged into the car.

Somebody crooned, Oh, you little turtles, you poor little turtles, you don't know what's in store for you. Do they, girls? A loud cackle followed.

Jesus Christ, thought Ani, this is like those creepy made-for-TV movies with the evil sorority sisters. What were they going to do to her? She had heard horror stories about the fraternities: naked rituals with hot dogs in a flooded basement; "boot punch," where pledges were forced to drink liquor that had been vomited by upperclassmen; pledges driven to a distant women's college and handcuffed naked to the sinks in a dormitory. Since this group was named after a turtle, there would probably be some water involved. No matter what they threatened, Ani would not remove one article of clothing.

The car careened around town until Ani had no idea where they were. When they came to a halt she was linked by hands with two other recruits and led through the woods, which she recognized by the crunching twigs beneath her feet. Ani entered a building still blindfolded and was made to sit on a crowded couch.

Okay, girls, you can take off the blindfolds, they were told.

Ani slid off her blindfold and glanced around at what she suspected to be a college-owned cabin on the river. She recognized the faces of everyone in the room and knew most of the names. Ani sighted Gretchen Woodbridge among the women at the front, each of whom was wearing a forest-green union suit and holding a long-stemmed white rose.

My real name is George Washington, said Lizzie, who looked like a very tall elf. George continued, You are among the best women in the class of 1982. You were chosen on the basis of your commitment to this school. As a member of Terrapin you will be expected to wear something green on your person from this day forward. Messages from Terrapin will be sealed with a green dot and shouldn't be opened in the presence of nonmembers. When you say goodbye to a fellow member you will say Tootle-oo. You are not to tell anyone that you are a member of Terrapin or divulge any of the details of our activities. Only at graduation when you are carrying a white rose will anyone but your sisters know that you have been a member of this group. Let us now stand to sing the school anthem.

Ani rose to her feet with the rest of the women but couldn't join the singing. She still didn't know the words to the anthem, except for the chorus. And she disliked the chorus.

When the song had concluded, Lizzie said, I, George Washington, welcome you, Megan Lord, to Terrapin. Next year Megan will take the name George and lead this group.

Lizzie strode over to Megan, a thin, serious girl with long blond hair, and handed her the rose.

Gretchen Woodbridge stood. My name is John Adams. Belonging to Terrapin has given me an opportunity to serve the local community as well as the college. My rose is for Katie O'Brien. Welcome, Katie.

My name is Thomas Jefferson, said Maisie Zimmer, a senior Ani knew from women's studies classes. I have found Terrapin to be a wonderfully supportive and loving sisterhood. These women will continue to provide me with sustenance and comfort for the rest of my life. This rose is for Ani Silver.

As soon as Ani arrived back at the house that she, Elena, Asa, and one of his friends were sharing that term, she peered into Asa's closet-sized room. He was asleep on the narrow mattress amid a jumble of dirty clothes and climbing gear. The fact that he was in his bed and not hers indicated that he was in a bad mood so she decided not to wake him.

She lay on her futon, rolling in the blankets like a rotisserie chicken. What should she do? How could she possibly enlist in such a strange group? She would have to wear something green every day for the next two years. She would have to call herself Thomas Jefferson. But how could she say no to the enveloping arms of an exclusive community of women? Finally Ani heaved off the bedclothes and crossed the hall to Elena's room.

Elena said, Oh, it's beautiful. *My real name is George Washington.* It's so perfect I can't stand it. Can you believe somebody sat around and thought this shit up?

What should I do? Ani asked.

You should join. How else am I going to find out what they actually do? Come on, Ani, be a sport.

You want me to hang around with a bunch of women who pretend they are American presidents and prance around in union suits? In a group that's named after a turtle? I don't think so, Elena Torino.

The next day Ani called Lizzie and told her that she was declining the invitation. Freed from the bond of secrecy, Ani recounted the evening's events to Asa, who wasn't the least bit interested in the details, not even the fact that Gretchen, his not-so-secret crush, was there. Ani told a couple of other friends and a women's studies professor she knew would appreciate the story, but not many people at all considering how many she was tempted to tell.

Lizzie sought Ani out in the library. Ani, we've heard you've been betraying our secrets. If you spoil this for us, I promise you we will make your life miserable.

I only told my boyfriend and a few close friends, Ani explained.

If you know what's good for you, you'll shut up, Ani, Lizzie said menacingly.

No problem, George, Ani replied. My lips are sealed.

Ani hadn't wanted to be a member of Terrapin any more than she had wanted to marry Asa. There, she had admitted it. In her secret heart she was relieved that their relationship was over. When she had seen Peggy Willard's social stationery—engraved with the name Mrs. Benjamin Willard—Ani had recoiled in horror. Ani had feared she herself would be transformed into a brittle woman, riven with jealousy and insecurities, whose name was Mrs. Asa Willard.

"Mommy," Sydney called from her room. "Mommy, where are you?"

Ani took the stairs two at a time and made the child's doorway in a flash. "Hey, Sydney, your mom isn't back yet. How you feeling?"

"I don't feel well at all."

Little Sydney was flushed with sleep and fever. Ani pulled the child onto her lap and felt her forehead.

"What do you think, Syd? Aspirin. A little juice. Then I'll read you a book."

"Can I have some ice cream?"

"Sure bet." Ani felt sorry for Sydney. With parents like Tacey and The Asshole, what chance did the poor kid have?

without the wind, no leaf will move

Ani lurked at the lobby door, peering out into the dark wet street. As the rain poured down, a frantic mouse ran on a wire wheel inside her belly. The wheel squeaked as it turned, making the sound that she associated with long hours and sometimes days of waiting for Asa. She lifted her sweater cuff to check her wristwatch. Eleven minutes after five. Van was eleven minutes late. Well, her watch was actually three minutes fast, so he was only eight minutes late. And she had come downstairs ten minutes early, which had made the span seem longer. In the street, a black sedan rolled by without stopping.

Maybe she was mistaken about the date and tomorrow was the morning he was coming for her. No. This was the day she had written in her calendar. She laid her cheek against the door's cold glass, staring at a streetlight's reflection in a puddle on the sidewalk. The man in the blue coverall should be appearing soon to sweep the gutters with his tall twig broom. Perhaps her telephone was ringing at that very moment: Van calling to say he had decided to go to Corsica alone.

A gray Peugeot pulled up and Van stretched to push open the front passenger door. Ani leaped through the downpour, tossing her pack into the backseat. She shook the rain from her hair.

"Some morning for a drive," Van commented, as he pulled away from the curb. "Did you have breakfast?"

"No," Ani answered.

Van hadn't shaved in a few days, so there was a dark mask spread over his jawbones and cheeks. Ani recollected the Van of her childhood, but for a moment she wondered what she knew about this inscrutable man.

117

"I downed an espresso and picked up a couple of croissants. The bag is on the backseat," he said.

She grabbed one and pulled off a long flaky strip of pastry. "You want some?" she asked.

"No, thanks."

They left the city and rolled onto the highway. The windshield wipers kept up a steady rhythm that soon made Ani drowsy. She had been up late, taken by one of those frenzies of indecision that required trying on each item of clothing before stowing it in her bag. The dilemma about whether or not to pack the diaphragm had been difficult to resolve. Bringing it was presumptuous; why did she think she would have any need for it on this trip? But then she might kick herself for leaving it behind if the occasion arose. In the end she decided to follow Elena's dictum: Take birth control with you the way you do a toothbrush.

When finally she climbed into bed, she had waked repeatedly during the night to check the clock, worried that she might over-sleep.

"You mind if I rest for a while?" Ani asked Van.

"Why don't you push your pack onto the floor and lie down on the backseat," he suggested.

When Ani opened her eyes again the skies were clear and the terrain mountainous. Her spirits had lifted as well. An adventure was unfurling around her like a colorful banner. Perhaps she would have an exciting life after all. She sat up and climbed through the bucket seats to the front.

"How long was I out?" she asked.

"About two hours," he said.

"Sorry to be such dull company," she said.

"No worries. I'm not much of a conversationalist when I drive."

They stopped briefly at a small-town café for lunch before heading south again. They chatted amiably, or rather Ani noticed that she chatted and Van gave short, companionable replies. Making

an effort to check her patter, she stared out the window at passing farms. Rolling clouds cast long shadows over broad plowed
fields and farmhouses with red tile roofs.

On the southern outskirts of Lyon they heard a loud Klaxon
and saw a white police sedan draw up behind them. Ani glanced
at the speedometer and noted that they were well within the limit.
She had no idea why they were being pulled over, unless the car's
taillight was broken or something like that.

"What's the problem?" Ani asked Van.

"We'll see," he said grimly.

Van halted the car at the side of the highway. The officers asked
them to step out of the car with their identity cards. While Ani
rummaged in her bag for her passport and *carte de séjour,* Van
reached into his jacket's interior pocket for his documents.

One of the cops stood a few paces back inspecting their papers.
The other one looked at Van contemptuously. Nodding his head
toward Van, he asked Ani, "What are you doing with this dirty
Arab?"

Ce sale arabe were the exact words.

"Why did you stop us?" Ani asked the flic. "Do you check every sixth car?"

The cop gibed, "We do it by the smell, mademoiselle."

Ani was appalled. She glanced at Van to see his response, but
Van's eyes were on the rutted mud at their feet. His eyes flickered
up briefly to meet hers with a sharp warning. She pressed her lips
into a line and stared into the distance.

In less than five minutes they were on the road again, but Ani
was jittery with rage.

"That racist pig," she said. "I can't believe he said that!"

Van's knuckles were white on the steering wheel. "Ani, next
time, if there is a next time, don't wise off to the cops. Sarcasm
can land you in jail." His voice was honed to a fine edge.

"What was that all about anyway?"

"Stupidity on my part. I should have shaved," he said.

"What? That asshole said it was because we smelled like Arabs."

"No. They pulled us over because *I* smelled like an Arab. And if I had shaved, the smell wouldn't have been so strong."

"What kind of weird thing is that to say?" Ani asked.

"Ani, understanding their racist ideology doesn't mean that I agree with it."

They drove in silence for a long time. Van's face was expressionless. Ani wondered if this counted as their first official fight. Their first official fight as friends.

By the time they reached Marseille the tension had ebbed. They decided to have a meal of fish and chips at a sidewalk restaurant in the Vieux Port. Van said he wanted to pick up a few things for the trip. He left Ani sitting in a café reading and writing in her journal. When he returned he was beardless.

"Well, you certainly smell better," Ani said. "Quick visit to the barber?"

"Stopped by a friend's apartment."

"You have friends in Marseille?"

"An Armenian has friends everyplace," he said.

The ferry was called the *Cyrnos*. After leaving the car in the hold they climbed to the passenger deck and installed themselves on a banquette upholstered in green vinyl. As the boat trundled out to sea, Ani dozed while Van read some Armenian newspapers he had picked up in Marseille.

Ani slumbered fitfully through the night, falling in and out of dreams. Asa and Ani sped down a rural pine-lined highway on a motorcycle. No helmets, just the wind on her face and through her hair, faster and faster as she held tightly to his waist. They crashed into a massive tree in a tangle of limbs and metal. She started awake. Van was still absorbed in his newspapers. She drowsed again.

In the morning as land appeared on the horizon, Van was sleeping. Ani went to the exterior deck. A dark-haired guy wearing a thick woolen sweater stood next to her at the railing staring over the water toward the island.

"Can you smell it?" he asked in French.

"Smell what?" Ani asked suspiciously.

"The maquis."

Ani sniffed the air. "No."

"If you came here in May you would notice it. The flowers are all over: yellow broom, rock rose, heather. It's the perfume of the island. When I smell it I know I'm home."

Ani returned to her seat. Van's head was tipped to one side, exposing his Adam's apple and a line of neck that Ani yearned to touch. His sleeping face was vulnerable and approachable. A longing radiated from the center of her body and pushed against all its borders.

Just then a voice from the loudspeakers announced that drivers should descend to their cars. The ship was arriving at the dock. Van snapped awake.

They parked near the center of Bastia and wandered through the flea market on the place Saint-Nicholas. At the terrace cafés old men were drinking coffee, playing cards, and arguing in a language that sounded to Ani's ears to be somewhere between Italian and French. As they walked around town Ani noticed the letters FLNC spray-painted in black on the facades of several buildings. She pointed them out to Van and asked if he knew what the initials stood for.

"Front de Libération Nationale de la Corse," he said.

"Nice accent," she said. "What exactly is this party?"

"In Corsu they call themselves Frontu di Liberazione Naziunalista Corsu. Corsican separatists. They want an end to French occupation of the island."

"How come you're so well informed?"

"It's my line. I know a lot about national liberation struggles."

"And my ignorance is as vast as a continent," Ani said.

"But you're willing to learn, aren't you?" Van asked.

"Always. Self-improvement is *my* line," she replied.

The sky was overcast as they made their way along the main highway. Ani held a map of the island on her lap, tracing with her finger the route they were following. A few kilometers from Saint-Florent, Van turned onto a dirt road that didn't appear on the map. The road grew bumpier and more rutted as they drove through scrub toward the water. When they stopped by the shore, Ani opened the car door to the scent of broom, resin, and ocean.

"I smell it," Ani said.

"What?" Van asked.

"The maquis. The perfume of Corsica," Ani said.

Van gestured toward the white mountain peaks in the distance and the hills dropping to the sea. "Beautiful, huh?"

They walked to the water's edge, where sea anemones clung to rocks. Shells and plastic debris dotted the shoreline. Ani kicked a pink tampon applicator aside.

"The French flush their toilets and it washes up here," Van commented. "We should get going. Pascal's expecting us for dinner."

Van's friends lived in an old stone farmhouse by the side of the road just north of Ponte-Leccia. Pascal Centuri had dark curly hair and a gap between his two front teeth. His wife Isabelle, her wavy chestnut hair tied up with a scarf, was visibly pregnant.

In French, Pascal said, "Let me show you the caravan. Bring your stuff out back."

Pascal led them through a rocky meadow where a donkey grazed on a patch of tufted grass beside a stream. Pascal gestured that they should enter and they stepped into a mini-camper, which had a foldout bed, a small kitchen table, and a sink with no water. The bed was a little wider than a single, but not much.

After Pascal returned to the house, Ani and Van moved gingerly around the camper, trying not to bump into each other.

Van crouched low over his pack. His back was to Ani as he said, "You take the bed. I'll unroll my pad and bag right here on the floor."

At dinner, Pascal and Isabelle sat at either end of the long wooden table. The benches were crowded with their friends, Louis and Flore from Aléria, and neighbors whose names Ani didn't remember. She and Van were seated across from each other in the middle. The Centuris served lamb stew with beans, a delicious sheep cheese, fresh bread, olives, and lots of red wine. Pascal, who was proud of the Corsican cheese and wine, refilled everyone's glasses assiduously.

Van put his palm over his glass, shaking his head.

"You can trust a woman who doesn't drink, Ardavanian. But a man who won't drink? Who can trust him?" Pascal protested.

"Do you trust me?" Van asked.

Pascal smiled. "With my life."

"Then take that bottle away, my friend."

After the meal, pear brandy and cognac were passed around. Pascal insisted that Ani try both. When Pascal recited Corsican poetry, Ani countered with an Elizabeth Bishop villanelle. Several more rounds of brandy followed. Liberal toasts to the Armenian cause and Corsican liberation were made. The Corsicans sang what seemed to be nationalist standards; Van rejoined with a few Armenian patriotic tunes Ani had never heard before. Pascal appeared to be singing along in Armenian, which made perfect sense to Ani at the time. She herself joined the choruses in both languages with gusto.

At about three o'clock in the morning when Van steered Ani through the moonlit meadow toward the caravan she was tipsier than she had ever been.

"Van, have you noticed that I talk a lot more than you do?" Ani stumbled over a stone.

Grabbing for her arm, Van steadied her. "I have."

"Do I get on your nerves?"

"You don't get on my nerves." He opened the caravan door, helping her up the steps.

"Sometimes it bugs me that I rarely know what you're thinking. Do you ever say what you're feeling?"

Van led her over to the bed and sat down next to her. "I'm feeling that you had too much to drink."

"I have this incredible urge to put my nose right up against your neck." Here Ani leaned into him and inhaled the fragrance of his skin, the scent of Van Ardavanian.

She felt his fingers stroking the hair at the back of her neck. She closed her eyes and saw a spinning black pinwheel. Then there were two black pinwheels, and four.

Ani groaned. "Oh, no, I'm going to be sick. We better go outside. . . ."

Van jumped, hustling her out of the caravan and toward the stream. As they reached the bank Ani doubled over and dinner came churning up. Most of it landed in the rushing water but Van's running shoe took the rest. Ani vomited until there was nothing left in her stomach.

"I am so sorry, Van. Your sneaker. I'll buy you a new pair. I have never done this before. Have you ever been sick like this?"

"In high school."

"I didn't taste beer until college and I still don't like it. The only alcohol in our house was in the vanilla extract. Oh, no, I'm going to be sick again. Sorry."

Ani heaved again, but all that came up was bile that burned the back of her throat.

Ani woke the next afternoon wearing her nightgown in the caravan's bed. Van must have removed her clothes. She checked: her bra was gone and her underpants were on. Every molecule in her body had been poisoned and her head throbbed like a thumb that had been hit with a hammer.

There was a note on the table reading, *Gone kayaking with Pascal. Hope you're feeling better. See you later. V.*

After a half hour of staring at the rust-spotted ceiling, Ani decided to trek to the house for a shower. When she opened the door the donkey stuck its gray bristly head into the caravan and brayed loudly.

"Shoo," Ani admonished. "Move, *eshek.*"

The donkey grabbed at Ani's nightgown with its big yellow teeth. Ani jumped back and slammed the screen door. The donkey blinked at her through the screen. Defeated and exhausted, Ani climbed back into bed.

About an hour later when Van smacked the donkey's rump it ambled away. Van entered the caravan with a cup of tea and two slices of toast.

"I thought you might want this." He sat on the edge of the bed.

"Just tea."

"It's some herbal mix Isabelle swears by," Van said. "How you feeling?"

"Let's not talk about it. How's your shoe?" That was one detail Ani remembered clearly.

"A little stinky, but otherwise unharmed."

"Great," she said. "I didn't know you kayaked."

"One of my many hidden talents," he said.

"Was I hallucinating or was Pascal singing in Armenian last night?'

"His mother's Armenian."

"Those Armenians sure get around." Ani nibbled at the toast's crust, then dropped it on the plate. "I feel like shit."

He ruffled her hair sympathetically. "Pascal and I are driving into town this afternoon. We'll be back by supper. Isabelle's expecting you at the house when you're up to it."

The hangover's nasty film rinsed off in the shower, although the headache was still lodged behind her left eye. When Ani sat down at the kitchen table, Isabelle gave her a couple of aspirin and a glass of mineral water. She also set a bowl of potatoes in front of Ani and thrust a peeler into her hand.

"That was a big one," Isabelle said, placing her palm on her belly. "Probably a knee. Six more weeks and we get to meet this new family member."

"Do you think the baby's a boy or a girl?"

Isabelle shrugged. "No idea. My mother is certain it's a girl, and my mother-in-law is predicting a boy. We'll be happy either way."

Ani turned the potatoes onto the table and began to peel the first one into the bowl. As Isabelle chopped onions, the knife clacking against the wooden board, Ani wondered how old Isabelle was and how long she and Pascal had been married. How many years would it be before Ani should be married and carrying a child? Whom would she marry?

"How do you know Van?" Ani asked.

"Pascal met him in Lebanon," Isabelle replied.

"What was Pascal doing in Lebanon?"

Isabelle pushed back a wisp of hair with her forearm, waving the knife in her hand. "He was there for a couple of months doing this and that. Van told us you knew each other when you were kids."

"He came to my fifth birthday party."

"He must have been a cute little boy."

"When I was ten, half the girls in my class wanted to kiss him," Ani said wryly.

"And what about the other half?" Isabelle asked.

"They were still playing with dolls."

"And you?"

"Me? I was playing with dolls and pretending I didn't want to kiss him," Ani answered.

"You two are driving to Ajaccio tomorrow?" Isabelle asked.

"That's the plan. Then Van wanted to go to Bastia."

"But you'll come back to us before you leave," Isabelle said.

When Van and Pascal returned, the four of them sat down to dinner. Ani didn't touch her glass of wine.

"You Armenians don't know how to carry your liquor," Pascal ribbed her.

"You're as Armenian as I am," Ani reminded him.

"Yes, but I'm also a Corsican, and we know how to drink," he replied.

After the dishes were washed, Van and Pascal fitted together with wooden pegs the pieces of a cradle that Pascal had carved. Isabelle sat by the window working fine white wool on silver needles. Ani wished she had something practical to do with her hands. She thought of centuries of Armenian women who had embroidered towels, crocheted lace doilies, and woven carpets. They had shorn the sheep, carded and spun the wool, gathered plants to dye the wool, and put it to the loom.

Ani worried that if a nuclear war threw humanity back to the time before the Industrial Revolution she would have no handy skills whatsoever. She had come to rely on machines—airplane, radio, hair dryer—that she would never be able to repair, let alone reinvent. Awful to imagine a world without flush toilets and tampons. She would plant a garden and snare small animals. She would have to get over her squeamishness about animal parts. By necessity she would learn to pluck steaming entrails from a rabbit.

It was late when Ani and Van walked silently through the field to the caravan. She heard the stream rolling over stones. She smelled the olive trees and maquis and felt the firmness of the rocky earth beneath her feet. Ani looked up at the cloudless sky and thought the moon looked like a white melon on a black platter. The stars were a scattering of seeds. She wanted to tell this to Van, but he seemed preoccupied.

Inside the caravan, Van silently prepared his pallet on the floor. He was focused and efficient. In the dark with her back to him Ani removed her blouse, quickly pulling on an oversized T-shirt and stepping into a pair of baggy sweats. Not exactly sexy sleepwear, but there didn't seem to be much call for lace and satin or a pink feather boa with matching mules.

"Night, Ani," Van said. The zip of his sleeping bag was emphatic.

"Good night, Jim-Bob."

"What?" he asked.

"Remember the end of *The Waltons,* how they all say 'Good night, John-Boy, Good night, Mary Ellen'?"

"Never watched that show."

Of course he had never watched that show. Ani lay down on the mattress and dragged her bag up over her. Their second night in this caravan and he still hadn't tried to kiss her. What was all this pathetic hankering for his touch? It would be weird to kiss somebody whom she had known since kindergarten and who was practically a cousin. Although, according to Grandma, in Armenia in the old days people married their cousins frequently. That was why *Digin* Pauline had crossed eyes: her parents were first cousins.

Well, we're not in Armenia, Ani, and he's your fourth cousin thrice removed, or something even more distant, but it doesn't matter at all because he's not interested in you.

"What's the matter, Ani?" Van asked. "You're sighing."

Ani blurted, "You forgot something."

"What did I forget?"

"To kiss me good night."

When he laughed, Ani winced. Why had she said that? A wave of crushing embarrassment tumbled her under. It was like the time when she was eight and someone tapped her on the shoulder at the public pool to tell her there was a rip in the back seam of her bathing suit.

His sleeping bag rustled, the zipper whisked open, and he was standing at the side of the bed.

Ani turned onto her side to make room for him. "Squeeze over, squeezebox."

"What's that?" He lay on his side with his head on her pillow. Ani talked fast. "I think it's from Ma and Pa Kettle. There was this series of movies: *Ma and Pa Kettle Go to Town, Ma and Pa Kettle on Vacation, Ma and Pa Kettle at Waikiki.* I watched a lot of old movies with my mother. They used to say 'Squeeze over, squeezebox.' About ten of them slept in the same bed."

He kissed Ani, stopping the torrent of words. Needles of light shot down Ani's spine and raced along her limbs. He tasted like cumin and apples; he smelled like cumin and apples and the black earth in the back garden.

Van slipped his hand under her shirt and ran a finger along the curve of her breast.

"Is this okay with you, Ani?" Van asked.

"It's okay." She breathed in his scent again. The traces of his fingerprints on her skin, his voice in her ear. His mouth was molasses on moleskin in the blackest night.

He slid his hand under the band of her pants.

"I don't have my birth control handy," Ani whispered.

"I've got a condom."

"How resourceful of you."

"A Boy Scout is always prepared."

"I never made it past Brownie. I think I still have that beanie and orange tie someplace at home. I got a homemaking badge. One of the requirements was making butter from heavy cream."

With his index finger he stilled her lips. "Did anyone ever tell you you talk too much?" he asked with mock seriousness.

Forget the question marks. She could climb inside here and rest out of the wind. A small fire would make light and warmth for the night. Pine branches sent sparks flying over their heads like exclamation points.

The next morning Ani woke from cramped sleep with a crick in her neck. She couldn't believe Van Ardavanian was lying next to her. There was a shadow of a beard on his open face. His eyes were closed, and the long straight lashes fanned above his cheekbones. Ani wanted to lay her head on his chest and feel its warmth and solidity.

Then panic seized her. What if Van told his grandmother that they were lovers and his grandmother told her grandmother? Amid a circle of pilling cardigans there would be the clucking of tongues, wagging of heads, and a loud chorus of *amot kezi, amot kezi.* Could she climb over him, sneak out of the caravan, and hitch a ride to Bastia? She'd stow away on a ferry to Marseille and take the TGV back to Paris. Seemed unlikely.

Alternative plan: maybe they could pretend it never happened.

be neither sweet and swallowed nor sour and spurned

After breakfast Ani and Van headed south in the car. In the backseat was a wicker hamper of food that Isabelle had pressed on them as they left. They drove on winding roads lined with terraces bordered by ancient stone walls. Wooden beehives sat in the middle of the terraces. Ani stared out the window, the landscape a sad sweet thing like the frail leaves of an old book dipped in syrup.

Van paused several times as flocks crossed the road accompanied by craggy-faced old men. The sheep walked on their haunches like women in high heels. The goats were bearded and sarcastic. We own this road, they said, and you are merely passing through history. Our history. Ani wondered if the gray shepherds spoke Italian, French, or Corsican.

This was the kind of place people should go on their honeymoon, where the landscape's beauty is sharp and melancholy. It made you feel that life hadn't changed much in a thousand years. It reminded you how short your own life was and how small you were on the face of the spinning planet. Suddenly an image of herself turning in Van's embrace flickered through her mind. It made her weak.

"Reminds me of Armenia," Van said.

"When were you there?"

"A few years ago." His terse reply didn't invite further questions.

Higher up the mountain a snowstorm fell upon them. Slowly wending through the blizzard, they stopped at a small ski lodge at the summit for coffee and hot chocolate and then drove down the mountain, heading toward Ajaccio. A few hours later in the port town the azure ocean glittered under a brilliant sun. They parked the car on a street lined with expensive boutiques.

"First it's nineteenth-century peasants and now we're in a fancy resort," Ani commented.

"There is a certain grimness in the contrast," Van replied.

Entering the lobby of a modern building, they took the elevator to the sixth floor. The apartment, which belonged to one of Pascal's friends, had white walls and spare, angular furniture. There were two rooms, a small kitchen, and a bath. Van said he had some errands to do so Ani set herself up on the balcony with a book. It didn't occur to her to ask where he was going.

When darkness began to fall, Ani set the glass-topped dining room table with dishes she found in the kitchen and the provisions from Isabelle's hamper. She rummaged in the cabinets, coming up with a pair of candles and some matches. She turned off the lights and lit the candles. It was so romantic. There was too much expectation in that kind of light.

When Van arrived, the floor lamp was on and the candles back in the drawer.

"You get everything done?" Ani asked.

"Yup," he answered.

"Isabelle packed a banquet. She even put in a bottle of wine."

"Looks good," Van said, taking a seat at the table.

"Do you want some wine?"

"No, thanks."

Ani stared at the roast chicken on her plate and felt her stomach ball up on itself. She listened to the accusatory clink of his fork and knife against the plate.

It was all her fault. She was the one who had asked him for a good-night kiss. If she had just kept her mouth shut he wouldn't be walled off behind a stone grill of silence. She drained the mineral water in her glass and poured some more.

Van and Ani cleared the table and stood in the narrow kitchen at the sink. She washed; he dried. When they were done Van strode to the living room and unfastened the ties of his sleeping bag, spreading it on the couch. Ani marched to the bathroom with her toothbrush, her gums soon suffering from her vigor. In the bedroom she jerked on her nightclothes and flung herself onto the bed.

Van called from the living room, "Good night, Ani." He flicked off the lamp.

"Good night, *Baron* Ardavanian," Ani called back.

The electric alarm clock glowed on the bedside table. Ani watched the second hand glide around and around the dial. One night on the metro Ani had met a young fireman—*un pompier*—from Toulon. They ended up strolling along the rue de Rivoli and across the Pont des Arts to the Left Bank, stopping at a café for a hot drink. Didier told Ani that women would call the fire station looking for someone to come by. On the many slow nights when there were no fires one of the guys would be happy to oblige. Ani was incredulous, but Didier solemnly insisted that it was true. She wondered if what had transpired between her and Van was the equivalent of a *pompier* house call or what Asa referred to as a "mercy fuck." Ani cringed at the thought.

"Hey, Ani." Van called from the next room.

"Yeah?" she asked.

"Are you okay?"

She was not going to repeat her mistake. "I'm fine."

Something in her was broken. Her heart was like a piece of defective machinery. It made her fall in love with the absolutely wrong person, one she would never please, one who would always find her wanting. First Asa Willard, whom she had made into a kind of god and worshiped at his frostbitten feet; now Van Ardavanian, her supposed friend and so-called compatriot. He was too fierce in his judgments and expectations. In his own way, he was more of a puritan than her grandmother was. Ani should never have had sex with him.

Ani continued running down the list of men in her brief and narrow sexual history. Captain Will, for all his chivalry, had never

called her Ani but only Nelly, after a black-maned horse. He had
never really known her and had treated her like a transient, if
cherished, character in the drama of his life.

Damn. She had filled her belly with mineral water at dinner.
She needed to pee. To get to the toilet she would have to pass
through the living room.

Ani tiptoed by Van, who was stretched out on his side with
his face to the couch back. Ani grimaced. Well, at least somebody
was getting a good night's sleep.

As she passed the couch on the return trip, Van turned over.

"Still awake?" he asked.

"Yeah," she said.

"Me too." He sat up and patted a spot next to him.

She sat down. Two feet of dark air churned between them.

"Ani, we should talk."

"Okay," she said. Let him start.

"How do you feel about what happened last night?"

"How do you feel?"

"Well, you seem like you're mad at me. So I guess it wasn't
such a great idea."

"*I'm* mad at *you*? You're the one who wasn't talking to me all
day."

"Ani, you weren't talking to me."

"Well, we seem to be having a conversation now. What do you
think is going on?"

"Listen, when I invited you to come on this trip I had no idea
how things would turn out between us. I had some business to
take care of in Corsica and I thought you—"

"What kind of business? I thought this was a vacation."

"It's just a figure of speech. I wanted to visit Pascal. And drive
around the island. I thought we'd be good company."

"But now I wrecked it all," Ani said miserably.

"No. It was my fault. Neither of us is in a position to start
something like this."

"Why not?"

"You're on the rebound. And I'm not in the right place either."

"Because of Maro?"

"Maybe that's part of it. It can't be something casual because neither of us is like that. And because we're friends. My work is the main thing right now. I don't want to get distracted."

"Okay, my friend," Ani said. "Let's not get distracted. Let's maintain a hawklike focus on our objectives."

"Don't get pissed off, Ani. Be fair. Admit that you're confused too."

"All right," she said grudgingly. "But promise you won't say anything to your grandmother."

He laughed. "Is that what you're worried about?"

"At this hour of the night I have all kinds of irrational fears," Ani said. "I'm going to bed." She stood.

He tugged on the hem of her shirt. "You forgot something."

She sat back down. "That's my line. Are you asking for trouble?"

"Just a good-night kiss." He ran his finger down her neck.

"We're both asking for trouble," she said, leaning into his kiss.

The next day they drove to Bonifacio, an old town where white cliffs faced south over a shimmering aquamarine sea. The sky was clear, and Van pointed out Sardinia in the distance. From there they drove to the outskirts of town, where a small roadside house looked over the sea. It belonged to another of Pascal's friends, and Van again had the key. The house was little more than a cabin; in the bathroom there was no tub or shower, only a toilet and a small washbasin.

Van said he wanted to go running, so Ani headed out for a walk. She was joined by a big dignified dog that came from a neighboring house. Ani and the dog traveled beyond the pavement onto a dirt road leading toward the ocean. Sometimes she followed the dog; sometimes the dog circled around to follow her. They made their way up a small hill, bushwhacking a bit. There was an abandoned shack at the top with a weathered wooden door. On the narrow path leading to the road someone had abandoned his shoes in their steps, and the old boots were filled with cobwebs.

The next day they returned to Ponte-Leccia, where Pascal and Isabelle served another feast. After dinner, Ani and Van walked in silence across the stony meadow. This was their last night on Corsica. The moon cast shadows on the ground, and the donkey brayed mournfully as they passed.

In the caravan she dropped onto the narrow bed. He lay down next to her, turning toward her. Their faces were a hairbreadth apart, his gaze so intent that it scared her.

Pulling back slightly, she whispered, "What's the secret password?"

"Bonaparte," he guessed.

"Think dessert," she said.

He was smiling now. "*Pakhlava?*"

"Close," she told him.

"*Khadayif?*"

"Bingo!"

She kissed him, trying not to think of anything beyond that moment and the feel of his hands moving along her body.

On the ferry to Marseille they sat side by side watching gulls swoop outside the windows. Ani noticed that although Van didn't lack passion in private, his public displays of affection were minimal. Asa hadn't been much for kissing on the street, but he often had his arm around her as they walked, and he pulled her onto his lap even in the library. Ani glanced at Van, imagining sidling into his lap and the look of consternation this would provoke.

It reminded Ani of her grandparents, whom she knew were devoted to each other in their own old-fashioned way. She had never once seen Baba and Grandma hold hands, let alone kiss, but they were completely dedicated to each other in their daily habits. She made his meals. He drove her to her appointments and to church. They never spent a night apart.

Van reached out and tugged lightly on a lock of Ani's hair. "I'm really sorry about this, Ani, but I have to make a detour to Switzerland. I'll drive you as far as the station in Lyon. You can get the train back to Paris."

This announcement felt to Ani like a slamming door.

"What do you have to do in Switzerland?" she asked.

"It's for work. When I called in yesterday they told me. It came up at the last minute." His face was impassive. "I'll cover the ticket. I know you were counting on driving back together."

"You don't have to pay for the ticket," said Ani. "I have plenty of money. I didn't spend a franc in Corsica."

The drive to Lyon was tense and silent. Ani scanned Van's opaque face. His gaze was fixed on the road ahead, and she wondered if he was feeling anything at all. He was like a closed market stall, all its wares behind a thick metal shutter that the proprietor rolled down at the end of the business day.

This was the old loneliness.

Baba and Grandma were grocery shopping on Saturday afternoon. Ani stood in the hall outside the closed door of the bedroom she shared with her mother.

When Ani knocked, her mother said, Don't come in. I need to be alone. Why don't you go play on the swings?

Instead Ani pressed her ear to the wooden door and listened to her mother's muffled crying. Then there was silence. Had her mother fallen asleep? Had her mother stealthily slipped out the window and run away? She would have no mother and no father. She would be altogether abandoned. Ani squeezed her hands into a prayer chapel and asked God to keep her from being an orphan. Just then Grandma had bustled into the kitchen calling, Ani, come see candy I bought you at store!

Ani wasn't a kid anymore and nobody was going to bring her fruit slices from the candy counter at the Star Market. She knew the adventure was over. She had seen the island of Corsica and smelled the maquis. The sex had been ardent, but that was behind them now. She would bravely say goodbye and not look back.

She pressed her heart smaller and smaller. It was a lump of coal, the kind they always threaten you with at Christmas. In one television episode of *Superman*, Clark Kent had secretly squeezed a bit of coal with such force that it was transformed into a glittering diamond. Ani's heart was that hard.

When the car stopped outside the train station in Lyon, Ani reached into the backseat for her pack. As she opened the car door, Van firmly grasped her forearm.

"Ani, don't look so sad. I'll call you as soon as I get back to Paris."

Her heart dissolved like sugar in a glass of tea.

"When?" she asked, hoping her tone didn't sound as desperate as she felt.

"A week, ten days at the most." Here he drew her hand to his face, brushing his lips across her knuckles in the most extravagant gesture he had yet made outside of bed.

in a foreign place the exiled man will have no face

On Saturday afternoon, fifteen little girls in pastel dresses drifted into the Bartons' apartment like so many artificial flowers. Sydney, as befitting the birthday princess, wore a rhinestone tiara and a pink satin dress. She had informed Ani how much the dress cost in French francs and in dollars at the current exchange rate. Ani supervised the games—pin the tail on the donkey, musical chairs, and a treasure hunt for prizes and candy. Finally Tacey and Ani herded the girls to the table for cake and ice cream.

In her room that evening Ani perused acceptance letters from graduate programs. The one from Seattle—an application she had made when she thought she wanted to live with Asa—she discarded. The other three she lined up on the table, unable to decide in which city to cast her fate. She felt like a bobbing cork in the ocean searching for a shore. Elena was in New York, and this seemed like as good a reason as any to go there. It was the university where her father had gone to law school and the neighborhood where she had spent the first four years of her life. She filled out the requisite forms and sealed the envelopes.

In the morning she dropped the letters in the yellow postal box affixed to the wall across from her building. Somehow the thought of the crowded metro or the jammed autobus filled her with dread. She didn't want to brush up against someone else's sorrow or be hemmed in by the pulse of other lives. So she walked to the university, reading melancholy on the faces that she passed.

When she turned to the mirror in the evening she half expected to see herself grown transparent. But there she was, substantial as ever, with sad gray eyes, pale skin, and black hair.

It had been ten days—she counted them on the calendar again—since Van had dropped her at the train station in Lyon.

What did it matter? She would be leaving Paris in less than two months. She didn't need Van. Life would unroll ahead of her like a long narrow carpet that she would walk one step at a time. Come September she would immerse herself in her studies. She would sit in classes all day, read French novels all evening, and then lounge with Elena eating brownies at midnight. She would eventually find someone else to love.

Day eleven, or rather night eleven, minutes after Ani had shut out her light, the phone rang and she knew it was Van before she lifted the receiver. He was outside the Palais-Royal metro station at a pay phone.

Darkness leaked from beneath the concierge's door in the front hall. When Van strode out of the shadows she opened the door, putting a finger to her lips. In the elevator Ani crossed her arms and watched the floor indicator rise. When the elevator door opened on the top floor she marched up the hall with Van behind her. Inside her room he dropped his pack, slung his coat over the back of a chair, and turned to her soberly.

Seconds later she was in his arms. His face was soft from a recent shave and his mouth was a warm shock of syrup.

"Wait a minute, wait a minute," Ani said, as much to herself as to him. She pulled back from his embrace. "I want you to answer me something."

"What's that?" he asked.

"Am I distracting you from your work?"

He sat heavily on the couch. "It's almost midnight, Ani. Work hours are over. I got back to town, dumped my clothes, shaved, and headed here."

"What were you doing in Switzerland?" Ani sat down beside him, their knees touching.

"A business trip. Meetings." There was a thread of annoyance in his voice.

"Could you be a bit more specific?"

With studied patience he said, "I told you this already. The Armenian Refugee Aid Association. ARAA."

She scanned his veiled countenance. His answers were gruff and perfunctory. Yet she believed he was sincere. She loved the black crescent eyebrows in his olive face and the strong line of his nose.

"I missed you," he said. His lips curved slightly into a smile. The smallest smile. The light was faint, but in it was the promise of a pleasure she couldn't decline.

In the morning Ani dragged herself downstairs to see Sydney off to school, leaving Van asleep. The bed was empty when she returned. There was a note on the table saying he had gone for a run and would call from the corner. He had left his wallet on the bookshelf, along with a pen and some coins. The wallet was brown leather, worn at its corners, the kind that folded in half.

Searching another person's wallet—invading a private space— wasn't a nice thing to do. Ani had sometimes been driven to this kind of prying when she was living with Asa and he had gone emotionally underground. Once when she found a girl's name and number scrawled on a strip of paper, Ani had flushed it down the toilet. These were her other sins of stealth: reading letters from his friends, skimming his journal, and eavesdropping on telephone conversations.

When she was little she used to sneak into their room and explore the top drawer of her mother's dresser: a fake pearl necklace, a pair of white kid gloves, and a velvet clutch with a golden clasp. In the very back of the drawer she found a small laminated black-and-white photograph of her parents on their wedding day. They were on a corner in Manhattan, beetle-roofed cars frozen in the street behind them. Violet wore a white skirt and jacket with a white hat topping her upswept black hair. Her lips were dark with lipstick and she was radiantly happy. David Silver wore a black suit, a white shirt, and a black tie. His arm was around Violet's slim waist, his eyes turned toward his bride.

Nancy Kricorian

Ani wished her mother would secretly know that Ani was rummaging in the drawer and leave her gifts of knowledge. Ani wanted her father's driver's license, or his birth certificate, or a love letter he had written to Violet. She even imagined her father writing to her from heaven and sending the note by angel courier. The angel would slide the envelope into the back of the drawer where Ani would find it.

Dear Ani,
Behind my mansion there is a pond and on its surface I watch
reflections of the earthly world. The mirror that you stand before
is a window through which I can observe you. When I see tears
on your face I want to reach out and brush them away. . . .

But every time she looked Ani held the same photograph, always the same.

Not knowing exactly what she was seeking, Ani opened Van's wallet. In its folds were several hundred-franc notes and a few coins. There were no cards of any kind, nothing with his name on it. He must have left his identity papers in one of his pockets. She searched his jeans and came up empty. In one jacket pocket she found a metal key ring with three keys and in the other a *carnet* of yellow metro tickets. No passport.

When Van called from the corner, Ani went down. Madame Spinelli stood framed in her doorway as Van crossed the threshold in his sodden running clothes with a brown *boulangerie* bag clutched in one hand. The woman glared at Ani disapprovingly, disappeared into her apartment, and closed the door.

That afternoon Ani talked with Tacey, preempting anything the concierge might have to report.

"I've got a new boyfriend," Ani said.

"The Communist?" Tacey asked.

Ani fought back exasperation. "My friend from Watertown. He stayed with me last night. Madame Spinelli saw him."

"I heard," Tacey said dryly.

"Is it okay with you if he stays over some nights?"

Tacey paused to consider. "Where does he live?"

"On the boulevard Voltaire."

"You'd probably be late all the time if you slept there, and that would be a bother," Tacey mused. "Just as long as John doesn't know anything about it, I suppose it's okay. I'll speak to the concierge."

Ani was baby-sitting until midnight on Friday. After Sydney was asleep, she let Van in and sent him upstairs to wait. On Saturday they lazed in bed until afternoon.

They strolled to the Pompidou Center and sat outside on the plaza near the fountain watching people walk by. Later they walked to the place de la Bastille for supper at a brasserie.

Van spilled some salt on the black tabletop, then traced a spiral in the white grains. He seemed sad and pensive.

"What are you thinking about?" Ani asked him.

"Mount Auburn Street," he said. "Is Kay's Market still there?"

"Of course. Randy's Bowl-a-Way is gone, though. There's some law office or something there. And you remember Lucy Sevanian's dad's tailor shop?"

"Sure."

"He sold it," Ani said.

"You and Lucy were like salt and pepper shakers," Van commented.

"She was my best friend from third grade to senior year," she said.

"Almost as long as we've known each other."

"Except Lucy and I have drifted apart," Ani said, a little sadly. "I haven't seen her since freshman year."

"When Lucy and I were eight there was this boy named Robert Uzkonian in our class. He drove Lucy crazy. He always wanted to hold her hand and sit next to her. Lucy couldn't stand him. There was something the matter with him. He drooled. He banged his wrists together so much that the teacher made him sit on his hands.

"One day when Robert was absent, Mrs. Van Dee sent Lucy outside to check on the weather. While Lucy was gone the teacher told the class not to speak to her when she came back. We were to stand around in groups, talking to each other, and if Lucy tried to speak to us we were supposed to turn our backs on her."

"What was that about?" Van asked.

"She was giving Lucy a lesson in unkindness. Lucy completely ignored Robert, and now she would know how it felt."

"What happened?" he asked.

"When Lucy came back she went to the teacher's desk and the teacher pretended she didn't see or hear her. Then Lucy came over to me. We were friends. We sat together. We traded from our lunches. I saw the teacher, who was staring at me, daring me to defy her. And I turned my back on Lucy. I think that was the worst thing I've ever done in my life."

"The worst?"

"Well, I've shoplifted. I've lied. I've fornicated. But betraying my best friend?"

"I don't know if there are many eight-year-olds who could have done different. Did you and Lucy ever talk about it?" Van asked.

"No. I gave her my cupcakes and cookies at lunch for a week. It was a kind of penance."

The waiter cleared their plates.

"You want tea?" Van asked.

Ani checked her watch. "We better get going. It's past eleven."

"Come to my place," Van said.

"I have to be at the Bartons' early."

"We'll put you in a taxi by seven," he assured her.

In Van's building they rode the elevator to the penultimate floor, climbing a flight of narrow stairs to the top. Ani followed Van down a long dingy hallway where the paint was peeling and plaster had come out in patches. Ani stopped to use the communal WC that stank of urine and cheap cologne.

Van's tiny whitewashed room contained a simple desk, a wooden side chair, a washbasin with a mirror above it, a tiny fridge, and a set of yellow cabinets that looked like refugees from someone's kitchen. Ani noticed that the top doors on the cabinet were padlocked. A bare lightbulb hung from the ceiling and a gooseneck lamp sat on the desk. Over the desk was a shelf on which there were a few books: a French dictionary, some tattered paperbacks—mostly history and political science, Ani noted, no novels or poetry—and a serious-looking clothbound book with Armenian lettering on its spine. The walls were otherwise bare.

The bed, which on closer examination turned out to be two stacked foam mattresses, ran the length of the wall opposite the door. The white sheet was neatly folded over a navy wool blanket. Above the bed the room's only window looked out on an inner courtyard.

"It's like a monk's cell." Ani kicked off her shoes and sat down on the bed.

He sat down next to her, prying his sneakers off one at a time. "I was aiming for that. When I moved in it was a dank closet filled with broken furniture and stacks of magazines."

The mattress was wide enough for sex, but sleeping was another matter. Ani dozed in snatches, unable to find a comfortable position. Finally, around two-thirty, Van pushed the desk and chair against the door, making enough space to separate the mattresses and lay them side by side. They were both wide awake by then, so Van lit a candle and put it on the shelf under the mirror. He stretched out on the bed with one arm behind his head while Ani leaned against the cold plaster wall and pulled his feet into her lap. She began to massage one of them.

"Hey, you're good at that," he said.

"I took a massage workshop when I was in college. I learned all the homely arts: massage, knitting, and self-defense. Some friends and I got a nurse from the women's health center to come and show us how to do pelvic self-exams. Everyone had a hand mirror. The party favors were plastic speculums."

"Don't think I've ever seen one of those."

"They look kind of like duck beaks. Elena and I used to put on puppet shows with them. Just for ourselves, of course."

"Is she your best friend?"

"She's the one I talked to about everything. She's in New York now. That's part of the reason I decided to go there."

"When are you leaving?"

"June fifteenth."

"You going back to Watertown first?"

"For the summer." She pulled his other foot into her lap.

"I haven't been home in four years. Maybe I'll fly back with you," he said, almost wistfully.

Her mind leaped from that statement to a wedding at the First Armenian Church. Her grandmother and his grandmother sat together weeping with joy into their pressed white handkerchiefs. Baba led her down the aisle toward the altar, where Van waited in a black tuxedo. No. That was all wrong. A two-minute town hall ceremony presided over by a justice of the peace. Then a party at the Armenian Cultural Center. The Armenian Cultural Center? What was she thinking? It was better than the VFW hall. How about the Sheraton Commander Ballroom? Maybe a party in the backyard. The lilacs were in bloom and the forsythia leaves shone a handsome green.

"That would be great," was what she said.

"Do you know what yesterday was?" he asked.

She was disappointed that he had changed the subject. She was hoping for a firm commitment on the trip home. "Sunday?"

"April twenty-fourth."

"Damn. Forgot to write Martyr's Day on my calendar." Her tone was more flippant than she intended.

Van didn't respond for a minute. Then he asked, "Did your grandparents talk about it?"

"Forbidden topic in our house. I always had the idea it would kill my grandmother."

"My grandmother used to give lectures in churches and clubs. She's a smart woman. She doesn't do it anymore, though. It kind of tired her out."

"She gave me a book for high school graduation," Ani said.

"Which one?"

"It was called *The Murder of a Nation.*" Ani could still see the inscription written in a looping hand on the title page: *Souvenir to Miss Ani Kersamian Silver from Aunt Sophie Nahabedian.*

Van said, "The Morgenthau. She had a box of those in her closet."

The night she had received the book Ani had cracked open the spine as she lay in bed. Skimming a few pages, she was put off by the fusty prose and so began to flip through the captioned photos. FISHING VILLAGE ON LAKE VAN: *in this district 55,000 Armenians were massacred*; A VIEW OF HARPOOT: *where massacres of men took place on a large scale*; THOSE WHO FELL BY THE WAYSIDE. This last showed a row of decomposing bodies strewn along the edge of a dusty road. Ani had closed the book and turned out the light.

That night she had dreamed she was preparing for a long journey. She packed some clothes, her Bible, a toothbrush, and a box of saltines in a cardboard suitcase. She stopped in a thrift shop to buy a raincoat for the trip. The black slicker she tried on had metal buckles and yellow fluorescent stripes on it, like a fireman's coat, and it came down to her ankles. As she examined herself in the full-length mirror, a saleswoman came up behind her and said, I wouldn't wrinkle my nose up at that coat if I were you, honey. It will come in handy when you're digging trenches in the rain.

In the dream Ani had realized she was being sent to a Nazi concentration camp. When Ani turned she saw her grandmother gesticulating at her from the sidewalk through a plate glass window. As Ani watched Grandma metamorphosed into a little girl in a long brown dress caked with mud. Two policemen grabbed the child by the arms and dragged her away.

April 24 was Genocide Commemoration Day. Now it had an official name. When Ani was ten she had opened the church bulletin one April Sunday to see the listing *Commemoration of the 1915 Massacres, Mr. Torkom Norabedian.* After the invocation and the hymn, Pastor Duke announced that instead of his regular sermon Mr. Norabedian, one of the church deacons, would speak.

The Massacres had never been explained to Ani, but she knew from bits of conversation she wasn't supposed to have heard between her mother and grandfather and occasional vague references from her grandmother that in the old country the Turks had murdered lots of Armenians and forced even more to leave their homes. But no one was supposed to talk about the Deportations, especially not in front of Grandma.

Mr. Norabedian declined the pastor's offer of ascending to the pulpit and stood instead on the same level as the pews at the front of the church. He was a thickset older man in a gray suit. His thinning hair was grizzled, his skin was ashen, and everything about him was gray. Even his stiff, craggy voice had smoke in it as he started to speak.

In 1915, the Turks came into our house and said to my father, Give up your God and we will let you live. But my father wouldn't give up his Jesus, so they threw him in the fireplace in front of us—my mother, my grandparents, me and my sisters and brother—and they burned him alive. And the Turks held my mother and made her watch her husband burn. When I saw my father die I wanted to tear the eyes from my head.

Mr. Norabedian's voice broke and tears began to roll down his face, but he kept talking over the moans of the old women in the front pews.

He said, But my eyes saw more. The Turks used bayonets to cut babes from the bellies of pregnant women and then tossed the bloody babies into the air and caught them on the ends of their bayonets. This was a game and they laughed. They tied young girls to trees and raped them, one man having his way after the next, until the girls were torn open and bleeding to death. I still hear them screaming.

Tears streamed down his craggy face. He went on.

Some girls threw themselves into the river. Some mothers threw their children into the rushing water and jumped in after them. Better to go to God than to be defiled by the Turks or die like a dog by the side of the road. The land ran red with our blood.

Ani was glad that the small children were downstairs in the Sunday school room because these stories might give them nightmares. Next to Ani her cousin Mike was doodling with a small pencil on a collection envelope. He had drawn a row of bayonets. Ani gazed at her grandmother's small pale hands, which were clenched tightly in her lap. Then the girl glanced up at the old woman's pallid, stonelike countenance.

Ani turned away, blinking rapidly. She didn't think Grandma should be hearing what Mr. Norabedian was saying. His voice kept spilling out the horrible story and wouldn't stop. After a while it sounded like a saw rasping through wood. She stared at the white numerals on the hymn board and repeated the numbers: 115, 89, 236, 115, 89, 236.

Finally they did sing hymn number 236.

Then, as he did each week, the pastor blessed the congregation with these words: *Now unto Him that is able to keep you from falling and to present you faultless before the presence of His glory and with exceeding joy, to the only wise God our Savior, be glory and majesty, dominion and power, both now and ever.* Amen.

Ani repeated the phrases in her head. To keep you from falling. To present you faultless. Falling. Faultless.

"Ani? Are you listening?" Van asked.

Sliding his feet onto the mattress, Ani crawled to the other end of the bed and took his head into her lap. "Sorry. I was thinking about something. What did you say?" She applied pressure to his temples.

"I said it's like the culture and language were pulled up by the roots and tossed into the desert to wither away. The plan was to exterminate the Armenians, drive out the Greeks, and assimilate the Kurds. Only the last was unsuccessful. So now they're razing Kurdish villages. According to government policy there are no Kurds, only 'mountain Turks.' You can be thrown into prison for speaking Kurdish."

Ani heard what he was saying, but his words dropped through silent air until they hit bottom with distant echoing splashes.

Van stopped talking.

She said, "My grandmother used to tell me about angels and spirits. Satan was a fallen angel. In the old days there were *devs* as big as mountains that came out at night to make trouble. There were evil spirits that liked the dirt in corners, which was why you had to sweep carefully. There was a hearth angel who lived in the fire. We didn't have a *toneer* or an *ojakh,* so I thought the angel lived in the pilot light of the stove."

As she talked, Ani slowly massaged Van's face, pressing deeply into his tense jaw muscles until she felt them begin to slacken.

She continued. "There was a small blue and yellow flame inside the oven that burned night and day. Sometimes I would open the oven door and peer into the hole to check on the flame. As long as that pilot light was burning I knew nothing bad could happen in our kitchen. I also believed that my pink blanket had magical powers to protect me from Satan. I would pull the blanket over my head at night before I fell asleep so that not even the tip of my nose was showing."

Finally Ani lay down beside him and listened to his breathing as it grew deep and regular until she drifted off herself.

It seemed like five minutes later that the alarm went off. Van reached across Ani to slap the clock quiet, then pulled her closer.

"Sleep some more," he murmured.

Ani rested her head on his shoulder. A minute later she rolled over and looked at the alarm clock. "Oh, shit. It's almost seven. I won't have time to shower and change."

She jumped up, pulling on her skirt, and nudged Van with her foot. "Come on, get up. The door's barricaded. We have to move the furniture."

When Ani arrived in the Bartons' kitchen Sydney was lining up the pancake ingredients on the counter.

"Your hair is sticking up on one side and it's flat on the other," the little girl observed.

Ani told her, "It's called bed head."

"You have a new hairdresser?" Sydney asked slyly.

"You're too smart for your own good, little lady." Recognizing that the sentence and tone came straight from Violet Silver's repertoire, Ani laughed.

The following weekend the Bartons were away. Van arrived on Friday night with a day pack and a toothbrush. They cooked meals in the palace kitchen and made forays to the local greengrocer, cheese shop, and bakery for supplies. On Sunday evening when they emerged at dusk to seek out dinner there was a guy lurking in the passageway near the front entrance.

"Van, *bos yegoor,*" he said, in a gravelly voice. Wearing a black leather jacket and jeans, he had a beard and mustache and looked to be in his mid-twenties.

Van told Ani, "Wait for me in the garden. I'll be three minutes."

"Van!" Ani protested.

"Go on, please. Hratch is a friend. I have to talk with him and then we'll go."

Ani glanced at the guy and shrugged. "Okay."

Hratch addressed her in a brighter tone. "*Kisher pari,* Ani."

She reluctantly walked through the passageway to the garden, where she righted a metal chair and sat in a pool of light spilling from the nearby arcade. Ani didn't like that Hratch knew not only her name but also where she lived when she had never even heard of him. As a matter of fact, she didn't know any of Van's friends, except for Pascal and Isabelle. He didn't know any of her friends either. They met each other in a separate world outside of her daily contacts at work or school.

It seemed like a lot longer than three minutes before Van appeared.

"Come on," he said, lacing his arm through hers. "I'm hungry."

"What was that all about?"

"He was trying to get in touch with me all weekend."

"Give him my phone number, will you? All we need is for the concierge to see him skulking in the alley like that."

The next morning after Van had padded out to the hall for his shower, Ani went for his pack. It had been in the back of her mind to do this since she had searched his wallet. Out of a front compartment she pulled Van's U.S. passport and a pocket spiral notebook filled with Armenian words she couldn't decipher. She reached into the main section of the pack, pushing his clothes to one side. Toward the bottom her hand brushed a zipper on the back inside face. From this hidden pocket she extracted a small booklet. It was a Cypriot passport with a white slot in its dark blue cover. The name on the outside was Yannis Antoniades. The photo inside was of Van.

There were any number of reasonable explanations for why Van had false papers, although Ani couldn't think of them at the moment. She could just ask him, Hey, Van, why do you have a passport in the name of Yannis Antoniades? When he questioned her about how she had come across this item, she would answer, Oh, I was sweeping the floor and by accident I knocked over your pack and the false passport fell out.

She remembered how grim-faced he had been when the cops had pulled them over outside Lyon. Was he a drug runner? Wasn't Marseille some kind of drug hub? She remembered the unspecified "errands" he had done in Marseille and in Ajaccio. But she couldn't believe that Van—who didn't drink alcohol, who disdained cigarettes, who lived an austere life in a tiny rented room—could possibly be a drug dealer.

Then what the hell was he doing with a false passport?

She replaced the booklet, arranging his pack exactly as she had found it. She would say nothing, but she would monitor him closely with the invisible threadlike antennae of her doubts.

ARAA, that's where Van said he worked. The Armenian Refugee Aid Association. How would that read in French? Association pour l'Aide aux Refugiés Arméniens? Ani paged through the telephone directory in the central post office until she found the listing.

As she dialed, Ani decided that if Van answered the phone she would hang up immediately, but there was no answer. At least there was such an organization with an office in Paris. Since Ani had found the Cypriot passport she had begun to worry that nothing he told her was true.

Ani had scrutinized his face for signs of deceit. But there didn't appear to be anything counterfeit about him. He seemed genuine. Was it a facade behind which another life—another Van—existed?

She wished she had access to some pot. Most of the time that she smoked—always with Asa—it had made her feel like a chipped teacup on an empty shelf. Occasionally, though, the altered habits of perception it provided had been enlightening. Everything was a half inch off-kilter, nudging ordinary sights, smells, and sounds into strangeness. One time she was able to watch and listen to beautiful, outwardly invulnerable Asa and hear not only the words he was saying but also the anxieties and insecurities that lay behind them. It allowed Ani, if only briefly, to recognize the power she had over him.

Knowledge is power.

While on the ferry from Corsica, Van had said, Knowledge is a kind of power, but force is also power. You can know many things and not have the ability to alter them because they are braced by violent force.

What gives true power? Ani had asked.

A gun, Van had said, jokingly aiming and siting his finger at her temple.

Ani's Van was a kaleidoscope of memories and images, starting with their first meeting when they were small children. His smile burned like a candle's flame in a dark chapel. His touch melted her as though the scaffolding inside her body were made of wax. She had refused to allow the gesture of a gun to her temple be a part of how she understood him. But now she found herself resifting his words, especially the ones she had pushed aside.

She wouldn't see Van again until the end of the week. She was grateful for the machinery of daily life that kept her occupied—lecture, seminar, and dance classes. Through it all, though, her thoughts of Van were like a string of beads she worried in a jacket pocket. Late on Friday night long after Sydney had fallen asleep, Van finally arrived in the front hall of the Bartons' apartment carrying a duffel bag.

Ani rested her head on his shoulder and breathed in. She sighed deeply, his presence dispelling her frantic doubts.

Van laughed. "What do I smell like?"

"Spices of the Orient. Earth in Baba's garden. October apples."

"As long as it's not unwashed gym socks, I guess we're okay."

She sent him upstairs to wait for her.

When the Bartons swaggered in several hours later Tacey's lipstick was smudged and John's face was florid.

"Sorry we're late, Ani." With her words, Tacey blew a puff of whisky breath into Ani's face. "First of all, the play was dismal. Lots of nonsensical screaming and dashing around the stage. If it had to be modern they should at least have been naked. But no, they wore these hideous costumes. Then there was dinner and then these clients dragged us off to a bar and we lost all track of time, right, Johnny?"

He was already halfway up the stairs to the second floor. "Shut up, Tacey, and come to bed."

She dramatically whispered into Ani's ear, "If it wouldn't mean losing all my credit cards, I think I'd divorce the bastard." She put her hand over her mouth in a theatrical gesture and laughed raggedly.

When Ani slipped in, Van was sitting on the couch reading *Libération,* the table lamp beside him shedding a circle of light in the otherwise dim room. This picture was transported immediately into the house of Ani's memories—the particular quality of the lamplight, the serious concentration on Van's handsome face, the sense of possession it gave her to find him waiting for her.

Van looked up at her with panther-dark eyes and she felt a whirlpool spin behind her ribs down through her belly and below. She didn't want to talk about anything at all. . . .

Hunger drove them out into the world after sundown the next day. They went to a bistro on the rue des Petits Champs. Van turned Ani's palm up on the table. He traced her lifeline, which wrapped itself around the mound of her thumb almost to her wrist.

"You have a long life ahead of you, Ani. I'd guess you'll live to be ninety years old."

"Can I see yours?" Ani asked.

He turned his palm up, placing his fingers over hers.

"Is this it?" she asked, running her finger along a crease in his open hand. She wanted to pull his fingers to her lips.

"That's it. Not long, not short. But I don't really believe in this stuff," he said. "Maro was into palmistry and tea leaves. You're more sensible than that, aren't you, Ani?"

"Sure. My superstitions are random. Except for believing that dreams are messages."

"Messages from whom?" he asked.

"Messages from yourself," she told him.

They were up late on Saturday night and slept until noon. Why put clothes on when you could lie around under the sheets with books and a bottle of mineral water to pass back and forth? Ani opened the final volume of Proust while Van read Fanon. Every now and then one of them would read a line out loud.

On Monday, Ani readied herself for the morning routine chez Barton. While Van stuffed his duffel he told her he was going out of town for work for a few days. His tone was casual, but the news had the same effect on Ani as a window shade unexpectedly snapping open. After the initial start from the noise there was the moment of adjustment as stark light poured in the window.

A trip. A business trip. What kind of business? And under what name are you traveling, Mr. Ardavanian?

Attempting to sound equally casual, Ani asked, "Where are you going?"

"Belgium."

"Are you taking the train?"

"Driving with a friend."

His sentences were clipped and telegraphic.

"Are you going with Hratch?" she asked.

"No. Another friend." He hefted the duffel to his shoulder. "So. I'll see you Friday night?"

"Friday night? I'm not sure. I might be busy on Friday." Her tone was chill.

He dropped the bag to the floor and turned to face her. "Give me a break, Ani. It's my job."

Ani blurted out, "And what exactly is your job, Mr. Yannis Antoniades?"

She watched as awareness spread across his face. Following seconds behind was wrath.

"You shouldn't have done that, Ani. You shouldn't have gone through my stuff. How am I going to trust you if you do things like that?"

"How are you going to trust *me*? You're the one with the false passport."

"Listen, Ani, I work for a relief agency. I have to travel all over. I go to Israel, Lebanon, and Syria. You can't use the same passport."

"What exactly is your job description?"

He glanced at his watch. "Shit, Ani. I don't have time for this. Can we talk on Friday?"

"Are you a drug dealer?" Ani asked.

Van laughed, his face suddenly sunny. "Is that what you're worried about? Listen, Ani, look at me. Do you really think I'm a drug dealer?"

"No. I guess not. But there are a lot of things you aren't telling me, Van. I know that much."

"Ani, I promise, when the time is right, we'll talk. Trust me."

"I'm supposed to trust you?" she asked.

"That's right," he told her firmly.

The next day Ani dialed the ARAA number again. This time a woman answered the phone and gave Ani the office's hours of operation. A half hour later Ani entered a cobbled courtyard on a narrow street in the Ninth Arrondissement. She climbed a flight of worn wooden stairs and knocked on a heavy door with a gold knob in its center.

"*Entrez,*" a woman's voice called from inside.

Ani opened the door and stepped into a small cramped office where two desks were squeezed into the corner and bookcases lined the other walls. One of the desks was empty and at the other sat an Armenian woman in a brown cardigan and a beige dress. She reminded Ani of the organist at her grandmother's church. Her raven hair was set in waves around her head, and her jet eyebrows were plucked into sleek arches.

"May I help you?" she asked Ani.

"I just wanted to look around. I was curious about your organization."

"We have offices in six countries. We help Armenian refugees and immigrants. There are difficulties sometimes with the papers. Or with finding work or permanent lodging. We have a network of churches and businesspeople to go to for assistance. We also have a library of books in Armenian that people can borrow. Over there are back issues of our newsletter." She pointed to a bookcase full of yellowing periodicals. "Are you Armenian?"

"My mother's Armenian."

"Where are you from?"

"The States. Watertown."

The woman's face softened. "Watertown? I have cousins there. The Mardigians? You know them? They live on School Street."

"I don't know them, but my grandparents probably do. They know everybody."

"Where are your grandparents from?"

"My grandmother's from Mersin. My grandfather's from Marash."

"My people are from Erzurum."

Ani had no idea where any of these places were on the map or how far Marash was from Erzurum. For Armenians, being from one place or another seemed to signify something about what kind of life your people had lived because of geography and climate. The same way that to say you were from Watertown meant one thing and to say you were from Fresno meant another.

"Do you work here alone?" Ani asked. She wanted to find out if the second desk was Van's.

"I'm the only full-time employee. We have a few part-time people and some volunteers."

So Van didn't work here—at least not full-time. She wondered if he was even on the payroll. Should she ask the woman what Van did here? Then when he got back from Belgium he'd find out that she had been snooping.

How am I going to trust you, Ani?

Damn.

She wished she had time to sit down and read through some of the newsletters, but she was due at Sondage's seminar in half an hour.

On Friday night the Bartons reached home earlier than usual. Van hadn't yet arrived and Ani was worried that he would ring the front bell. Instead of returning to her room she sat on the step outside the marble entrance hall with its gilt and crystal chandelier. She was wearing a sweater, but hours after the sun had gone down the stone was cold. She wrapped her arms around her legs and put her head to her knees, willing Van to appear.

Vhat you doing, you crazy girl? Sitting outside freezing you vorik?

That was Grandma's voice. Ani smiled. She was freezing her *vorik* with only a thin cotton skirt and her *vardik* underneath.

And Baba? What would Baba say? He'd come up with some gnomic phrase.

When Ani was in the third grade the teacher had required everyone to stand in a circle and hold hands while they spouted adages. *What's good for the goose is good for the gander. A stitch in time saves nine. A penny saved is a penny earned.* Ani tried to bring new and unusual ones, polling her family for suggestions. Violet had proposed a few that had gone over well with the teacher. Grandma's offerings, however, tended toward inappropriate Bible verses, such as *A virtuous woman* is *a crown to her husband: but she that maketh ashamed* is *as rottenness in his bones.* Ani knew enough not to repeat this at school.

The first time Ani offered the class a Baba saying she could tell by the look on the teacher's face that it was a failure. *If you are overly happy, go to the cemetery; if you are overly sad, still go to the cemetery.*

What does that mean, Baba?

You've got to think about it, *anoushig.* Use the brain God gave you.

For someone who's supposed to be so smart, you have no common sense, young lady, Violet chimed in.

It wasn't fair to have her mother say only that.

I saw your friend Lucy Sevanian the other day at the post office.
She asked after you. She told me she's expecting a baby in June.
Her husband is that nice Kevorkian boy from Belmont. Do you
remember him? The one with the red sports car.

That was something Violet had put in her last letter to Ani. She
had also written, *We are all looking forward to seeing you very soon.*

Ani would be leaving Paris for home in four weeks. Then in
September she would be a small wooden boat setting forth on a
great wide sea. At least she didn't have to worry about where she
would be living in New York. Elena had reserved a room for her
in her university apartment.

What place did Van Ardavanian have in any of this? He hadn't
said another word about returning to Boston with her, and she hadn't
the nerve to ask him. She tried to keep within the borders of a narrow garden bed, yanking up weedy expectations as they grew. She
fought off fantasies of an ordinary life with him: dishes in the sink,
potted plants on the sills, evening news in the shared bed. Love was
a dandelion growing from a crack in the pavement, with fierce green
leaves and an improbable sunshine of a flower. More likely, though,
Van would vanish wraithlike into the mysterious world of Armenian refugees, bullet-pocked landscapes, and false passports.

"What are you doing out here?"

She looked up. Van had materialized before her, solid as a stone
pillar.

"Come on." He pulled her to her feet.

When he put his arms around her and she leaned into him,
without warning she began to cry.

"It's okay, Ani. Everything's okay," Van reassured her.

Nothing was okay, though. Sadness welled up inside her like a
spring creek flooded by rain. Cold gray water churned over rocks,
sweeping along twigs, leaves, and old losses, large and small.

"Come on, let's go inside. We'll make some tea." He led her to the back entrance of the building, taking the keys from her chill fingers.

By the time they reached her room her breath came in ragged gulps, but the tears had stopped. She went to the washbasin and splashed water on her face. In the mirror she saw an ugly fish with swollen eyes and a down-turned mouth.

Van came up behind her and put his hand on her shoulder. "The tea's ready."

"Okay." She dried her face with a hand towel.

"I missed you," he said.

She stared at him in the mirror. What made this any different from the running, chasing game she had played with Asa for three years? The bereft waiting and the fear she felt were the same. *Maybe, Ani, the similarity is more about you than it is about either of them.* That thought was like peering out a porthole at a storm-lashed sea.

She turned and when his arms enfolded her, drawing her in, it felt like refuge. As long as she stayed in the present—the pressure of his fingers on the small of her back, the sound of his breath in her ear—everything was okay.

The next night they ate at a small Vietnamese place in Beaubourg. Ani wasn't feeling particularly talkative—she had been quiet most of the day—and Van took up some of the conversational slack.

When his espresso arrived he asked her, "Do you ever think, Ani, about the voyage this coffee has made to get here?"

"You mean from the kitchen to the table?" she asked.

"From beans grown thousands of miles from here to the drink in this cup. What country do you think they're from? Colombia?"

"I guess."

"Do you have any idea what a Colombian coffee picker's life is like?"

"From your tone, I'm guessing it's pretty wonderful."

"I'll spare you the details. I look at the waiter here and think about the American war in Vietnam and the decades of French colonialism that preceded it. What happened to his family? How did he get here and who was lost or left behind? And even your red cotton shirt, Ani. When I look at it I'm reminded of cotton workers suffering from brown lung."

"So everything's contaminated?" Ani asked.

"No, not contaminated, interconnected. It's a system for circulating money and power, keeping it in the hands of the rich and the powerful."

"What good does that kind of insight do you?" she asked.

" You have to see it before you can try to take it apart," he told her.

As they walked back toward Ani's place, Van took Ani's hand in his and she felt his vision seeping into her consciousness. She didn't resist.

The *clochard* passed out on the sidewalk gripping a dark bottle was connected to the well-heeled couple with distaste marked on their faces as they stepped over his legs. The woman's gold and diamond bracelet was a circle of dollars around her wrist, a circle that had been wrested from grime-covered miners who had dug up the metal and the gems. A tired retail clerk peered longingly into the glowing window of a closed boutique. The elegant clothes in the display had been sewn by immigrant workers who leaned over their machines until their backs ached. Other rich people passed, their faces repulsive with self-satisfaction.

Ani withdrew her hand from Van's hold, momentarily breaking the telepathic link.

"Do you see the world this way all the time?" she asked.

He touched her temple with his forefinger. "Ani, what you see is all yours."

She was in no mood for the palace's servant quarters.

"Come on," she said, abruptly turning on the sidewalk and catching his hand. She pulled Van behind her.

"Where are we going?" he asked.

"Your place."

As Ani helped rearrange the furniture so they could lie down for the night she almost regretted her choice. She had forgotten how small the place was. If discomfort was virtue, Van's room earned him a crown in heaven. At least, though, it wasn't squalid. Poverty was one thing and filth was another. If Van didn't get paid for his work at ARAA, it was no wonder he lived in this white-washed closet. But he must have some source of income.

She had wondered about Asa's money as well. The year between his college graduation and starting law school he hadn't held a job of any kind. When he was a student Ani assumed that his parents were bankrolling him, but while he was just hanging around, she thought they might expect him to support himself. He treated her to dinners out and rented cars for weekends away. He flew to visit friends in Denver. He never seemed short of cash for the best weed or single-malt scotch and was generous with his friends.

At one point Ani had said, It makes me nervous seeing money going out and none coming in.

He laughed. Just because you don't see it doesn't mean it isn't coming in.

What does that mean? Are you dealing drugs or something?

I have a trust fund, Ani.

Money that made money so he didn't have to. She should have suspected something of the sort, but since she had never before been close to anyone wealthy, it wouldn't have occurred to her. She had been torn between wishing she had been so provided for and think-ing that there was something sordid and wrong about it.

Van Ardavanian, however, didn't have a trust fund. His father was a washing machine repairman. But she knew if she started quizzing Van about his finances, a mask would come down over his features, leaving her forlorn. She would wait for him to speak. Better to spread a cotton sheet over the yellow foam mattresses and lie down beside him under the cracked pane of his single window.

a traveler's departure lies in his own hands,
his return in the hands of God

Van seemed edgy when he arrived at her place the following Friday. In the middle of a conversation he fixed his eyes on a spot in the air to the left of her, his brow furrowed. When she asked him if he was okay he shook himself like a wet dog and dredged up half a smile.

"Got a few things on my mind," he said.

"Anything you want to talk about?"

He shook his head. "Not now."

On Saturday she dragged him off to the Porte de Clignancourt flea market, where she bought plastic neon Eiffel Tower earrings for Elena and an embroidered apron for Grandma. She found nothing for her mother and Baba, but there was still time. Her departure was twenty days away. Van hadn't said another word about flying home with her, and somehow she couldn't bring up the topic herself.

Ani felt the unasked questions floating between them like fishhooks when they had sex that night. A certain level of mystery and uncertainty was sexy, but it had been pushed to the point where alienation had taken over for her. Van was so preoccupied that Ani didn't think he noticed anything amiss, but she watched the proceedings with skepticism. The mechanics of the sex act seemed rather absurd. She fell into a restless sleep where she was a small figure wandering a vast plain of dreams.

As the morning's white light poured in the windows Ani noticed the dark hollows around Van's eyes. He hadn't slept well himself. She offered to give him a back rub and began to work the stringy and tense muscles in his neck. He groaned as she pushed her thumbs into his shoulder muscles.

"Is that too hard?" she asked.

"No. No. That's great."

When she got hungry, she threw on some clothes and dashed around the corner to the *boulangerie* for some croissants. By the time she got back, Van had showered and dressed. He sat on the couch, his face set with grim determination.

"Ani, come sit down."

She did as he asked.

"We need to talk," he said.

She waited.

"Before I tell you, I need something from you," he said.

"What?"

"I need you to swear you won't repeat anything I say."

Ani asked, "I can't tell anyone? Ever?"

"That's right," he said gruffly. "Can you do that?"

"Keeping secrets is hard for someone who talks as much as I do, Van. You know, if I didn't love you, I wouldn't even bother trying. Okay. I won't repeat a word." There, she had said it. She had told him that she loved him.

He took a deep breath, bowing his head and running his hand through his hair. "Okay. This is the condensed version. I'm part of an underground army committed to armed resistance against the Turkish government. I can't tell you the particulars."

"Army?" Ani asked.

"Army," he said.

"Like with guns and grenades and tanks?"

He laughed grimly. "No tanks as yet. But no harm in thinking big."

"That explains the passport."

"Yes."

"And you don't actually work at ARAA?"

"No."

"Okay," Ani said. She wondered if she was supposed to be shocked, because she felt oddly calm, as though she had suspected as much all along. "Anything else you want to tell me?"

"I have one more operation to carry out. If things go as planned, I'll fly back to the States in a few weeks."

The implication was that his trip might coincide with hers. "For a visit?"

"Maybe longer. I'll have to see. I love you, Ani. But I'm not sure what's next for me."

There. Now he had said it too, but rather than pounce on the pronouncement, however qualified, she would stick to the topic at hand. "What kind of operation?"

"I can't give you the details. I've told you more than I wanted to. But I thought I owed you some kind of an explanation. I don't like lying to you."

"Well, that's good to hear. It would be hopeless if you enjoyed deceiving me," she said sarcastically. "When does this operation take place?"

"I'm leaving tonight."

"Do you have a gun in that bag?" she asked, pointing to his pack.

"No."

"So is it in the locked cabinet in your room?"

"At the moment."

"Have you ever killed anyone?"

He shrugged. "In Beirut."

She was afraid to ask whom he had killed and how. Last year Baba had read an article to her—Grandma was nowhere around at that moment—from the local paper about an Armenian group that blew up a Turkish-owned gift shop in Cambridge. She wasn't particularly intrigued by the news, but Ani had noticed that there wasn't a trace of disapproval in her grandfather's tone, which she had found strange at the time. She wondered if this had been the work of Van's group.

"What's the name of your organization?" she asked.

"I don't want to tell you that now," he said tersely.

She asked, "Are you planning to kill someone?"

"No, Ani. I'm not planning to kill anyone. Just for your information, I don't believe in targeting innocent civilians. The goal is to publicize the Armenian cause and to inspire young Armenians to join us. We have to choose our targets carefully."

"Only guilty civilians?" Ani asked.

"Enough, Ani," he admonished.

"What's the long-term goal, Van?"

"Combat in the hills of the historic homeland."

The whole thing was surreal. The boy she had grown up with—the boy who had shown her how to whistle through an acorn cap—was dreaming of combat in the hills of Anatolia. Although it was obvious he was more than dreaming. She imagined there must be a training camp with target practice and lessons in tactics. How many people were in this army? Who was its leader? What was their philosophy? The only clandestine organization she had any experience with was Terrapin, the secret senior society with its ridiculous green union suits.

"Are there women in your group?" Ani asked.

"There are some women."

"Do they have guns?"

"Ani, no more questions," he said.

"What are you planning to do, Van?"

His face muscles tightened. "That's it, Ani. No more."

"Oh my God, this is completely insane." She squeezed her skull with her hands. "I can't believe this conversation. What planet are you on, Van?"

"Same planet, Ani, just an alternate reality," he replied.

When they made love that afternoon it was like a desperate farewell in a wartime melodrama. She wished she could lock the door and throw the key out the window into the garden, keeping him with her where he would be safe. She heard police sirens and imagined men lined up against a stone wall and shot. All around Paris there were plaques commemorating Resistance fighters who were executed by the Nazis. On the subways there were special seats reserved for *mutilés de guerre.* Those mutilated by war.

"Van, can't somebody else go?" she asked.

"Don't, Ani." He placed two fingers across her lips. "Don't make me regret telling you. I'll come here the first night that I can. It could be as early as Tuesday. Remember that I love you."

After he left, each minute had a thousand tiny feet and the hours stretched like a desert highway. The sun dragged itself into the sky, and soon thereafter Ani went downstairs.

Sydney asked, "What's the matter with you, Ani? You're not listening to me."

"Sorry, Syd. What did you say?"

"I said would you please pass me the maple syrup."

Ani complied.

"Thank you," Sydney said.

Ani glanced at the clock. It was 7:45 A.M. How was she going to make it through another forty hours?

Sydney sighed in exasperation. "I said, Thank you, Ani. Now you're supposed to say, You're welcome."

Ani jumped up from the table and asked with false cheer, "So what do you want for lunch today?"

Tuesday crawled by on hands and knees until it was 10 P.M. Ani sat at her table staring at the orange phone in front of her, willing it to ring. And then it rang.

"Ani? Your friend told me to call." It was Hratch. His voice was low and full of grit, and his English heavily accented.

"Is he hurt?" she asked.

"No. There were two witnesses, so he had to leave. He said next week go to American Express and look for a letter."

"How can I get in touch with him?" Ani asked, but Hratch had already hung up.

Ani never fell asleep that night.

Just after dawn she dressed and slipped down to the palace apartment. She waited on the fawn-colored couch in the Bartons' living room as light gradually took over the garden. Finally she heard the newspaper drop to the mat outside the front door.

After pulling in the *Herald Tribune,* she scanned its columns for something she hoped she wouldn't find. But there it was on page three—a four-sentence news item.

BRUSSELS, May 24—In the early hours of the morning two bombs exploded in front of the Turkish Embassy's Information Office and a nearby Turkish-owned travel agency. The travel agency's director was wounded in the attack. In a phone call made several hours later, the Armenian Secret Army for the Liberation of Armenia (ASALA) claimed credit for the bombing. ASALA, a leftist terrorist group with ties to the Popular Front for the Liberation of Palestine (PFLP), was responsible for the September 1981 takeover of the Turkish Consulate General in Paris.

She tore the page out of the paper, although there would be no need to look at the article again. The words were seared into memory. She folded the page smaller and smaller, then tucked it into the back pocket of her jeans.

When the Bartons drifted into the kitchen for breakfast, Ani mechanically performed the morning routine, listening to the pleasantries she thought impossible until they came out of her mouth. The sight of the food they were eating made her queasy, so she stood at the counter sipping a cup of tisane.

After the Bartons left, Ani went to her room, where she sat on the couch. She imagined that the French police would momentarily be pounding on her door. Madame Spinelli would triumphantly lead the flics to the top floor and down the hall to her room. They would handcuff Ani and escort her to the Palais de Justice. She would be marched to a grimy interrogation room in a turret. There a sneering investigator would question her for hours about Van Ardavanian and the Armenian Secret Army for the Liberation of Armenia.

But Ani didn't have any answers for him. What did she know about ASALA?

The bombs had gone off in the early hours of the morning. What was the travel agency director doing at his desk at that hour? Ani was sure that Van had been counting on the offices being empty. He didn't intend to hurt anyone. He was aiming for property damage to the Turkish Embassy's Information Office. It was full of colorful pamphlets about vacationing in Turkey. No reference was made to Armenians or the Armenian homeland in the photo captions. The pamphlets flew into the air when the bomb went off, raining down like confetti in the street.

A law-abiding citizen had a responsibility to report whatever little she knew to the proper authorities. Was she law-abiding? Think of that NO TRESPASSING sign outside the train yard in Denver. Or the sign behind the bookstore cash register: SHOP-LIFTERS WILL BE PROSECUTED TO THE FULL EXTENT OF THE LAW. Think of all the illegal drugs she had ingested over the three years she had been with Asa. It had never occurred to her that she should report Asa to the police for having a stash of pot or a bag of hallucinogenic mushrooms. But none of those things had resulted in bodily harm to anyone else.

Her mind circled around the injured man. If he was badly hurt in the attack, he must be in the hospital. His wife was at his bedside. He was wrapped in gauze. There was a coin of blood on the bandage around his head. Did they have children? Were the children crying at home with the grandmother?

"*Vhy babum,* Ani. Vhat kind of trouble did you make?" It was Grandma's voice, the one inside Ani's head.

Well, Grandma, you're the one who wanted me to find a nice Armenian boy. How could he be both a "nice Armenian boy" and a "leftist terrorist"? Whatever he was, she would not betray him.

Where was Van? Maybe he was in Venice wearing a false mustache and dark glasses, riding gondolas up and down the canals. Maybe he was in Nicosia or Beirut or Yerevan. Where did a secret army keep its troops and store its ammunition? Who paid the soldiers' salaries? Ani envisioned Van in fatigues with an assault rifle slung over his shoulder. He was handing out pay envelopes to a bunch of similarly clad Armenian men.

The next week Ani headed toward American Express as Hratch had instructed. As Ani walked the avenue she felt that at any moment violence might tear through the fabric of the ordinary afternoon. A man raised his hand to strike his whining son and the child cringed. On the corner cops were hassling African street vendors. There were troopers with black bulletproof vests and submachine guns standing outside a synagogue.

After entering the office, she descended to the basement mail desk and waited in line. Wiping her sweaty palms on her jeans, she willed her heart to slow its frantic thrashing. When her turn finally came, the man at the desk handed her a padded envelope with her name written on it. The package, which bore Dutch stamps, had been postmarked four days earlier in Amsterdam. Ani tucked it into her bag and hurried home.

Ani slit the end of the package to find a small worn clothbound pocket English-Armenian dictionary. Inside the front cover Van had inscribed: *To Ani, with devotion, from Van.*

There was no letter, no apology, no explanation, and no promise of his return. Was there some kind of coded message inside the dictionary that she would have to decipher? Half the entries were printed in the Armenian alphabet, which she couldn't even read.

Two days later in the Bartons' kitchen as Ani sorted her dirty clothes she picked up a faded denim work shirt that Van had left behind. She was tempted to seal it unwashed into a Ziploc bag. She held it to her face and shut her eyes, reinventing for a moment Van's presence: his mouth on her skin, his breath in her ear. Her throat tightened and tears smarted into her eyes. She cast the shirt into the washing machine and opened the newspaper to scour its pages—in vain—for mention of Van, the wounded man, or ASALA.

She counted ten days on the calendar until her flight home. She calculated ten days and ten nights to be two hundred and forty hours to fill. She should deduct eight hours a night for sleep, but she wasn't sleeping much. She'd drift off only to awaken several hours later, her mind muddied with crazy thoughts. Satan was lying on the floor under the bed, planning to reach his arms around to grab her ankles. Van was hurt. He had dragged himself to her building with his last bit of strength. His blood was pooling on the tiles outside her door.

She turned on the light. There was no devil. There was no blood. There was no rat on the shelf chewing open the box of crackers. The clock's face was set in a mocking smile. Wasn't it laughable, really, how naive she was?

Had there been a secret agenda on the trip to Corsica? Maybe his friends there were actually members of the FNLC and he was sent by his group to make contact with them. There was a connection between these groups, these national liberation struggles, as he called them.

Of course his face had gone ashen when the cops stopped them outside Lyon. Of course any dealings with the police would be dangerous for a member of ASALA.

When Ani saw Van again—if she saw him again—she would conduct a formal interrogation.

She had to go to sleep. She would make herself sick otherwise. She numbered her breaths, one count in and one count out. The breath through her nostrils made this sound: *he is lost, he is lost, he is lost to you.* With each exhalation she pushed the thoughts out of her head until it was empty, empty of everything but dark space.

The alarm clock knocked her awake. Daylight. Sydney's breakfast and lunch to be made. After Sydney was hustled off to school, Ani packed her course books and notes into yellow postal boxes. She stood in a long line at the post office waiting to send the boxes to herself by boat. On the street she drifted slowly while a stream of people jostled past her on the way to the important business of their lives. She walked through the Palais-Royal garden, where in the blue sky clouds paraded like headless sheep.

The day before her flight home, Ani took Sydney for a farewell ice cream at the gilt café on the place Colette.

"I didn't want vanilla ice cream," the child whined. "I said I wanted chocolate."

Ani, who had heard the child order vanilla, exchanged sympathetic glances with the waiter as he took the offending dish away.

Sydney pouted. She kicked the table stand. "I hate this place. It's not nice at all. You should have taken me to Fauchon."

"Do you think maybe you're just in a bad mood because you don't want me to leave?" Ani asked.

"You are so stupid," Sydney said. Then she burst into tears.

Ani, without warning, felt the banks of the river overflow. She took Sydney on her lap and kissed the child's wet cheek.

"It will be okay, sweetie," Ani said, through brimming eyes.

But how would anything be okay again? Sydney would have to stay in the palace apartment with her selfish and bigoted parents. And Van had become an ambiguous, scary figure and then vanished.

That evening Ani opened Van's pocket dictionary and flipped through its small pages again. She couldn't decipher the Armenian letters, but in the center of the book there was a section in English filled with conversations and phrases that a recently arrived Armenian immigrant might need in America. The entries were broken into categories such as AT THE POST OFFICE, LOOKING FOR A TENEMENT, and AT THE GROCERY STORE. The final category was labeled FOR THE EMIGRANTS.

What is your name?
My name is Mardiros.
What is your last name?
My last name is Giragosian.
How old are you?
I am thirty years old.
Where were you born?
I was born in Harpoot, Turkey.
What is your occupation?
I am a carpenter.
I am a blacksmith.
I am a watchmaker.
I am a tailor.
I have no trade. I am a student.
Are you married?
No, sir, I am single.
Yes, sir, I am married.
What is your wife's name?
My wife's name is Mariam.

Mariam was Ani's grandmother's name. And Baba was called Mattheos.

Ani saw them suddenly, a young man in a black cloth coat standing beside his diminutive dark-haired wife. They were at Ellis Island being questioned by an immigration official. The man tapped his pencil impatiently on the desk. Mattheos repeated his last name slowly and the man wrote the letters down. He showed it to Mattheos.

Is that it? the man asked.

Yes, that's it, Mattheos said.

Mariam, following the proceedings skittishly, didn't understand English, so Mattheos translated for her. She gave the name of her town and the approximate year of her birth.

The vision faded.

Had Baba known English when he arrived? How had he learned it? Why did they come to America? When they emigrated, whom had they left behind?

Her grandparents drew a curtain of silence over their early lives. And Ani, growing up amid Old World shadows, had never thought to ask.

where a nail was driven, there will always be a hole

Violet's black hair was shot through with silver and the lines on her face were deeper than Ani remembered. Grandma, wearing a white summer hat and a pink paste brooch in the shape of a dahlia, was thin and pale. When Ani hugged Baba she noticed he was now wearing a hearing aid.

Grandma said, "*Meghah!* Skin and bones. They didn't feed you nothing, Ani?"

"Ma, leave her alone," Violet admonished. "You look tired, honey. Haven't you been sleeping?"

"*Ahrr,*" Grandma said, pulling an Almond Joy candy bar out of her purse and shoving it into Ani's hand. "I made *manti* for supper. And fresh *madzoon.*"

They left the airport with Baba at the wheel and rolled up their windows as they entered the yellow tiled tunnel. They drove along the glittering Charles River, where small sailboats and sculling shells raced over the water. Sunbathers were strewn on long towels in the grass along the riverbank.

"You see those girls in bikinis," Baba said. "They cause lots of accidents. I read about it in the *Globe* the other day."

"They don't cause accidents, Pa," Violet said. "Men who can't keep their eyes on the road do that."

Along Mount Auburn Street, Ani saw the same storefronts, made strange by her absence but bathed in a wash of recollections. There was the corner grocery where she and Van had picked small enamel tiles off the crumbling facade while waiting for their grandmothers. She saw Van's shadow falling over the school field. His feet had trod every block of pavement along this street.

They pulled into the driveway on Spruce Street. In Baba's vegetable garden the tomato plants were staked up with broken hockey sticks. Grandma's zinnias and marigolds were blooming. Mr. Narboni called a greeting over the hedge and the Kersamians stopped to chat with him. After a few minutes Ani excused herself and walked up the back steps, lugging her bags.

In the hall Ani let herself be swept away by the distinctive combination of smells—lamb and onions, lemon furniture polish, Grandma's liniment, Violet's perfume. The atmosphere of her childhood rose up around her like a dense cloud. A slide show flickered past: Baba's hands tying the laces of Ani's shoes; Ani at the kitchen table with Grandma rolling out snakes of yeasty dough; Violet calling from the front porch as Ani rode her bike down the darkening block.

In the kitchen the white Formica kitchen table with silver legs and the matching red and silver chairs gleamed with memory. White sheers stirred in the windows over the sink. Ani moved through the front rooms, her eyes catching homely objects: a bowl of waxed fruit on the sideboard, a porcelain figurine of a girl driving a flock of geese on the end table, a gold Depression glass bowl filled with hard candies on the polished coffee table. She wanted it always to stay the same—like a museum of bygone days—so that no matter how complicated or confused her life should be, there would be a place of rest and comfort.

Nostalgia.

An aching in the heart for the homeland.

Was this Ani's homeland?

As soon as the family passed under the lintel, Grandma would shout from the kitchen that Ani should shut the front door before all the dust blew in from the street. Violet would loudly tell her mother not to shout. Baba would settle into his old wine-colored armchair and snap the newspaper open in front of his face. After a few minutes he'd fall asleep, and his snores would rumble through the apartment.

She carried her suitcase to the basement room. On the wine crate that served as a nightstand stood a framed color photograph that Asa had given her. Wearing a red bandanna and green shorts, Asa was stretched over a craggy cliff face while a red rope dangled from him like an umbilical cord. Ani considered tossing the picture, frame and all, into the trash basket but instead wedged it into a corner of the old footlocker where she stored toys and souvenirs. She searched until she found the white cigar box—Van's gray quartz stone was still in there and her father's marbles. Replacing them inside, she closed the trunk's lid.

From her suitcase Ani pulled an envelope filled with small slips of paper and a few folded notes that Van had written. It was funny how few physical mementos she had from their five months together: just these bits of paper with his handwriting and the pocket dictionary. Van Ardavanian had slipped in and out of her life like a magician. She imagined him walking backward on the sand, erasing his footsteps with a palm frond as he went.

The next morning Ani walked to the bicycle shop on Mount Auburn Street and bought a used three-speed Schwinn and a wicker basket. She pedaled up Boylston Street, around the back of the junior high school, past the front of the elementary school, and down Hazel Street. As she approached the Ardavanians' house on Dexter Avenue she slowed the bike. There wasn't anyone out front, but a light shone in the downstairs living room. She wanted to knock on the door and ask if she could see Van's bedroom. Had they kept it as a shrine, with a pair of bronzed baby shoes on a shelf next to his sports trophies? Would he have left a Red Sox pennant tacked to the wall or a poster of Che? Ani picked up speed and turned toward home.

She started a summer job in the children's room at the East Branch Library. Ani loved the cool basement room with its low tables and small chairs. This was where she had learned to read. As she shelved the young adult novels she offered suggestions to a twelve-year-old girl—an Armenian girl, Ani guessed, from the look of her—who was picking through for something good. At the end of her first shift she climbed the cast-iron spiral staircase to the adult reading room, where she paged through back issues of English language Armenian newspapers. She was looking for mention of ASALA and its "operations."

As she read the coverage of ASALA's September 1981 siege of the Turkish Consulate in Paris, she scrutinized the photos carefully. A Turkish security guard had died of a heart attack and one commando was wounded, but the rest of the hostages were released. Next she scrolled through microfilm of *The New York Times* for the same dates and found several articles. One of the reports explained the context for the present-day attacks against Turkish targets by citing the past:

> In the period around 1915, Turkish authorities scattered the Armenian nation, killing 1.5 million people according to most historical accounts and driving others from their homeland in Eastern Anatolia.

Ani checked out a stack of books on the Armenian Genocide, squeezing them into her bicycle basket. Carrying the cache of books to the basement, she sat cross-legged on her bed and read until the letters blurred. She attempted to take the information in with dispassion. This was something that had happened decades before in a distant and foreign place to people she didn't know. Despite her resolve, a little knot of grief worked its way from the pit of her stomach up to her throat.

The number 1.5 million was repeated again and again. The only way she could take in the enormity of it was to choose one person out of that 1.5 million and try to list the losses and terrors that particular person had suffered before dying a gruesome death. Then multiply it by 1.5 million. Add to that the hundreds of thousands who somehow survived with the horrors etched in their heads and who dispersed themselves over the globe like the seeds of a rare plant slated for extinction.

This sum of suffering was totaled without figuring in the fields confiscated, the vineyards appropriated, the houses occupied, looted, or burned, the handwoven carpets carried off, the dish sets smashed or stolen, the pocket watches and earrings traded for scraps of food, the words torn from mouths and not passed to the next generation and the one after.

Violet called from the top of the stairs. "Ani, dinner time." When there was no response to her second call, Violet descended.

Ani didn't hear her mother until Violet was standing over her.

"Mom, you scared me," Ani said, springing up.

Waving her hand at the books on the floor, Violet asked, "What are these?"

"Books," she said.

"Ani, I can see that. I mean, what are you reading them for?"

"Research," Ani replied.

"You've been acting strange since you got back. Are you depressed?"

Ani knit her eyebrows, considering for a moment. Was that the right word to describe her current state?

She answered, "I don't think I'm depressed. Depressed is when you can't get out of bed because gravity weighs too much on you. I think this is called *bummed out*."

"Maybe you're still sad about Asa. But I don't think shutting yourself up in the basement with morbid books is going to help you, Ani, I really don't."

"Mom, this has nothing, I mean *nothing,* to do with Asa."

Her mother couldn't have been further from the truth. But who could blame Violet? Ani had promised Van not to tell, and now that he had dematerialized she felt she couldn't even mention his name for fear the whole story would come spilling out.

"Just do me a favor and don't leave those lying around where your grandmother might see them. A friend of mine is coming over for supper tonight. Someone special I want you to meet."

"Who?" Ani asked.

"Nick Mavrides. He lives at the top of the hill. His wife died three years ago."

So her mother had a boyfriend, a Greek widower. Good for her, thought Ani. "How did you meet him?"

"He's a patient at the office," Violet said. "And he's a contractor, for your information."

"How did you know that was my next question?" Ani asked.

Nick Mavrides was a little taller than Violet and a little older, although not much, and had a full head of short graying hair and a small potbelly. He brought yellow garden roses with their stems wrapped in aluminum foil for Grandma.

Grandma carried the roses into the kitchen, saying to Ani in Armenian as she passed, "Look what Violet's Greek boy gave me."

"I understand you're just back from Paris," Nick said to Ani, after they were all seated at the table.

"Uh-huh," Ani responded.

"When I was in the army stationed in Germany, I went to Paris on leave a couple of times. Great city," he said. "New York's a great city too. Maybe sometime this year your mom and I could drive down to visit you at school. One of my sons lives in New Jersey, on the other side of the bridge. We could stay with him."

"That would be nice," Ani said. She looked across the table at her mother, who was beaming happily.

After supper, as Ani toweled the dishes, she asked Grandma, "You like Nick?"

"Good boy. Not like *Baron* White Cadillac."

"Do you think it's serious?"

Grandma nodded. "Sure. Last time he brought me candy."

Ani returned to her reading, but Baba knocked on the basement window, beckoning for her to come outside. Baba's vegetable garden glistened in the sun's last rays.

"Can you spray your grandmother's flowers?" Baba asked, handing Ani the hose. "Your mother told me you're reading about the Massacres."

"That's right." The long family tradition of silence almost kept her from saying more. "What happened to your family, Baba?"

Baba sat down heavily on the picnic bench, running his fingers through his thick white hair. "We lived in Marash. My father was massacred in the street so my mother was left alone to care for four children. My brother Vahan was the oldest. Next my sister Satenig, and then me. The smallest was Tovmas. Because we were Protestants we were under the protection of the American missionaries, but one day a deportation order came for Vahan and me. We took it to the missionaries. They went to the governor, who told us to ignore it and move to another house. My mother's family had already been deported so their house was empty. We moved there."

The story poured out of him as though he had told it a thousand times, yet Ani had never heard him say a word about it before. Maybe he had told himself this story again and again. Maybe he had been waiting all this time for her to ask.

He continued. "Everyone was hungry all the time. People ate anything they could put their hands on: a dog, a cat, any poor bird you might get with a slingshot. Vahan and I went out to the fields with a basket, a string, and a stick. We made a trap and caught sparrows. Can you imagine that? Such a tiny bird, hardly any meat on its bones. We spent the whole afternoon catching them. But compared to the others, we were kings. They were driven out into the desert where there wasn't so much as a crumb. They died like flies. Some of the orphans were picked up from the desert by the missionaries and brought back to the orphanage.

"That's how your grandmother came to Marash. She had no family left. When she first got there she must have been about fourteen, maybe fifteen, but she was so tiny with her bones sticking out all over that she looked to be nine years old. You wouldn't have liked to see it, Ani. She wouldn't talk to no one. I was working for the missionaries, fixing things. They had a car and a truck, and I learned how to repair them. I would see Mariam sitting to one side by herself, and little by little I came closer to her. I carved a whistle from a piece of wood and gave it to her. I made up a song for her. She one day finally smiled at me. I wanted that girl to be my wife, but I had to wait until she was a little older.

"Finally Mariam said she would marry me. We guessed she was about sixteen. The American *badveli* married us with my family there. My uncle was in America and they decided that Mariam and I should go there. We would send for my mother and my sister and brothers later. A few months after we got to Watertown we heard that the French and British troops had left Marash. After that the Armenians still in Marash were deported and massacred. The American missionaries had no power anymore. My whole family was killed."

Baba's story stopped there. He was staring past Ani, his eyes fixed on the past. Ani noticed that the hose was at her feet spilling water into the grass. She reached to turn off the spigot.

"What about Grandma's family?" Ani asked.

He shrugged. "She told me about their house in Mersin. She had a brother and younger sisters who were twins. Her father was a tailor. She would only say that they all died except her. She doesn't like to talk about it, Ani, and after so much suffering, why should she? She wants to forget the misery she saw in that place. No one's eyes should have witnessed that. America is very far from there. Come on, *aghchigess,* that's enough of that terrible tale. Let's go inside."

The next day Ani found an old tape recorder on a shelf in the hall closet. She bought new batteries and a cassette tape, testing the machine to make sure it worked.

Late on Saturday afternoon, when Grandma was settled on the back porch couch reading her Bible, Ani sat down next to her with the tape recorder.

"Ve missed you," Grandma said.

"I missed you too," Ani replied.

"I heard that boy Esau give you trouble," Grandma said.

Ani didn't bother to correct her. "Dumped me."

"He don't know nothing. Spit from you mouth. You are jewel for prince." Grandma picked her pocketbook up from the couch beside her. "You need dollar?"

"Thanks, no. I don't."

They sat in silence for a while.

"Grandma," Ani ventured, "you know, I was wondering about your life in the old country."

Grandma examined her wedding band.

"Baba told me about his family. Do you have any stories from your childhood you want to tell?" Ani asked.

The old woman stared at her turned-up palms, which were resting on her lap.

Ani went on. "You could say it into this tape recorder when you're alone. All you have to do is push this red button here. You push it down and talk. The microphone is built in."

There was no response.

"So you push this one to start"—Ani pressed down the RECORD button—"and when you're finished you push down this one at the end."

Gesturing toward the grapevine growing up over the porch railing, Grandma said, "Those *yaprak* are too tough to cook. If you vant me to make *yalanchi* you have to get jar at Kay's Market."

Ani stood, leaving the tape recorder on the seat next to her grandmother. "Okay. I'll pick some up."

"Let me give money." Grandma pulled a small plastic change purse from her apron pocket, opened it, and pulled out a crumpled ten-dollar bill. "Buy some *banir.* And halvah if you vant. You like that."

After Ani came home with the groceries, she checked the porch. The tape recorder was nowhere to be seen.

better to go into captivity with the
village than to go to a wedding alone

A month after Ani arrived home from Paris, a bomb exploded in a suitcase at the Turkish Airlines counter in Paris's Orly Airport, killing five and wounding fifty-six. It was on the front page of the morning paper. When Ani saw the photos of the bewildered blood-spattered travelers, her stomach lurched and the nerves under her skin contracted into little pins of pain. The Armenian Secret Army for the Liberation of Armenia had claimed responsibility for the attack.

Not Van. It couldn't have been Van. He would never do something like that.

Why would ASALA do it? As far as Ani could see, the people who had been killed had nothing remotely to do with the death of 1.5 million Armenians. Their only fault, if you could call it that, was to have bought a ticket to Istanbul from the Turkish national airline.

The queasiness that Ani felt was worsened by the small part of her that thrilled at the idea of revenge. Let them suffer. Let them know how we suffered. Our blood ran in the gutters, our dead filled the streams, our women wept for their murdered husbands, and our mothers watched their children starve. The pain of my people sears my heart.

This kind of thinking frightened her.

If you wanted revenge for what had been done to your grandparents, whom should you target? What was the difference between an innocent victim and a guilty one? If you were guilty, did that make you not a victim? Who was guilty now?

Ani distractedly shelved the picture books in the children's room of the library. Every time she thought of Van, her stomach wrenched into a little ball. Was it possible that he had re-

186

turned to France? Maybe he had been ordered to plant the bomb at Orly by the head of his organization. No. She couldn't tolerate that thought. He must be thousands of miles away,on Cyprus or in Lebanon. The bomb in Brussels had been bad enough.

Can you explain it to me? Can you tell me how you can be so sure about what you believe that you can put explosives outside a travel agency?

She imagined his explanation.

You are in a war zone, Beirut for example. You are responsible for protecting a neighborhood. You learn how to take the weapons apart and put them back together. You hear the planes overhead and the shelling. There is fighting on the street. You see someone you know shot and killed by a sniper. One day you kill someone in combat. Eventually the war inhabits you. Then you translate it outward.

Go on, Ani urged. Don't stop there.

You can see the same forces at work everywhere. Different faces but the same body, like some mythical monster. You look around and see what is happening to people, your people, and think the only way to fix it is to fight the system.

And the system is a hapless tourist at an airline counter? Ani asked.

The beast chews up and spits out tens of thousands of people a day. Pick any spot on the globe and there are hundreds of dead bodies lying at its feet.

It's too big for me, Van. I can only see the individuals and not the pattern.

All you have to do, Ani, is connect the dots.

She heard his voice so clearly, but those were her words and not his. She didn't know where he was or what he was thinking. She only prayed he was safe.

When her shift in the children's room was over, Ani went upstairs to pore over the newspapers. Baba arrived and sat down next to her.

Baba pointed to the headline with his forefinger. "Now these boys are killing the wrong people."

"Who are the right people?" Ani asked.

"I never held a gun in my life. But if I was going to shoot somebody I think it would be those guys in the Turkish government who say the Genocide never happened. You know after the war, some Dashnaks went and hunted down those Young Turk leaders and shot them one by one: Talaat, Djemal, Enver, and a few other big murderers. Operation Nemesis it was called. I could be wrong, but I think even your grandmother's God gave his blessing to that. But this?" Here he tapped the newspaper and shook his head. "In the end I'm afraid this will be bad business for the Armenians."

Ani made photocopies of the Orly newspaper coverage, putting them into a manila file folder labeled ASALA. On her day off she went to the Boston Public Library to read the French newspapers, pained by the descriptions of the people who had been injured and especially those who had been killed in the bombing.

Among the dead: a small French boy and a Greek-American student who was about to leave on a flight to Istanbul with his Turkish fiancée. Surrounding the figures of the dead Ani imagined widening circles of family and friends, their mouths contorted with grief.

One of the books Ani had come across in her reading was by a Turkish writer who claimed her son had been killed by Armenian terrorists. The writer, in idiosyncratic English, described the Armenians as a "community of nonappreciatives." In the book there were photos of dead Turks who had apparently been killed by Armenian revolutionaries.

With pictures of corpses the captions always instruct you on whom to blame.

"Don't you think you're dwelling too much on this stuff, Ani?" Violet asked her. "If you're not depressed yet, you're certainly pushing yourself in that direction."

Ani groaned. "Mom, would you give me a break? Knowledge is power."

She heard Van again, his voice small behind her ear: No, actually a gun is power and a bomb in a suitcase gets you a banner headline. It's called *armed propaganda*. No one cares what happened to the Armenians, Ani. No one remembers what was done to us. We have to make them remember.

When she lay in bed she closed her eyes and saw Van on a street corner standing in a lighted phone booth. He hadn't shaved, his clothes were rumpled as though he had slept in them, and his duffel was at his feet. After he pulled a handful of foreign coins from his pocket, he pumped them into the slot and began to dial her number. The phone didn't ring and the image faded.

One afternoon about a week later, Baba was waiting in the car outside the library for Ani when she got off work. He gestured her in.

"Put the bike in the trunk. We're going visiting," he told her.

Minutes later they pulled up in front of the Ardavanians' house. They walked around the side to the cellar door, where Baba knocked. Vahram Ardavanian, a frail man wearing an ancient gray cardigan despite the summer heat, opened the door. Ani noticed milky cataracts around the edges of the old man's brown irises.

"Come sit down," Vahram invited them.

In the paneled basement room, a narrow bed took up one corner and there were stacks of yellowed Armenian newspapers against a wall. A frayed couch was covered with a crocheted afghan. As she sat down, Ani glanced at a cluster of photographs in gilt frames that were arranged on an end table. Four generations of Ardavanians were represented. Ani picked up a photo of smiling Van in his Red Raiders football uniform, holding his helmet in the crook of his arm.

Ani remembered watching Van loping down the long aisle in the high school auditorium as the cheerleaders chanted, *Van Ardavanian, he's our man, if he can't do it, no one can.*

"Can I get you something to drink?" Vahram asked. "How about some candy?" He lifted the cover of a yellow cardboard box filled with chocolates that had gone white with age.

"No thanks, Vahram," Baba said.

Vahram lowered himself carefully onto a wooden side chair. "I understand you saw our Van in Paris," he said to Ani.

What did Vahram Ardavanian know? She couldn't tell anything from the look on his face or his tone.

"We ran into each other on Christmas Eve," Ani replied. She kept her own voice neutral.

"He called yesterday," the old man said. "I was the only one home. He asked me to tell you hello."

Ani wanted to ask if there was any other message. Had he said, Tell Ani I love her?

"Where is he?" Ani asked evenly.

Vahram shrugged. "You never know with that boy. He doesn't say. We're just happy to hear his voice."

From the floor above, Sophie Nahabedian called in Armenian down the basement stairs, "Vahram, is Mattheos Kersamian there with you?"

"Come down, Sophie. Mattheos and his granddaughter are here," Vahram called back in Armenian.

The old woman slowly descended the steps, gripping the railing. "Hello, hello. Mattheos, don't get up." She settled carefully into an armchair, then smoothed the skirt of the paisley housecoat she was wearing over her dress. "We hear you saw our Van," she said to Ani. "How did he look?"

"He looked fine, Auntie," Ani responded.

"Was he eating enough?" the old woman inquired.

"Eating, sleeping, exercising. He's in good health," Ani assured her.

Auntie Sophie shook her head. "I pray every night that he will come home to us in one piece."

"Sophie, Sophie, don't start," said Vahram. "In a war there have to be soldiers."

"*Vhy, vhy, vhy,*" Auntie Sophie said. "The Turks murdered us, stole everything we had, and keep killing us with their lies. Now we have to give up our grandsons too."

Baba commented, "Some kind of war your grandson is fighting, blowing up innocent people in airports."

Sophie clucked her tongue.

Ani scrutinized her grandfather. Baba knew about Van's political activities and yet he hadn't said anything to her. But then, she hadn't confided in him either. Van's grandparents were chatting about Van's involvement in ASALA as though it were akin to joining the U.S. Army.

Van and these old Armenians, members of the same clan, were open with each other. Ani had made herself an outsider who couldn't entirely be trusted. Only when he was heading to Brussels and an operation from which he might not return had Van shared his secret with her.

"Mattheos, that blood isn't on Van's hands," said Vahram. "There's trouble in the group. Who knows how it will end?"

Baba said, "The Justice Commandos only go after diplomats and government officials. They get a better reputation that way."

Vahram waved as though shooing flies. "Those guys are thugs. They have no politics. They only don't want ASALA to get all the attention—"

Ani interrupted. "Who are the Justice Commandos?"

"Justice Commandos of the Armenian Genocide. It's a group the Dashnaks made to compete with ASALA," Vahram said. "Van and some other guys were against Orly. So Van is hiding from Mujahed *and* the police."

"He told you this?" Ani asked.

"Not in so many words. I pick up things here and there," Vahram answered.

Baba said, "Always with Armenians, huh, there's this group and that group, and this group splits into two groups and nobody is talking to nobody."

"The churches are the worst of it," observed Sophie.

"You put a priest in the middle and it becomes a riot," Baba added.

Vahram said, "At least in the church it's been a long time since anybody's killed anyone. They've become a little more civilized. I just hope Van can stay down until it gets calm. He wants to come home."

"I pray, I pray," said Sophie. "I pray for him night and day."

"Well, if he makes it home, give your God a little of the credit," Vahram said sourly.

"How is Mariam?" Sophie asked, changing the subject.

Baba shrugged. "She misses you. She said she has some *tourshi* on the back porch for you but you have to come get them."

"With this pain in my hip, it's not so easy to walk to your house anymore. I don't like to bother Aram and Alice for rides."

Baba told her, "Anytime you want, Sophie, you call me and I'll come pick you up."

Ani and Baba got in the car. Instead of heading down Mount Auburn Street toward home, Baba drove toward Cambridge.

"Where are we going?" Ani asked.

"You'll see," Baba replied.

Ani asked, "What do you think will happen to Van?"

"I don't know, *aghchigess*. He has a good heart, and I hope he comes home soon."

"What kind of job can you have after being an armed revolutionary?" Ani asked.

"When guys come home from a war they can go into any business they want. Dry cleaning, whatever," Baba said.

Ani couldn't quite imagine Van as a dry cleaner.

Baba said, "Listen, *anoushig*, don't look for trouble. No more mountain men or fighters, okay? Why don't you go out with a nice guy with a steady job, like a dentist or something? Your grandmother could use a new pair of dentures. Plus she would love to see you get married."

"To a nice Armenian dentist?" Ani asked.

Baba shrugged. "Why not?"

Ani didn't think she'd be the right kind of a wife for an Armenian dentist any more than she was a proper partner for an Armenian revolutionary. Van needed a woman with an assault rifle in one hand and the Armenian flag in the other—an Armenian version of the girl in the Delacroix painting leading the battle charge. Ani saw the two of them in dusty fatigues, bandoliers crisscrossed over their chests, as they moved with an armed column across the Anatolian plain. After the revolution they would settle by the shores of Lake Van and name their dark-eyed children after Armenian pagan deities.

Baba pulled into the Star Market parking lot.

"We're grocery shopping?" Ani asked.

"No. We're crossing the street."

They entered the Mount Auburn Cemetery through a massive granite gate.

"Are we here to visit someone in particular?" Ani asked.

"No. I come here to walk."

They strolled up the cemetery's main avenue, passing a row of marble crypts, tombs guarded by angels with long stone wings, and all along the way the names of the dead inscribed in stone. There were potted annuals, sculpted shrubs, rolling lawns, and the tall graceful trunks of century trees. It was a beautiful place, once you accepted the death motif as part of the natural order of things.

"Let's sit," Baba said. He was winded from the upward slope.

They found a stone bench under the shade of an oak tree.

"Who is Mujahed?" Ani asked Baba.

"He goes by the name Hagop Hagopian. He's the big boss in ASALA. I guess Van is on his bad side right now."

"How do you know so much about all this, Baba?" Ani asked.

"I know a lot of things, *anoushig*. But we can't mention it at home."

"I know."

The shadows of the leaves shifted around them in the breeze.

Baba stared into the distance. "I sometimes gave money for ASALA. When I went to play *tavloo*, I collected money for them too."

"You did?" Ani asked incredulously.

"They used to do better things. Like that Turkish Consulate takeover in Paris. That was a good one."

"Why, Baba?"

"Do you know what I dream about at night? I see my mother. She's lying in the dirt. She's dying. There is blood in the corner of her mouth. And my older brother is crouching in the ditch on a pile of rags and bones that used to be people. He is thin like a scarecrow. He says, *Mattheos, you should have brought us with you.* And my sister. My sister—"

Baba stopped. He put his hands over his face. His shoulders were moving up and down as though he were crying, but he didn't make a sound.

After supper, Ani and Violet sat on the front steps watching the neighborhood kids play kickball in the street. A passing car put a brief halt to the game. One of the boys held the ball under the crook of his arm while the kids watched the offending vehicle roll by. The kids spilled back into the street.

"Did you hear the latest about Brenda O'Malley?" Violet asked.

They both glanced at the O'Malleys' house directly across the street.

Ani saw an image of Brenda's freckled face circa first grade. "What about her?"

"Well, she and her boyfriend had a big blowout. She came home with a twin under each arm and a black eye."

"Who is her boyfriend?" Ani hadn't thought about Brenda O'Malley in years. They hadn't been friends beyond second grade.

Violet said, a grimace of disapproval on her face, "Her boyfriend is that awful Vinny DeRenzo."

Ani had a recollection of Vinny as a thuggish, long-haired guy wearing a dungaree jacket with a pack of Marlboros poking out of the pocket. Four years out of high school, he showed up at the Thanksgiving football game their senior year with a Doberman puppy on a leash as a kind of bait. Brenda O'Malley had been among the girls gathered around the dog.

Violet continued. "He has no interest in providing for them. It's a shame. Poor Gloria has Brenda and the babies to support now that they moved back in. I told you about Lucy Sevanian, right? Did I mention that she sent you an invitation to her baby shower? You were in Paris so I called with your regrets. The baby must be about three months old. You should call her," Violet said.

Ani had no interest in calling Lucy, who, at the age of twenty-four, was installed in a split-level ranch house in Belmont complete with husband, infant, and, Ani supposed, her own vacuum cleaner and washing machine.

New York City—in Ani's imagination a vast canyon of tall buildings with an underground network of fast trains where people rushed from one engagement to the next—would be her salvation.

Ani had called Elena, who told her she didn't need to bring or buy a bed. Elena's previous roommate had dropped out of graduate school and returned to Ohio, leaving behind an almost new mattress and box spring. Ani had wanted to know whether to bring twin or double sheets.

Elena said, "A twin? Nobody should sleep in a twin bed except for children and monks. It's a double. I can't wait for you to get here. I want you to meet my new lover."

Ani thought it strange the way Elena said *lover.* Maybe it was a New York thing or a graduate student affectation. *Boyfriend* must be considered too juvenile a word. Ani would soon find out. She'd be leaving for New York in less than ten days.

"What's up with you and Nick?" Ani asked her mother.

"What about us?"

"Are you guys going to get married?"

"Maybe," Violet answered. "We haven't talked about that yet."

They sat in silence for a while. The streetlights came on and the kids drifted home, some of them hearing their names shouted from up the block.

Violet said, "When you were a toddler we used to take you to the campus every evening after supper in the summer. There would be lots of other families with small children. Your dad would bring a ball for you to kick around and you loved to throw it in the fountain. You liked to slide down the stone balustrades until you wore holes in the seat of your pants."

"Where was our apartment?" Ani asked.

"Overlooking Morningside Park," Violet replied. "I still remember the phone number, isn't that funny? Almost twenty years later and I still remember the number. The phone was installed the day we were married. We went to city hall because we didn't want a religious ceremony. We had what they called in those days a *mixed marriage*. Odd expression, don't you think?"

Do you feel twice blessed or doubly cursed?

Van had once asked, If you cut yourself off from your people, then who are you? A person is nothing alone, he had said. We are only something together.

At the time Ani understood his words without knowing what they meant. Now she could feel how a thousand family stories made her who she was. She could faintly sense the pull of invisible satin laces that bound her to the Armenian people. What about her father's family? Would it be possible to knot or splice together the severed ties?

"I was thinking about trying to contact the Silvers," Ani told her mother.

Violet drew her eyebrows together, her mouth twisting into a frown. "Oh, Ani. What for? After we got married they sat shiva for him. He was dead to them long before he died. They never wanted anything to do with us either. You'll only get yourself hurt."

"I thought you said his sister used to call him once in a while."

"Occasionally. And if I answered the phone she pretended not to know who I was when she asked for him. We sent her an announcement after you were born and she never sent even a card. Can you imagine not acknowledging your own brother's child?"

"Mom, that was a long time ago. I'm a grown-up. They're my father's family. They're my family."

"I've never wanted to tell you this, Ani, but when your father and I had been dating for about six months, his sister came to see me. I didn't tell your father about it. She found out where I was living and knocked on my dorm room door. She had come to tell me that David would never marry me because his family wouldn't accept me. And she also told me—contradicting the first thing she said—that if he did marry me, the Silvers would never have anything to do with him or me and any children we might have. No contact. No money. No nothing. We wouldn't exist for them."

"Mom, that was decades ago. I'm going to be living in the same city. Wouldn't it be weird if I walked past one of them on the street and didn't even know it was my blood relative? I have to at least try."

Her mother looked heavenward and sighed. "Between the Massacres and the Silvers, you're really trying to torture yourself, aren't you?"

Violet shrugged in defeat. She went into the house and came back with a faded cloth address book. Ani watched as her mother copied onto a blank index card the name Leah Kantrowitz and an address on West End Avenue in Manhattan.

Violet said, "Your father's sister. I have no idea if she's still at this address. Before you call her, Ani, you should think about what you want. Don't expect much."

In the basement room, Ani pulled out the framed black-and-white photo of David Silver. She recollected little from the years they had lived in New York. She wondered if returning to the same neighborhood would be like taking a stick to the bottom of a pond, stirring up fragments of memory from where they had settled long before.

Ani glanced at the address on the piece of paper her mother had given her. She wanted someone to tell her stories about her father when he was a child or to repeat a joke that he used to tell. Maybe she'd be invited to meet her grandparents, if they were still alive, and her cousins. They would all crow over her and say how much she looked like her father. Maybe, though, Leah Kantrowitz would shout into the phone, *We want none of you!* and slam the receiver down.

Ani began to pack her things for the move to New York. She had expected that her mother would be getting weepy about losing her baby again, but Nick seemed to provide distraction. Grandma was the one Ani worried about. The old woman seemed sad and preoccupied, sitting in her armchair staring into space.

"You're eating like a bird, Grandma," Ani scolded her at suppertime.

The old woman complained, "Tasteless. *Anham eh.* Old age. Taste buds dry up."

"You want to go for an ice cream?" Ani offered.

"No, honey, I'm too tired," Grandma said.

The next night Ani convinced Grandma to accept her invitation. Ani drove Baba's car up Mount Auburn Street. The windows were rolled down and an August breeze blew in, pulling wisps of Grandma's gray hair from her bun and sending them flying around her head.

Ani brought the car to a halt in the parking lot of Dairy Joy. Grandma called it "Jeddy Doy."

"You want a marble cone?" Ani asked.

Grandma nodded. "Sure. Let me give . . ." She reached for her wallet.

"This is my treat," Ani insisted.

Hearing that Grandma had been half starved during the Deportations explained a lot. Little wonder that she slammed the string cheese on the dining room table, announcing, *Four dollars a pound.* It had seemed like an indictment of some kind, but Ani now realized it was actually a profession of love.

After the famous expression *amot kezi* and the numbers one to twenty, the first Armenian that Grandma had taught Ani was the phrase "I love you," *kezi geh sirem.* Grandma had said that to Ani from time to time—never to anyone else—but more than with words Grandma expressed her affection through small gifts: quarters, dollar bills, homemade yogurt, tiny meat dumplings that took hours to produce, fruit slices, and chocolate bars. This was Grandma's economy of love.

Ani and Grandma sat at a picnic table with ice creams that dripped in the late-summer heat. A crowd of high school kids sat at the other table, smoking cigarettes and flirting noisily. Ani didn't know any of them. When she was in high school she would have died rather than be seen in public with her old Armenian grandmother. Grandma's polyester flowered dress was hanging off her thinning shoulders, and there were several rhinestones missing from the tips of her cat's-eye glasses.

"You going to come visit me in New York?" Ani asked fondly.

Grandma swatted at the air with her free hand, dismissing Ani's idea. "I'm too old for that. You come home."

"Of course I'll come home," Ani assured her.

"Not too long," Grandma said sternly.

"Soon," Ani promised.

"You are my girl," Grandma said. She patted Ani's hand and said in Armenian, "Intelligent, beautiful—"

"*Khelatsi, keghetsig,*" repeated Ani, adding, "*yev khent.*"

Grandma laughed. "Crazy too."

Ani thought she had to be crazy to still be pining for Van. Was it folly to believe he loved her and not only that he loved her but that he would return to her? How would the ballad of Ani and Van finish: with biblical weeping and gnashing of teeth or with formulaic wedding bells?

She was named for the Armenian city of a thousand churches that was now in ruins within Turkish borders. He was named for a lake and a city that were no longer Armenian and, despite his quixotic plans to the contrary, would never again be Armenian.

"*Aghchigess,*" Grandma said, laying a hand on Ani's arm, "I'm tired, honey. Let's go home."

Around midnight, Ani lay on the futon in the basement listening to the sounds of the oscillating fan as it moved through its arc. She stared above her at the thickness of the night. When she was little she used to hang her head over the side of the bed and gaze at the hall light, imagining what it would be like to walk on the ceiling. She had liked seeing the world upside down, including her mother's bottom lip, which then appeared as her top lip and moved strangely over her sharp teeth as her mother had said, Put your head on your pillow, young lady, and go to sleep. . . .

"Ani," her mother called. "Wake up."

Ani sat up in bed, shielding her eyes with the back of her hand. Violet stood framed in the door, light falling in behind her.

"What's going on?" Ani asked.

"It's Grandma. She's having a heart attack."

Ani followed her mother up the cellar stairs to the kitchen. They went to the hall, where Grandma, whose hair was undone, was seated at the telephone table. Her face, Ani noted, was the same color as a frozen turkey defrosting on the counter. The muscles in her neck stood out like wires. Her head was large and strange. Her mouth worked the air as though she were trying to talk, but no words came out and she grimaced in frustration.

Baba, who was pacing the tiny hall, stopped to pat Grandma on the shoulder. In Armenian he said to her, "Don't talk, Mariam. Don't try to talk. Save your strength."

Violet shouted, "The ambulance will be here any minute, Ma!" as though deafness were the problem.

Grandma closed her eyes, resting her head against the wall.

It felt like forever that they waited under the hall's bleak light.

Finally the fire truck and the police cars arrived, followed closely by the ambulance. Many tall uniformed men stood around, their large hands empty. Ani looked down, noticing how short her cotton nightshirt was. She glanced up and saw a cop ogling her legs.

The paramedics loaded Grandma onto a stretcher. Baba and Violet trailed behind them to the sidewalk. By that time Ani was in the corner of her grandparents' bedroom. She curled up in the small armchair with her cheek against the faded flowered slip-cover. Ani saw behind her eyelids her grandmother's gray face, stricken with the speechless animal terror of great pain. Ani couldn't imagine anything lonelier than that—except death.

When Ani arrived at the door of her grandmother's room in the cardiac ward the next afternoon, her mother and grandfather were in the hall conversing with the doctor.

Ani kissed her grandmother's cheek, which was as smooth and soft as an apricot. She was relieved to see that the old woman, although pale and weak, was smiling.

"How's it going, Grandma?" Ani asked.

"*Akh,* food here is terrible, *aghchigess. Anham eh.* They don't let you get no sleep neither. Every five minute, take temperature, check this, check that."

Baba and Violet entered the room.

"You two, I want to talk to Ani. You leave," Grandma said in Armenian, as she waved them away wearily.

"I'll go to the cafeteria and get you some chocolate pudding, Ma," Violet said.

After they were gone, Grandma said to Ani, "Get pocketbook."

Ani fetched the black leather handbag from the sill, where it was propped between two vases filled with flowers. It was from the forties, with a stiff handle and a gold clasp.

Ani handed the bag to her grandmother. "I don't need any money, you know."

"No money." Grandma snapped open the clasp.

Ani perched on the edge of the bed, watching her grandmother rummage in the purse.

"You looking for an Almond Joy?" Ani asked.

"*Ahrr,*" the old woman said, as she thrust a cassette tape into Ani's hand. "Don't say nothing about it to nobody."

Ani wondered how long Grandma had been carrying the tape around. "Not even to you?"

"That's right. Nothing to nobody."

"Okay," Ani said. "Can I keep it?"

"It's for you. Why anybody would want, *chem keedehr.*"

The old woman closed her eyes. Her face was pale and drawn.

Grandma opened her eyes and asked, "When you getting married, Ani? I want to see you wedding before I die."

"I've got to start from scratch, Grandma, so it might take me a while."

"Good riddance to Esau. What you need is nice—"

Ani interrupted. "Nice Armenian boy."

Grandma smiled weakly. "That's right, honey."

"I'll work on it," Ani said.

A nurse came in bearing a large arrangement of pink roses and white lilies. "These are for you, Mrs. Kersamian. Aren't they beautiful?"

"Thank you, honey. Very pretty," the old woman said.

"Is this your granddaughter?" the nurse asked, as she placed the flowers on the windowsill. She extracted the card and handed it to the old woman.

"This is my Ani," Grandma said proudly. She glanced at the card, tossed it aside, and sighed. "When you dying even people who don't like you send flowers."

The nurse clucked her tongue. "Mrs. Kersamian, you are not dying. The doctor says you will be going home in a few days."

"Don't worry," Ani assured the nurse. "She's been saying that she's dying for as long as I can remember. Right, Grandma?"

"*Bidi mernim,*" Grandma responded on cue.

"That's Armenian for *I'm dying,*" Ani explained.

Violet came in with the pudding and Baba beckoned for Ani to join him in the hall.

Baba said, "I forgot to tell you in all the commotion. Vahram called last evening. They heard from Van a few days ago. He's in Canada."

This news jolted through her. Van in Canada? He was on the same continent. He had now contacted his family twice and she hadn't heard a word from him since Paris.

"Did Van ask Vahram to call us?" Ani asked.

"I don't know, *anoushig*," Baba said, shrugging. "I thought I should tell you. But Canada isn't so close. Plus, you're supposed to be looking for that Armenian dentist, right?"

The bike ride from the hospital to home wasn't far, but the late-afternoon sun was fierce and the air thick. Ani didn't want to think about Van. She didn't want to know that he was on the same land mass only hours away. She didn't want to twist his nose and yell at him for all the anguish he had caused her. She didn't want to smell sweet loam and spices. She didn't want to kiss him.

When Ani arrived at the house, she located the tape recorder on the shelf in the hall closet and went downstairs to her room.

She rewound the tape and as it began to play she heard her own voice for a moment: "And when you're finished you push down this one. . . ." Then there was a patch of scratchy air between when her grandmother had turned on the machine and when the old woman started to talk.

Ani closed her eyes and listened to Grandma's small, affectless voice begin.

"The Turks told us to leave our house. All the Armenians left their house. We had only clothes on our back. We start walking."

There was a pause.

When Grandma's voice started again it was smaller still.

"My mother fell by road."

Silence.

"We left her."

Silence.

"My sisters died because we didn't have nothing to eat."

Silence.

"My father died of broken heart."

Silence.

"A Kurd took my brother."

There was a long silence as the tape rolled on. It seemed that the fragmented, telegraphic narrative was finished.

But then Ani heard her grandmother's voice, barely above a whisper.

"Jesus says love your enemy."

Pause.

"What they did to us I never can forgive."

better to be the village cat than a foreign aristocrat

These were the things that Ani hated about the city: cockroaches that scuttled into cracks when she flicked on the kitchen light; the crash, whine, and grind of buses, ambulances, and garbage trucks at all hours of the night and day; litter spilling out of over-filled trash cans where rats nosed about at dusk; and the rank smell of urine at the far end of the subway platform.

She counted the beggars panhandling up and down the avenue near the university. There were at least two on each block—people with dirt-streaked faces and grimy clothes. Hardened city dwellers walked past, deaf to their pleas, but Ani looked at each and every one. She said, "Sorry," after she ran out of change. One man, his face twisted with hatred and his red and swollen ankles showing over unlaced oversized sneakers, said, "You're not sorry, you god-damned bitch."

It was true. How sorry was she really? She wasn't sorry enough to do anything useful, such as volunteering in a soup kitchen or getting a degree in social work, or even something idealistic like joining the Spartacus Youth League, for which pale dour students handed out jargon-filled newspapers at the college gate. Workers of the world unite to throw off the chains of capitalist oppression. She tossed the newspaper onto a heaped trash receptacle and headed up the stone steps to a seminar on nineteenth-century French literature. Now that was a useful topic.

After class she dashed across the campus toward the subway station to meet Elena on the platform. It had turned out that Elena's lover was a young woman named Daisy, a former varsity soccer captain who was in a training program at some big Wall Street investment firm. Daisy lived in Greenwich Village and they were headed to her apartment for dinner.

Ani asked, "What do your parents think about Daisy?"

Elena's mother was a devout Catholic.

Elena replied, "I thought I'd wait until Christmas to drop the bombshell."

Ani found it baffling that Elena had disavowed all her previous heterosexual encounters as "inauthentic." Elena claimed that she was now and had always been—even before she knew it—a lesbian. Ani wasn't convinced. She remembered Elena's passion for her college boyfriends. Elena said this was the effect of a lifetime of brainwashing, which she had now overcome.

Elena had posted on the refrigerator in their apartment a list of the famous women who had been lesbians. There was a second column with a question mark above it for women who were rumored—but not yet confirmed—to belong to this group. It reminded Ani of the way her grandparents could catalog the name of every Armenian, half Armenian, and quarter Armenian who had attained any degree of acclaim.

Ani and Elena slid into seats in the train's second-to-last car.

"How was the day?" Ani asked.

"Kind of sucked. I spent all afternoon in the library, and none of the books I needed were on the shelves. I put recall notices on all of them, but I'm sure professors have most of them, which means it will take months to get them back. How about you?"

Ani answered, "I think we're going to suffer horribly through our twenties, and then settle into dull complacency in our thirties."

"Are you depressed?" Elena queried.

Ani asked, "Do I seem depressed?"

"Well, you haven't had sex in months. You've made sure that you're up to your eyeballs in work. You have big dark circles under your eyes."

This seemed to Ani like the moment to unburden herself—to tell the sorry tale of her failed love affair with Van Ardavanian—but she couldn't bear the scalding light of Elena's anthropological curiosity. And, more importantly, she had pledged silence.

Ani asked, "Does it seem to you that almost everyone on campus is wearing black? It's like they're all on their way to a wake."

"Black's in fashion," Elena responded. She was wearing black jeans and a black sweater.

"But what is the fashion about? What's behind it? I think it's a generation in mourning," Ani observed.

"In mourning for what?" Elena asked.

"Oh, I don't know. The demise of the planet. The threat of nuclear war. The end of love."

"You *are* depressed," Elena stated, as they stood to exit the train.

They walked along the narrow tree-lined street past brick townhouses.

Elena said, "You know, you can go to the student health service and talk to a shrink for free. Then they refer you to another shrink for treatment. The one I'm seeing now has a sliding scale. It's almost affordable."

As she listened, Ani noticed Elena making eye contact with a woman who passed them on the sidewalk.

"You're seeing a therapist?" Ani asked.

"Oh, my God, Ani, everyone I know in New York has a shrink," Elena replied.

Ani watched as two older women with matching leather jackets went by. When Elena raised her eyebrows at them, they smiled in return.

"Why do you do that?" Ani asked.

"Do what?" Elena said.

"Make weird faces at women on the street."

Elena laughed. "It's a secret signal we use to acknowledge members of our tribe."

While Ani wasn't interested in joining this particular tribe, belonging to one sounded like a good idea. There were millions of people in the city. Someone had told Ani that if everyone in Manhattan came out of their apartments at the same time there wouldn't be enough room on the sidewalks for all of them. Yet Ani had only one friend and twelve acquaintances. When Elena stayed at Daisy's over the weekend, Ani might go for two days without having a meaningful conversation.

Daisy's second-floor apartment had five spacious rooms with tall windows. Daisy, who was dressed in a black cashmere sweater and black jeans, gave Ani the tour. There were matching dishes and a complete set of flatware in the gleaming kitchen. Daisy's bedroom featured a queen-sized bed with a brass headboard.

Daisy gestured at the other bedroom door. "That's Jackie's room. She's a slob, so we keep the door closed."

"Wow," Ani said. "You've arrived. This is real life. Our furniture is all stuff that Elena dragged home on trash day."

"That's because Daisy has a job and brings home real money," Elena said, ruffling Daisy's cropped blond hair.

While Daisy was in the kitchen, Ani and Elena set the dining room table for four.

"Who's Jackie?" Ani asked.

"The ex," Elena said curtly.

"Her ex-girlfriend lives here?" Ani asked incredulously.

"Listen, Ani, we're all grown-ups now."

Ani couldn't imagine giving that kind of leeway to a recently split heterosexual couple.

Jackie breezed in as they were carrying serving platters to the dining room. She had a pretty oval face, short black hair, and there was a silver ring through her right eyebrow. She too was wearing a black sweater and black jeans.

"Jackie, this is Ani," Daisy said.

"Hey, Ani, are you my date for the evening?" Jackie winked at Ani.

Ani tried to keep her face immobile but felt the flush creeping up her neck.

"You slut," Daisy said.

When Daisy and Elena laughed, Ani realized it was all in jest and she smiled stiffly.

Ani took the subway home alone, surprised to find the car almost full at midnight. Two Polish carpenters with their tools in canvas bags sat next to Ani. Across the way was an older black woman wearing a nurse's aide uniform and reading a copy of the *Watchtower*. At Times Square a ragged white man with a matted beard and dirt in the creases of his face entered the car and started shouting at his fellow passengers as the train hurtled through the dark.

He yelled, "Cesspools, you're all fucking cesspools. Do you understand that? Not a grain of decency in a single one of you. Like fucking animals. Do you hear me? Fucking animals, all of you."

When she stepped onto the platform at her station, Ani felt the knot behind her forehead loosen slightly. She walked across the campus, past the gleaming facades of the neoclassical buildings. The moon sat in the satin sky like a crooked bowl. God ladled sadness into the bowl until it spilled from the heavens like bitter milk. Ani caught the milk in her cup and drank it down.

Where was Van? She wished she had pierced his nose with a golden ring and threaded a silken cord through it. She could lead him around like a prized calf. Except maybe the ring should be through the heart. Her heart had been ground to a fine meat that could be mixed in a bowl with onions and parsley for baking onto a *lahmejun*. Love was at its core a kind of cannibalism.

The next morning Ani went to the Armenian language class she had signed up for, despite the fact that it had no relation to the degree she was meant to be taking. The class met four times a week and was led by a thin bearded graduate student from Beirut named Zaven. The four women students all spoke some Arme-

nian, and the other three already knew the alphabet, so Ani would
have to work hard to keep up.

That afternoon Ani skipped a lecture sponsored by the French
department and sat in instead on an Armenian history seminar.
In the departmental office, Ani slid into a seat at a carved mahogany table with twelve students around it.

Professor Avedikian, who was short and portly with iron-gray
hair and a white goatee, strode in and took his place at the head
of the table. He lectured for two straight hours, speaking deliberately in impeccable English with a slight hint of an Armenian accent. As the minutes went by he slowly turned the
yellowed leaves of his notes without once appearing to consult
them.

After the lecture Ani headed to the student health service for
a consultation. The therapist was a tall woman with frizzy
shoulder-length brown hair and a row of silver bangles up one of
her forearms.

"What brings you here?" she asked, her long face calm and
expectant.

Ani twirled a lock of hair at the nape of her neck. "Well, people
keep asking me if I'm depressed, so I started thinking maybe I'm
depressed."

"About anything in particular?"

"I'm kind of unhappy."

"And what do you think is the cause of your unhappiness?"

Ani blurted out, "I have no idea what I'm doing. My best friend
has joined a lesbian secret society. My college boyfriend dumped
me like last night's table scraps. The next boyfriend was a childhood buddy, practically a cousin, who lied to me about almost
everything and then disappeared. The Turks tried to wipe out my
grandparents and the rest of the Armenians like they were so many
cockroaches, and did a damned good job. My father was killed by
a hit-and-run driver about a block from here when I was four years

old. His family had disowned him when he married my mother and I've never met any of them, including an aunt who probably still lives on West End Avenue."

Ani observed the therapist's eyebrows rise into two peaks while the rest of her face remained impassive. "You sound angry," the woman said evenly.

"I'm not angry!" Ani shouted. "I'm depressed."

Ani called her mother to ask for money. She needed help paying for the course of reduced-fee analysis she had agreed to with Dr. Levin, the woman to whom Ani had been referred by the health service therapist.

Violet responded with concern. "Therapy? Four times a week? I told you that you were depressed. Can't you just forget about that heel? You're too good for him anyway. I don't like the idea of you all alone in that big city when you're feeling depressed. You're not thinking of doing anything crazy, are you? Should I come down and get you?"

"Mom, it's totally normal to see a therapist in New York. It doesn't mean you're crazy. Elena's seeing one. I bet half the French department is seeing somebody," Ani assured her.

Violet went into stage two of her response. "So this is some graduate student fad? You think I should send you my hard-earned money so you can be part of a fashion trend?"

Ani took to the process quickly. After a few weeks of lying on the beige couch, the white room had become a mountain kingdom isolated from the rest of the world. Ani was the empress of the country and Dr. Levin its religious leader. Ani could say almost anything that came into her head and her secrets would not escape their national boundaries.

But Ani didn't mention the bombing in Brussels. She had thus far kept the details of Van's political engagement extremely vague. But how was she supposed to keep her promise to him and let herself "free-associate" at the same time?

On Sunday afternoon, Ani was alone in the apartment with her stacks of books and articles. She found herself thinking about her father, who had emerged in her therapy sessions more as an atmosphere than a person. Without quite articulating to herself what she was doing, Ani went outside, walked around the block to the building where she had lived the first four years of her life, and rang a specific buzzer.

"Hello?" an older woman's voice said over the intercom.

"Hi. My name is Ani. I'm sorry to bother you. I used to live in your apartment when I was small, and I was wondering if I could come up and take a peek around."

Miraculously, the woman buzzed her in.

On the third floor a white-haired woman with watery blue eyes peered out from her door. "I'm Rosemary Brennan. Why don't you come in, dear."

Ani followed her down a long hall with bedrooms and a bathroom on the right and black and white checked tiles on the floor. She suddenly saw the wheels of a red tricycle going over the checked floor. Her red tricycle. Her dad was behind her, with his foot on the trike's back step and his hands next to hers on the silver handlebars. There were red and white plastic streamers at the end of each handle grip.

"Why don't you sit down," Mrs. Brennan said.

"Thanks," Ani said, taking a wing chair next to a window overlooking Morningside Park.

Ani saw her father sitting back in a deep blue armchair blowing smoke rings out the window. He looked up at her and smiled before fading away.

"When did you live here?" Mrs. Brennan asked. Her face was fair and narrow with deep smile lines. Her head trembled slightly as she talked.

"We left in August of 1965," Ani said.

Ani stood on the sidewalk scuffing the rubber toes of her blue sneakers while Baba put the suitcases in the back of the car. It was a hot day and there were rings of sweat under the arms of Baba's work shirt. Grandma sat on the stoop fanning herself with a section of the newspaper.

"We moved here in October of the same year," Mrs. Brennan said.

"I remember the floor tiles in the hall," Ani said.

"Yes, we replaced them about five years ago with the same thing that was here when we arrived."

"My father was killed by a hit-and-run driver."

Ani had never seen the body, which seemed like a merciful thing to spare a child, although it left her with the impression that he had walked out the door and vanished into the cityscape.

Mrs. Brennan said, "We heard about that from the neighbors. Six years later our son was shot on the corner of Morningside and 120th Street during a robbery. You never get over something like that, do you?"

"How old was he?" Ani asked.

She immediately regretted having asked the question. Would it be better or worse if Mrs. Brennan answered ten or twenty? Ten would be worse, because then the mother could never forgive herself for allowing her child outside.

"Nineteen. The police never solved the case."

"I'm so sorry."

The words hung on the air for a moment, wan and useless.

"Yes, well, I have another son. That's something to be thankful for," Mrs. Brennan said.

Ani used the bathroom on her way out. She stood at the sink running warm water over her hands and staring in the mirror. When she shut her eyes she heard the sound of water jostling in the sink as her father splashed his face. He applied the shaving cream to his cheeks like a white mask. The razor slowly unveiled his beloved face in long narrow strips. After the water had drained there were bits of white froth and tiny hairs in the basin. Her father leaned over to offer his freshly shaved face to her. It was smooth, damp, and warm under her palm.

In her apartment Ani lay on the lumpy couch staring through the barred window.

Nancy Kricorian

*My soul is weary of my life; I will leave my complaint upon myself;
I will speak in the bitterness of my soul.*

Strange the lines that came echoing back up the long halls of
memory. Mrs. Duke, the Sunday school teacher, had listened to
the Bible verses that Ani learned by heart, putting a star on the
wall chart by Ani's name for each.

But Ani, dear, Mrs. Duke had said, why don't you try some
New Testament verses?

*And I saw the dead, small and great, stand before God; and the
books were opened: and another book was opened, which is the book
of life: and the dead were judged out of those things which were
written in the books, according to their works.*

That wasn't quite what Mrs. Duke had in mind either.

Suddenly tired, Ani closed her eyes and drifted into sleep.

When Ani woke up, the sky was dark outside the window. She
went to her desk and picked up her address book. She pulled out
the telephone directory and found what she assumed was her aunt's
phone number.

"Is this Leah Kantrowitz?" Ani asked.

"Yes. Who is this?" the woman asked.

"This is Ani Silver, David Silver's daughter."

There was a sharp intake of breath.

"I'm in graduate school here in the city," Ani said.

"You must be twenty-three?"

"That's right." Ani wasn't sure what to say next. There was a
long silence.

Leah Kantrowitz sighed loudly. "After so many years. I'm sorry.
I have nothing to say to you." She hung up the phone.

Levin asked, "Were you disappointed?"

"Of course I was disappointed," Ani answered. There were tears
streaming down the sides of her face into her ears. "The problem

216

with this couch is that the water gets into your ears and then goes running down your neck."

Levin slid a tissue box toward Ani along the back of the couch.

"You probably buy these things wholesale," Ani said, pulling a couple of tissues out of the box. "Where were my grandparents from? What job did my grandfather have? Does somebody have a copy of the family tree? I can just see it, with my father's branch amputated at the elbow."

"The phone call might have been a shock to her. She may need some time to think about it. You could call her again in a few weeks. Or you could send her a letter."

"Are you actually giving me practical advice?" Ani asked.

Levin laughed. "Maybe I am. But we'll have to talk about that next time."

That night Ani wandered again in a big warehouse full of dreams. She scribbled them down in her journal in the morning and brought them dutifully to the session with Levin like a cat returning home with a dead mouse dangling from its jaw.

Ani said, "And then Van lobbed a bomb into the Willards' house. Asa and May and Asa's parents all ran screaming from the house as it exploded into flames. Baba was standing on the sidewalk outside, shaking his head, and he said, That crazy boy got the wrong house. The Turks live up the block."

Levin was silent.

"Aren't you going to offer an interpretation?" Ani asked. She had never given Levin the information she needed, however, to interpret Van and the bomb.

"Do you want me to?" Levin asked.

"Well, I mean, isn't that your job? It seems like you don't have anything to say about my dreams unless you can somehow figure an angle to see yourself in them."

"Is that what it feels like to you? That I'm only interested in myself?"

"Lord almighty, do you always have to answer me with a question?"

"You want me to give you answers?"

"This is hopeless," Ani said. "It's going to take years to get anywhere at this rate. How long is this supposed to take anyway?"

"Are you worried about how long it's going to be?"

Ani said, "For once, could you just answer the goddamned question?"

"Generally, it takes between six and twelve years."

"I might be thirty-five and still lying here on this couch?"

"Do you like that idea?"

"Well, it is kind of reassuring, because I have no idea what else I'll be doing."

"What do you imagine?"

"Okay. As I see it, there are several possible scenarios. One: I'll be an assistant professor of French literature at some New England college, married with two children, a Volvo, and periodic depressions. Two: I'll be helping to run a lesbian commune in western Massachusetts, supporting myself by doing bodywork and selling hand-painted greeting cards. Three: I'll be living in liberated Armenia near Mount Ararat, knitting woolen sweaters for Van and our five doe-eyed children. I'm still working on the fourth and final possibility. I'm open to suggestions, so if you have any sage advice, now would be a good time to offer it."

"A lesbian commune?"

"That would be the one you picked up on, and I'm sure it has something to do with you," Ani said sourly.

When she arrived at her building, Ani opened the mailbox in the lobby. There was a letter from her mother, but when she opened the envelope there was another envelope inside that her mother had forwarded. It had been postmarked in Montreal six days earlier. She hurriedly pulled out a sheet of onionskin on which these words were typed:

I was one of the birds who didn't seek for grain on the
   ground,
I would always fly, fly and avoid the snare of love.
But my snare had been set in the sea, though about that I
   knew nothing.
Every bird stood trapped by its feet, but I stood trapped,
   both feet and arms.

Nahabed Kouchag
(16th century)

The Canadian postmark, the Armenian verses with an oblique
and cryptic message from an anonymous sender: this was Van's
work. Since when had he started reading poetry? He was still in
love with her. Montreal was not so far away. He might appear on
her doorstep, in a day, or a week, or a month.

"Sorry, I'm late," Ani said, as she tossed herself onto the couch. "Listen, there's something I've been wanting to tell you."

"Yes?" Levin prompted.

"It's about Van."

He had lied to her and then abandoned her: that was the version she had told Levin. But confiding in a shrink wasn't like telling anybody else. Saying it out loud here would be okay. Everything Ani said within these four white walls stayed here, out of time and ordinary space.

"What about Van?" Levin asked.

"He planted a bomb outside a Turkish tourist office in Brussels," Ani said.

"Why?"

"It's an Armenian thing, you know. He's in this underground army, or he was in this underground army, but now he's hiding from the leader because there was a split after the bombing at Orly. I really don't know what he's doing now. Or what he's going to do next. But I got a note from him yesterday. He's in Canada."

"You never mentioned these details before," Levin said.

"I swore I wouldn't say anything to anyone. But I figure telling you isn't exactly like breaking the promise because you're a shrink. If he comes back—"

"You would want him back?" Levin interrupted.

Ani shrugged and sighed. "Maybe I shouldn't, but I do."

"It wouldn't trouble you that he was a terrorist?" the analyst asked.

Ani glanced at the shoes on the black ottoman. They were red leather pumps. What would a woman in red leather pumps know about revolutionary struggle?

"Revolutionary," Ani corrected. "One person's terrorist is another person's freedom fighter. When a revolutionary wins he becomes the hero and leader of his country. Look at Fidel Castro—or George Washington, for that matter. But anyway, there was this guy who was an assassin for the Dashnaks' Operation Nemesis in the early twenties. He hunted down and killed a couple of Young Turk bigwigs—you know, the guys who masterminded the Armenian Genocide. Then he married his sweetheart, moved to New Jersey, and became a successful businessman. I think he ran a dry cleaning store or something like that. On Sunday after church he was just the Armenian guy next door outside mowing his lawn."

"You think he was justified in killing?"

"Justified in killing the men who orchestrated the deaths of over a million Armenians? They planned it. They made it happen. What do you think? I mean, it's a bit murkier when you start shooting Turkish diplomats who weren't even born in 1915, but these other guys were guilty of genocide. They were role models for Adolf Hitler."

"You think Van might become the guy next door mowing the lawn?"

"I don't know. Maybe I'll get over it, but right now I still love him."

Ani returned to her apartment. She finished lunch and sat on the couch, the telephone resting on her knees. She willed herself to pick up the receiver and dial Leah Kantrowitz's number. What was the worst thing that could happen? Her aunt would slam down the receiver. She had done that before. Maybe this time she would shout something horrible and insulting into the phone before hanging up. Ani would survive that as well.

Ani's shoulders were bunched up near her neck, as though tensed in anticipation of a blow to the head. The line rang, one, two, three times.

The woman picked up on the fourth ring. "Hello?"

"Hello, Mrs. Kantrowitz?"

"Yes? Who is this?" the woman asked.

"This is Ani Silver." Ani winced, fearing the effect of this name. There was silence on the other end.

The telephone wire ran from Ani's ear, into the wall, out into the street, and then snaked in cables underground until it emerged in the basement of Mrs. Kantrowitz's building, climbed to her apartment, and inched into the live handle the woman held against her ear. It was practically an act of violence and stealth. Would Mrs. Kantrowitz refuse the connection?

"I hope you don't mind—" Ani began.

Mrs. Kantrowitz interrupted. "I've been thinking about you since you called. You want we should meet?"

Several hours later Ani, wearing a skirt and jacket as though dressed for a job interview, presented herself in a gilt and marble lobby on West End Avenue. The uniformed doorman with bushy eyebrows called upstairs to announce Ani's arrival, and a taciturn elevator operator dropped her on the seventh floor.

Ani wiped her feet on the woven straw mat outside her aunt's door. On the right side of the doorframe there was a small wooden bar with Hebrew writing on it nailed on a diagonal. Ani pressed the cream-colored doorbell button, and the jangling bell echoed inside the apartment. She heard slow footfalls coming up the hall and then the door opened.

Leah Kantrowitz was short and stout with straight chestnut hair that curled in at her shoulders. The eyebrows were a very different shade of brown. Mrs. Kantrowitz—"Aunt Leah" seemed a presumptuous form of address even in thought—wore a drop-waist tan dress that fell to just above her ankles.

"Come in, come in," Mrs. Kantrowitz said.

As Mrs. Kantrowitz turned to lead the way into the apartment, her hair shifted in one unit. It had to be a wig.

A lace-covered oval table and a chandelier of crystal teardrops dominated the dining room. From the west-facing windows Ani could see the avenue and a sliver of river glittering at the end of a side street. Most of one wall was covered with framed photographs spanning from turn-of-the-century black-and-white studio portraits to professional color photos of babies and small children who were probably Mrs. Kantrowitz's grandchildren.

"Why don't you take a seat. Would you like tea or coffee?" the woman asked.

"Just water, thanks," Ani said.

Mrs. Kantrowitz returned with a glass of seltzer and a plate of cookies, sitting down across from Ani, whose palms were damp and cold.

"You have his eyes," Mrs. K. said. "Same shade of gray. Otherwise you look like your mother. I met her once. That was all a long time ago." She sighed heavily, her eyes clouded with the past. Finally, she twitched her head slightly, awakening to Ani's presence. "What is it I can do for you?"

What could Mrs. Kantrowitz do for Ani? She could throw her arms around her and welcome her home like the lost sheep in the parable or like the prodigal son.

For this my son was dead, and is alive again; he was lost, and is found.

But that was the New Testament. This was an Old Testament world with a fierce and wrathful God.

What would her father's family do? Once you had been cast out, would they ever take you back? Would they tell you the stories that made up their family mythology? Would they initiate you into the rituals of their particular cult?

Ani made her claim modest. "We have only a few pictures of my dad when he was a kid. I was wondering if you could show me an old photo album."

"This I can do. Wait here," Mrs. K. instructed.

The woman went to the living room and came back a few minutes later with a large leather-bound book. The pages were of thick black paper on which the black-and-white photos were held in place with little gummed corners. Someone had taken great care in mounting the photos and in typing captions on slips of paper that were glued below each picture.

Mrs. Kantrowitz sat in the chair beside Ani, pointing out faces. "Those are my parents. They both died a few years ago, within months of each other. There's me, and my brother Sol. The baby there is David."

The baby's fair face was round and his hair dark. Ani also saw that her dad's countenance was a hybrid of his parents' features: eyes from his mother, nose and cheeks from his father. On the next page there was a photo of the extended family sitting around a table. Ani's father was perched in a high chair and there was a new baby in his mother's arms.

"That was our apartment in Washington Heights. Those are the Orlovskys, my mother's side. And the Silvers, my father's family," Mrs. K. explained.

By the last pages David Silver had grown to his full height and began to look like the photo Ani knew from his high school days. At his college graduation he wore a cap and gown, and about twenty family members were grouped around him.

Mrs. K. pushed out a heavy sigh. "After that we have no pictures of David. You must understand, for our family being Jewish isn't like a nationality. It's a religion and a way of life. When David married outside he turned his back on us and everything we believe in. He knew that, but he had to have this girl.

"My father was a hard man and a proud man. My mother might have been softer on David, but my father's wishes she respected. He was lost to us, and then—again he died. You see he was my little brother and on him I couldn't turn my back. I kept in touch. But the girl I couldn't forgive. Now I know it wasn't her. David wanted a different life." She was silent for a moment, staring into the distance.

Suddenly Mrs. K. slammed the photo album shut. "It is time for you to go."

The finality of the woman's tone hit Ani like a brick.

Ani's face contracted with stubbornness. This one visit wasn't enough. She needed more. She wouldn't let herself be put out on the sidewalk with nothing.

Ani asked, "May I please have another glass of water?"

Mrs. Kantrowitz said coldly, "All right."

While her aunt was in the kitchen Ani placed her palm on the embossed black leather cover of the album. She didn't want to think—she was tired of thinking. It was time to act. She gathered up the album, her coat and bag, and moved swiftly toward the door.

When Mrs. Kantrowitz returned with the glass of seltzer Ani was several flights away, dashing down the back stairs.

On the final landing, Ani stopped to catch her breath. It would look suspicious to the doorman if she were panting as she went by.

She imagined Mrs. Kantrowitz emerging from the apartment screaming, "Thief! Stop, thief!" She would stump down the stairs behind Ani brandishing a long kitchen knife.

Ani tucked the album against her body, arranging her coat over her arm in such a way that the book was camouflaged.

In the lobby Ani glided past the doorman, briefly making eye contact with him as he held the door. "Thanks. Have a good evening," she said.

"You should put on your coat, young lady. It's getting chilly," he called after her.

The avenue was darkening as she hurried away. Near the river the purple-blue sky was scarred with sooty branches. She didn't want the lonely river. She wanted a blur of faces hurtling past like comets. She turned to Broadway, with its brightly lit storefronts and Korean markets where sidewalk stands were piled high with fruit, vegetables, and flowers. The 99-Cent Store was garishly decked out with Christmas lights. Cars, trucks, and buses surged up and down.

A man marched by with an armload of dry cleaning in a plastic bag. A toddler wrapped to the chin in a crocheted blanket was wheeled by in a stroller. Ani passed a bar window lit with beer logos. Inside a row of men sat at the counter with glass mugs and cigarettes watching football scenes on the television behind the bar. An old woman wearing a hat with floppy cloth flowers on the brim peered with concern into Ani's face.

Why you steal that poor woman's pictures, Ani? Grandma queried.

I don't want to answer that question, Grandma.

You gonna give them back?

I don't want to answer that question either.

Leave the girl alone, Mariam, Baba admonished. Can't you see she's upset?

She's upset? Violet asked. I told her not to call that woman. I told her the Silvers didn't want anything to do with her. Why doesn't she listen to me?

Listen to you? All I ever do is listen to you. All of you take up too much space in my head. Next thing you know Van's going to chime in, and Elena, and Asa. At this rate, I wouldn't be surprised to hear from Dana Grimaldi.

And how does that make you feel? Levin asked.

Not you. I forgot about you.

Why do you think you forgot about me?

I'm not going to answer that question.

Do you want to see me make this quarter disappear? It was a man's voice.

Daddy?

Watch this, he said. He snapped his fingers and the quarter disappeared. Where do you think the quarter went?

Behind my ear, Ani replied.

Let's see, he said, reaching behind her ear. He pulled out the shiny quarter and placed it in the middle of her open palm. That's for you, Penny Bright.

That's what he called me, Ani thought.

That was the sound of his voice.

Ani glanced at the street sign and noted that she had put ten blocks between herself and her deed. She paused to pull on her coat and button it against the wind. With the back of her hand she wiped cold tears from her face. Then Ani Silver clasped the black book and strode forward with it into the rest of her life.

glossary of foreign terms and phrases

aghchig	girl
aghchigess	my girl
ahnbeedahn	useless, worthless
ahrr	take
amot kezi	shame on you
anamot	shameless
anham eh	savorless
anoushig	sweetie
assez bien	pretty well
badveli	pastor, minister
banir	cheese
baron	mister
bidi mernim	I'm going to die
bonsoir	good evening
boum	party
carte de séjour	residence permit
chambre de bonne	maid's room
char dghah	bad boy
char shoon	bad dog
chem keedehr	I don't know
chezokh	neutral, nonpartisan
comment ça va ce matin	how's it going this morning?
dahngahlakh	blockhead
Dashnak	member of Armenian Revolutionary Federation
devs	devils, evil spirits
digin	Mrs.
éblouissant	dazzling
eshek	donkey, ass
fromager	cheese seller
inchbes es?	how are you?
gamatz, gamatz	slowly, slowly; little by little
herya	Jew

Nancy Kricorian

hos yegoor	come here
Hunchak	member of Hunchakian Revolutionary Party
jagadakir	destiny
je t'ai demandée une question	I asked you a question
je suis fou	I am crazy
je suis au plus profond de l'abîme, et je ne sais plus prier	I am at the bottom of the pit and I don't know how to pray anymore
je veux follement te faire l'amour	I want to make love to you
je vous souhaite bienvenue	I welcome you
keghetsig	pretty
khelatsi	intelligent
khent	crazy
khadayif	pastry of shredded wheat, nuts and syrup
kesh chem	I'm not bad
kezi geh sirem	I love you
kisher pari	good night
lahmejun	meat pizza
lav em	I am well
madzoon	yogurt
manti	small meat dumplings
medz mairig	Grandma
meghah	exclamation of surprise
mutilés de guerre	disabled veterans
odar	foreigner, non-Armenian
ojakh	hearth
pakhlava	pastry of filo, nuts & syrup
pamplemousse	grapefruit
poghokagan	Protestant
pomme de terre	potato
pompier	firefighter
préfecture	police headquarters
primeur	greengrocer
quatre bises	four kisses
qu'est-ce que tu as dit?	what did you say?
Ramgavar	member of Armenian Social Democratic Party

tavloo	backgammon
toneer	fireplace
toun inchbes es?	how are you?
tourshi	pickles
vardik	underpants
vhy babum	alas my father (idiom)
vorik	bottom, rear end
yalanchi	stuffed grape leaves
yaprak	grape leaves
yavrum	darling, dear

acknowledgments

Thanks to Anne Carey, Dahlia Elsayed, Daniel Goldin, Tanja Graf, Katie Hite, Arsen Kashkashian, Susan Kricorian, and Markar Melkonian for reading early drafts of the manuscript.

For research assistance I would like to thank Peter Bilizekian, Bethel Charkoudian, Ani Garmiryan, Jean-Claude Kébabdjian at the Centre de Recherches sur la Diaspora Arménienne, Lena Takvorian, and especially Markar Melkonian.

Gratitude to my top-notch editorial team: Maria Massie, Elisabeth Schmitz, Lauren Wein, and Kim Witherspoon. James Schamus was once again my most faithful and trusted reader.